Published June 2024
Published by Indies United Publishing House, LLC

Cover art by Leslie A. Piggott

ISBN: 978-1-64456-716-6 (paperback)
ISBN: 978-1-64456-718-0 (ePub)
ISBN: 978-1-64456-717-3 (Mobi)

Library of Congress Control Number: 2024903702

INDIES UNITED PUBLISHING HOUSE, LLC
P.O. BOX 3071
QUINCY, IL 62305-3071

www.indiesunited.net

UNWRITTEN IN DEATH

UNWRITTEN IN DEATH

The Cari Turnlyle Series: Book 5

by Leslie A. Piggott

INDIES UNITED PUBLISHING HOUSE, LLC

Dedication

To my sweet family: thank you for all your love, support, and encouragement.

Table of Contents

Chapter 1

Cari Turnlyle rolled her chair under her desk and waited for the computer to boot up. Earlier this month, she had gone on vacation to the Midwest and was still getting back in the swing of things. While the time away was a good break from work, it hadn't been very relaxing. Her vacation had been complete with one concussion, which made returning to work immediately following the vacation more challenging than she'd expected. She experienced headaches off and on for the first two weeks and her eyes couldn't handle staring at a computer screen for more than a few hours each day. Cari hoped she would finally be able to put in a full work week this week. She looked at the stack of papers on her desk. Her boss, Mr. Ollaman, had left a pile of assignments while she was away.

The editor and chief of the Brenington Beagle, known for his shiny, bald head, was a bit unpredictable. Some days, he praised her work and desire to get to the bottom of a story; other days, he criticized her inability to let something go. He had encouraged her to take a vacation—her first one since starting at the Beagle a few years ago—but now he was complaining that she was behind on her work.

Cari sighed. She realized she was rubbing her locket while she fretted over her job at the newspaper. Her grandmother gave her the locket when she graduated from high school. It held a photo of them in a field of sunflowers from Cari's childhood. Cari wore it every day. It was like her security blanket as she made her way through life. She reached down to pull her cell phone from her messenger bag when the desk phone rang. The caller ID only said *transfer*.

"Brenington Beagle, this is Cari Turnlyle. How can I help you today?" she said as cheerfully as she could into the receiver.

"Oh, thank goodness. I wasn't sure they would really transfer me to you. I didn't know where else to turn. I need your help," a young, frantic voice said to her.

Cari blinked, trying to recognize the caller's voice. "I'm sorry. Do I know you?"

"Oh, no, probably not. I don't think we've ever met, but I read all your stories in the paper, and I *know* you can help me. Please," she said rapidly.

"Slow down. What is it you need help with?" Cari asked her calmly. She could hear the despair in the young woman's voice.

"It's my great aunt. I'm sort of her caregiver. I mean, I don't live with her, but I come by her house every day and bring her groceries...that sort of thing...I'm a junior in college..." the woman trailed off.

Cari wasn't sure where this was going. "Okay...?"

"When I got to her house last Wednesday, she wouldn't wake up! She was...she was...*dead*," the woman broke into sobs.

"Oh, no! I'm so sorry for your loss. Did you need a phone number for a grief counselor, or—" Cari started searching for counselors in the area on her computer when the woman interrupted her.

"No! I mean, probably, but that's not what I need from you. The police say she committed suicide. She would never! She's like a grandma to me. I've known her my whole life. She had plans. Travel plans. Concert plans. Lots of...plans! She wouldn't commit suicide."

Cari's eyes filled with tears upon hearing the woman's anguish. "I'm not sure how I can help. If the police said...um, did she leave a note?" she asked gently.

The woman sucked in a breath. "There was a note, but it was typed. She rarely typed anything. Someone staged this. You have to figure out who."

Cari chewed the inside of her cheek as she mulled over how to respond. "Again, I'm so sorry. I don't think I caught your name or your aunt's, for that matter."

The woman sniffled. "I'm such a mess. I'm sorry. My name is Dahlia Roust. My aunt is, her name, is, was, uh, Vivian Roust."

Cari typed the older woman's name into a search engine to look up her obituary. She didn't want Dahlia to feel ignored, so she tried to make conversation while she skimmed through it. "How old was your aunt?"

"She was my great-aunt. Anyway, um, she was seventy-six," Dahlia paused. "I know that sounds *really* old, but she was still very active."

Cari read about Vivian Roust's life: she had married young and was widowed a decade ago. She'd been a school teacher for a short time before becoming a homemaker and raising several children. Mrs. Roust was survived by numerous family members from siblings to great-nieces and nephews. It sounded like the woman and her husband had loved traveling as they made it to all fifty states during their forty years of marriage. Cari looked again at the pile of work on her desk. She was really swamped and this felt like a distraction she didn't need.

She tried to choose her words carefully. "Dahlia, I can hear how much you loved your great aunt. I'm so sorry you are hurting, but I don't think—"

"Please don't turn me down. I don't know who else to ask. You have to believe me; she wouldn't do this. Anyway, her home is just down the block. It's 231 Grand Avenue. Can't you just come and see for yourself?" Dahlia begged.

She looked at the papers and reminders in front of her and frowned. "I'm very sorry, Dahlia. I just can't do this for you. If you find something more concrete, you should contact the police again."

The call ended and Cari wiped a tear off her cheek. She hated turning the young woman away, but she really needed to get back on track. Rubbing her locket, Cari sighed. She returned the receiver to its cradle and grabbed her cell phone. Her grandmother always had good advice. Maybe she could guide her through this too. She pulled up the number and hit talk.

"Is that my Cari? How are you, sweet girl?" her grandmother's voice sang into her ear.

"Uh, I'm pretty good. I was just thinking about you and wanted to say hi," Cari told her.

"I was just telling my neighbor down the street about how you got engaged! She thought Bob's proposal sounded so romantic and said she could just picture you with tears in your eyes as you said yes to Bob and then the sweet kiss you shared afterward," Grandmother told her. "But it sounds like something is on your mind. Did something happen with you and Bob?"

Cari glanced at her left hand and cringed. She had also gotten engaged while on vacation but wasn't used to wearing the ring yet. She had forgotten to put it on that morning. It had only been a few weeks, but she always felt guilty when she left her apartment without it on her finger. "No, it's not Bob. He's doing great; I think he's going to make it the whole way in the 5k this weekend."

"Oh, wonderful! He must be so proud of himself," Grandmother exclaimed.

Cari grinned. "Well, I don't know that he's proud, yet. I think he's looking forward to the race just because it means it's almost over."

Her grandmother laughed good-naturedly. "You never know. Maybe this will be a new hobby for him. Now, what is bothering you, my dear?"

"It's…well, I just got a phone call from a rather frantic young woman. Her great-aunt died recently. She wants me to investigate even though the police already ruled it to be a suicide."

"Oh my. How terrible. It sounds like they were very close," Grandmother said kindly.

"I think they were. She said she was like her caregiver but didn't live with her. I don't know how to help her, though, Grandmother. There was a suicide note, but she doesn't believe her great-aunt wrote it."

"Oh dear. That is troubling. Did you agree to see her?"

"I told her I couldn't. I'm still swamped with tasks here from Ollaman. I feel so guilty, but what else can I do?"

"It was kind of you to take her call and listen to her. You can't fix everyone's problems, Cari," her grandmother said gently.

"Thank you, Grandmother. It just doesn't feel like enough."

* * * * *

Genevieve Viacorte looked over at her partner, Alex Runimoss. He was hunting and pecking away at his keyboard, trying to finish up their report regarding damage to state property. It was summertime, so school was not in session, but someone had graffitied the outside of a school gymnasium. They'd left behind their empty spray paint canisters, so it was only a matter of time before she and Alex caught up with them. Brenington had a small police force with only a few detectives. She was thankful to be paired with Alex even though he was a bit old-school sometimes and couldn't type a report to save his life.

"I see you staring at me, Viacorte. It should be you typing this thing up. I'm the senior detective here," he grumbled.

"You lost the bet fair and square, Alex. That puts the paperwork in your box," she laughed.

"Ugh! I still can't believe the Knicks lost in the finals…they were up three games!" he complained.

"Always risky to bet on the Knicks," she said as she twirled a pen in her left hand.

"Also, you got an entire four weeks off from paperwork when you were doing that FBI training thing. I was stuck here training another rookie—"

"So many tears for you. You're good at training rookies. Look how well I've turned out," she bragged.

Alex jabbed at a few more keys and then grabbed his mouse. "Finally. It's done. Clicking submit and it's out of my hair."

Genevieve chuckled, her hazel eyes bright in amusement. She started to say something snarky back when she heard their lieutenant's door open and then slam close. She saw him marching across the bay with a determined look on his face.

"Runimoss, Viacorte. I've got a case for you. Listen up," he barked in their direction. The LED lights glared off his bald head as he stomped over to them.

"That new author lady, uh, what's her name?" he asked while snapping his fingers.

Genevieve looked at him blankly. "Sir?"

Alex spoke up before he could respond. "Do you mean the lady who was on the Today Show the other day? Gayle Smith or whatever she goes by?"

"It was *a week ago* and yes, that's the one," he opened the file in his hand. "Gayle Smith, more famously known as Natasha Gillespie. She was found dead in her home this morning by her housekeeper."

Genevieve's head swiveled between Alex and Lieutenant Grusky. "What? I'm not someone who watches the Today Show. Who is this person?"

Alex turned her way with a smug grin. "She's a bestselling author, but no one ever really knew who she was until this past week. She was a guest on the show and announced to the world that she is, uh, was, Natasha Gillespie. Turns out, she's been living in Brenington this whole time."

Genevieve blinked several times. "You read books?"

Grusky cleared his throat. "If we could stay on task…"

"Sorry, sir," she mumbled. "What do we know about Ms. Smith?"

Alex jumped in. "Smith owned a fairly large house on the edge of town. She was in her late fifties or sixties and not married," he paused. "And my wife reads her books."

Grusky nodded in agreement. "We don't know a lot about her, but we need to go take a look. The medical examiner is at her home now, along with CSU. Right now, it's just a suspicious death. She appeared to be in decent health and as Runimoss said, she wasn't elderly. We're looking into next of kin, but it's possible the housekeeper already contacted them."

"Okay, LT. We'll head over there and see what we can find out," Alex told him.

Genevieve hopped out of her seat and grabbed the keys to the cruiser. "I'm driving."

* * * * *

Cari hurried back out to her car. She wanted to run back to her apartment and get her engagement ring. She mentally berated herself for forgetting to put it on…again. She knew it would hurt Bob's feelings if he found out she was forgetting to wear it. It wasn't that she didn't like the ring; she loved it. She just needed to get used to wearing it every day. She pulled out of her parking spot and steered the car toward her apartment.

Luck seemed to be on her side and she didn't have to stop at any red lights. She quickly parked her car and hurried up to her apartment. Thankfully, she didn't live far from her office and could hopefully get there and back before anyone noticed she was gone. She'd barely finished the thought when her cell phone rang.

Ollaman. She hesitated before answering it. What could she tell him if he asked where she'd run off to?

"This is Cari."

"Turnlyle! I thought you weren't going to answer there for a minute," her boss' voice boomed into her ear.

"My apologies, sir. I was meeting with someone about a potential story," she said, immediately regretting the lie.

"Potential story? Never mind that. We have a bigger story. I need you to get over to the north side of town. Brenington's new claim to fame, the infamous Natasha Gillespie, was found dead in her home this morning. It's been classified as a suspicious death. Get over there, uh, Michelle is sending you the address now, and interview anyone who will talk to you."

Cari blanched. "Oh, wow. Has it even been a week since she revealed her identity to the world? Have you read her books, sir?"

"Her books? I don't have time to read books, Turnlyle. Keep me posted. This is going to be big."

The call ended. Cari slipped her phone into her bag and hurried back to her car. The wind lifted Cari's curls into her face. She tucked them behind her ears again and sighed. Not only was she ignoring a young woman's cry for help, she was also lying to her boss.

Chapter 2

Genevieve tapped her pencil on the side of her notebook. The CSU team buzzed around her and Alex. She watched as one of them bagged a small medicine bottle from the nightstand.

"Chris?" she asked.

He looked her way and raised his eyebrows.

"What's the med you bagged there?"

"Looks like generic melatonin, but the bottle is empty."

Genevieve made a note. "Did the ME give a time of death yet?"

Chris nodded. "He's estimating around eleven o'clock last night."

She watched as a middle-aged man with slightly unkempt, curly hair checked over the woman's body on the bed. He nodded in the direction of two technicians who came around to move the body onto the nearby gurney. Dr. Green tried to smooth his hair as he ambled past them, commenting on his way by.

"That's just an estimate and no, I don't have a cause of death yet. No trauma, no injuries to the body that I could find. I'll have more for you after I do the autopsy."

She looked over at Alex. His large frame blocked the exit to the bedroom. She could tell he was annoyed and ready to get on with the next thing.

"Should we go wait for the sister downstairs?" she asked him.

"Better than watching other people work," he said despondently.

He stomped off down the stairs and she hurried to keep up with him. At six-foot-six, he was almost a foot and a half taller than her. The staircase made a gentle curve to the right, giving them a view of the home's entry level. It ended in a sitting room with pale, hardwood floors and cream-colored furniture. Genevieve saw one of their officers sitting with a woman on the sectional sofa and wondered if it was the sister. She could only see them from the back; the woman had straight brown hair with streaks of grey in it. She had it pulled back in a low pony tail.

Alex cleared his throat as he approached them. "I'm Detective Runimoss and this is my partner Detective Viacorte. We're very sorry for your loss. Could we ask you a few questions?"

The woman's eyes were red and rimmed with tears. Genevieve didn't see any resemblance between the victim upstairs and the woman on the sofa. Maybe they each took after a different parent.

The officer spoke up before the woman could respond. "This is the housekeeper, Myra McIlvain. She had a panic attack, but I think she's okay now. Ms. McIlvain? Would you be able to answer a few of the detectives' questions?"

She wiped her eyes and nodded. "I feel so ridiculous. It was just such a shock. I've been cleaning Gayle's, I'm sorry, Ms. Smith's house for over two decades. I never expected…"

Her eyes filled with tears again. She let the tears fall down her face and started to talk again. "I come once a week. The house is never dirty, but she knows I appreciate the work. I guess, she *knew*…I'm sorry. What questions do you have?"

Genevieve and Alex sat down in the over-sized chairs across from the sectional. She took out her small notebook and pen. After handing the woman a tissue, the officer patted her shoulder and saw himself out the front door. Alex waited for the door to close before asking his first question.

"Is Ms. Smith usually home when you clean?"

"Sometimes. It just depends on the week. I would say she is here more often than not."

"How do you typically enter the property?" Genevieve asked her.

"I have my own key and my own code to the alarm. The alarm wasn't set today, so I figured she was here. I actually thought there'd be more of a mess today."

"Why is that?" Alex asked as he leaned forward.

"She had a big party last night. She was celebrating her, I guess you'd call it, her new-found-fame as an author. All sorts of people were invited from what I understand."

"Were you invited?" he asked.

Her head drooped before she answered. "She begged me to come. I'm her employee, though. It felt odd coming to a party knowing I'd be cleaning up after it the next day. I thought I'd be out of place. I should have come."

Genevieve nodded. "Tell us about the party. Was it catered? Can you estimate the size of the guest list?"

Ms. McIlvain scrunched up her face. "It was catered. As for the guest list, I couldn't tell you that. Her publicist or publisher might know more."

Alex's head whipped toward the front door as it burst open. Genevieve hadn't heard the commotion until that moment. A petite woman with long, mousy brown hair scrambled inside and threw the door closed behind her. She started to lock it when the door opened again. The young officer from earlier stumbled inside, out of breath.

"You can't come in here. This could be a crime scene. Ma'am. Stop." He bent over at the waist as he tried to catch his breath.

The middle-aged woman glared at him as she adjusted the strap on her cross-body bag. "I very much can be here. This is my sister's home. I have every right to come inside. Where is she? Who's in charge here? I want to see my sister."

Alex had jumped to his feet as soon as the door opened the first time. He positioned himself between the woman and the foot of the stairs. Genevieve saw his jaw working to keep from laughing at the young man who had obviously been out-matched by someone at least two decades older. To be fair, she had to admit the woman clearly had muscular legs. She could see their shape easily as the woman was wearing spandex leggings and a long t-shirt.

Genevieve glanced at Ms. McIlvain. She didn't want the outburst to induce another panic attack. The older woman's face was a bit pale, but she seemed to be breathing normally. She nodded confirmation to Alex when he looked her way.

"My young colleague is right; you can't just barge into a house like this," Alex began but paused when the woman's nostrils flared. "What I mean is, we need to know who you are. It would have been better for you and my young friend here if you'd identified yourself rather than going off to the races to get away from him. You mentioned this is your sister's house. Are you Penelope Holbein?"

The dark eyes narrowed at Alex when he said the name. "I most certainly am not. That's my other sister. She couldn't make it and asked me to come in her place. And it's clearly better that I'm here. She would have waited outside and not been assertive enough to get the answers we're entitled to."

Genevieve stifled a groan but saw Alex roll his eyes. She spoke up before his sarcasm got them both in trouble. "Our apologies. Which sister are you?"

"Sharon. It's spelled just like it should be. Sharon Chiddy. I'm sure it's on your list of associates for Gayle." She looked up at Alex. "I take it you're in charge, handsome?"

His jaw flexed, making Genevieve mentally cross her fingers he wouldn't snap at her. "Detective Runimoss. I'm the senior detective with Brenington PD. This is my partner, Detective Viacorte. We're speaking with Ms. McIlvain right now. If you could wait outside with this officer for a few more minutes, I assure you, we'll be right with you."

"I'd like to see Gayle," she responded stubbornly.

"Out of the question. Please wait outside. We'll send for you when we're ready."

The young officer put a hand out to escort her, but Sharon pushed past him. She flipped her hair over her shoulder and closed the door in his face again. He sighed and opened the door to join her outside.

Genevieve looked back at Ms. McIlvain. "My apologies, Ms. McIlvain. You were talking about the party here last night."

"Oh, right. I've never met any of her family before. The responding officers found her *in case of emergency* contact on her cell phone and asked me if I recognized the name. Like I said, I hadn't met any of them, but I knew she has, uh, had a sister named Penelope. I'm pretty sure all her siblings were coming to the party. She was a little nervous about them all being together."

Alex returned to the chair. "Are they all as volatile as Ms. Chiddy?"

She considered his question. "I'm not entirely sure. Gayle would occasionally drink her coffee while I cleaned the house. She didn't talk about them a lot, but she did mention that they weren't exactly a close-knit family...I'm sorry, but what happened to her? It just looked like she was sleeping, but she was cold. She wouldn't wake up. She didn't have any health conditions that I know of. I know I'm rambling. It's just, well, she was a friend. I mean, I worked for her, but I cared about her too."

Genevieve pulled her lips into her mouth as she mentally formed her response. "I understand, Ms. McIlvain. We don't know what happened—"

"But why bring in detectives at all? You must know something."

Alex responded first. "We're just being thorough at this point. It could be just as you said that she passed in her sleep."

"But why? She wasn't old. She wasn't in poor health."

"And that's why we're here. To make sure nothing else happened," Alex told her.

"Ms. McIlvain, do you happen to have a list of contacts for Ms. Smith? Like doctors or other medical professionals she saw?" Genevieve asked her.

Ms. McIlvain shook her head. "No, I just cleaned the house. I wasn't a personal assistant or anything like that. I don't think she had one. I suppose all of that is on her phone or computer. I wish I could be of more help. I didn't know she was an author, so I guess I shouldn't feel bad that I don't even know if she ever went to the doctor. She was never sick."

* * * * *

Cari pulled up to the address Ollaman's secretary had texted to her. She saw Bob's car parked at the end of the block, along with several police cruisers and the medical examiner's van. It seemed like she was the first media person to arrive, but knew it wouldn't be long before the local news stations showed up too. Two officers stood in the driveway. Cari figured they were there to keep people like her from getting inside. She grabbed her messenger bag and got out of her car.

No sooner had she stepped onto the sidewalk than the front door of the house opened. A woman in tights and a bright green t-shirt stomped onto the porch with a uniformed police officer at her side. Cari could see the woman was angry and knew that meant she had a good chance of getting her to talk. She was thankful she kept her press ID in her messenger bag and pulled it out, hoping to catch the woman's eye. Sure enough, the woman looked her way and nudged past the officer into the yard. Cari gave her a quick smile and waited for her to cross the yard. She slipped her hand into her bag, found her digital recording device, and switched it on just as the woman reached her. She released the device and looked inside the bag for her notebook.

"I thought it was you," the woman said accusingly.

Cari took a step back as she flipped the notebook open. "I'm sorry?"

"You're the girl from the newspaper here. The one who writes all the crime stuff. Carmen or whatever."

Cari tried smiling again, unsure how she'd offended the woman already. "Yes, I'm Cari Turnlyle. I write for the Brenington Beagle."

"Right. Whatever. Who sent you out here? You have one of those police scanners or what?"

Cari cleared her throat. "I'm sorry, Ms., uh, I don't think I caught your name."

"I'm Sharon. Sharon Chiddy. I'm *Natahsa Gillespie's* sister," she said waving her hands in a sarcastic manner as she said the woman's name.

"Nice to meet you, Ms. Chiddy. I'm very sorry for your loss. Were you and Ms.—"

"Nice?! My sister just died. There's nothing *nice* about that. And it's Sharon, not Ms. Chiddy, got it?" Cari nodded while the woman continued her rant.

"I can't believe those jerk officers inside won't even let me see her," the woman barked haughtily.

"Oh, no. I'm sure that's…frustrating. Were you and your sister close?" Cari decided using sister rather than one of the dead woman's two names was the better option.

Sharon cackled. "Close? That's a good one. No. I clearly knew nothing about her. I didn't even know she could write in complete sentences, let alone finish an entire novel or a whole series for that matter. She never talked to me. She kept to herself. She had this whole life none of us knew anything about."

"By us do you mean your immediate family? You have other siblings? Are your parents still living?"

Sharon gave Cari an icy stare. "There's a whole bunch of *us*. I have three adult kids, not that you'd know they'd reached adulthood. They all still live at home and contribute zero to my well-being. My parents have been gone forever. Decades. They left us nothing. Siblings. Now there's an *us* for you. I'm the second youngest of six. Agatha Christie in there was the oldest. Twin brothers after her, then another sister, and the youngest is a petulant child—worse than my own kids. In order, that's Gayle, Gary, Michael, Penelope, *Sharon*, and Douglas."

Cari jotted their names down even though her recorder was most likely catching all of their conversation. "That is a big family. Do you all live in the area? You seem to have arrived here quickly."

"I live the closest, but we were all in town for her dumb *coming out* party last night," she grumbled.

Cari flinched at her emphasis on coming out, unsure what she was implying. "Coming out?"

Sharon rolled her eyes. "She's been in hiding or whatever, writing under that dumb pen name for the last two decades. Now, she's decided to retire, so she announced her real name to the world and then called it quits. Apparently, for good."

Cari felt certain her poker face had failed her with that last comment. "Right. You mentioned Gayle never spoke with you. Were you notified of her passing as the next-of-kin?"

"No, that would fall on Penny—Penelope. Gayle apparently liked her better than the rest of us, but Penny was eating brunch with her grandkids this morning and couldn't get here quickly. She called me and asked me to come instead."

"I see. You said the police wouldn't let you see your sister. Did they give a reason?"

"They're marking her death as suspicious. She'd love that. If she weren't dead already, she'd probably write another book about it. Suspicious death. People die all the time. Suspicious!" she huffed. "I outran that junior officer over there, though. I knew they might not let me in, so I parked around the corner and slinked up the side of the house. I made a break for it when I was within ten yards of the porch. He never had a chance. He was at a dead sprint and I still beat him," she bragged.

Cari chewed the inside of her cheek debating how best to respond. *Congrats on outrunning the law?* "Is there anything else you can tell me about your sister or her party last night?"

"Oh right, the party. It wasn't a *huge* party. I mean, there were certainly less than a hundred people here. You know, it was come and go. She signed some books, but it wasn't open to the public or anything. I think it was thrown together rather last minute. I guess it was catered. The food wasn't bad. They could have had better wine, though."

"Besides for family and I'm guessing her publisher, who else was in attendance?" Cari asked.

"I mean, I didn't stay that long. She asked each of us to be there. I thought we might see someone actually famous—you know her books have been turned into movies, right? So, I thought the producer might come, or some of the actors who have been in the movies. Nope. It was just a bunch of other no-name people who write books. And the catering staff. Pretty lame party, if you ask me."

A whistle from the porch took Cari's attention away from Sharon. They both turned to look. Genevieve stood in the open doorway of the home and was gesturing for Sharon to come her way.

"Oh, she thinks she's gonna get me to come over there by whistling at me, does she? Rude. But I do need to get back in there. Do you have a card or anything? I might have more to tell you after I talk to the whistler over there."

Cari handed Sharon a card and watched her stomp across the yard to Genevieve. She mouthed good luck to her friend and then got back in her car. She wasn't going to get anything from the officers in the driveway, but she'd gotten plenty from Sharon. She could find contact info for the other siblings back at her office. Two news station vans drove past her before she could start her car. She mentally wished Genevieve and Alex good luck and was about to pull away when a different middle-aged woman exited the house. The woman had on an apron, making Cari wonder if she was the housekeeper who had discovered the body. Before she could get into the car parked in front of hers, Cari sprang out of the vehicle, making the woman jump.

"Oh! Can I help you?" she asked uncertainly.

"I'm sorry. I didn't mean to startle you. I'm Cari Turnlyle from the Brenington Beagle. I'm writing a story about Gayle Smith and just learned of her untimely death. Did you work with her?" Cari asked gently.

The woman nodded slowly. "Not *with* her, but for her. I was her housekeeper. I cleaned her house every Monday. It didn't really need it that often, but that's what she wanted."

Cari noticed the woman's red-rimmed eyes. "I can see you were close to her. Have you known her a long time?"

Her eyes were shiny and Cari wondered if she was going to cry again. "I'm sorry. I'm…not up for talking right now. Perhaps another time."

"Of course, I understand. I'm very sorry for your loss. Would you give me your phone number?"

The woman dug into her apron pocket and pulled out a business card for cleaning services. Cari wasn't expecting something so formal but gratefully accepted it.

"That's my cell number on there. I had these made up to help keep my schedule full. If you know of anyone needing a house cleaner, I've got an opening," she said wistfully.

"Thank you, Ms., uh," Cari glanced at the card. "McIlvain. I'll call or text later and we can set up a time for lunch or coffee tomorrow."

The woman nodded and got in her car. Cari rubbed her locket as she watched her drive away. Ms. McIlvain was more attached to her employer than she was willing to say.

* * * * *

Alex felt his hand tightening around the pen as he listened to the victim's sister. He could see Genevieve was trying to conceal her irritation with the woman too. She refused to sit and paced around the room while she talked with them. Alex's jaw worked back and forth in frustration.

"…you see, no one really knew Gayle or Natasha or whatever we're supposed to call her. She was a recluse."

"Ms. Chiddy—" Genevieve started.

"For the *last* time, it's just Sharon. I hate that stupid name," Sharon retorted angrily. "Mr. *Chiddy* is not part of our lives anymore. He was not here, nor was he invited to the party last night."

Alex pressed her. "You're divorced?"

She rolled her eyes again. "Catching on quick, huh?"

"My apologies…Sharon. You mentioned the party and that several of your family members were in attendance. Who else was there?"

"Let's see," she stopped moving to count on her fingers. "Like I said, I couldn't talk my three children into coming even though I mentioned if we played nice with Auntie Gayle, she might leave us some of her millions."

Alex choked and coughed. "Millions? Your sister was a millionaire?"

Sharon rolled her eyes again. "How dumb are you? She was a *best-sell-ing-auth-or*," she enunciated each syllable. "She's sold thousands, probably tens of thousands of books. Of course, she's a millionaire."

Alex saw Genevieve scrawl something in her notebook and hoped she was making a note to look up their victim's actual net worth. This woman was infuriating. She was behaving like they were two dumb cops, and if he was being honest, he wasn't the sharpest tack, but Gen's mind could run circles around her. He decided to bite his tongue and let Gen take the lead.

"Of course. You were telling us who else was there." Genevieve prodded.

"You sure are pushy. Let me think. Her publicist. Or was it her publisher? Or maybe both? Hmm…about twenty no-name authors were here too. I got some of their business cards. I'm sure the dorks think I'll go buy their books now."

"Do you have the cards with you? Could we take a photo of them?" Genevieve asked her.

Sharon made a show of unzipping her cross-body bag and pulling out a designer wallet. "I put them all in here. Just a second."

They watched as she removed a large stack of at least twenty business cards from the side pocket. "Here they are. Should I spread them out on the coffee table here?"

"That would be great," Genevieve responded as she took out her phone to snap some photos. "Could we also get contact information for each of your other siblings?"

Sharon tossed the stack of cards onto the table and haphazardly spread them out. Alex felt a laugh starting to escape and forced a cough to mask it. He could feel Gen smirking at him even though her face remained blank. The woman was irritating, but Gen was able to keep her cool. She arranged the cards in an orderly manner and snapped a few photos. He looked back up at the woman who was scowling at them rather than offering any sort of contact information for her other siblings.

"Are you incapable of looking up anything for yourselves?" Sharon asked snottily.

When neither of them responded, she huffed and pulled out her cell phone. "Are you going to write these down, or what?"

"Or what…" Alex breathed almost imperceptibly. Genevieve cleared her throat and spoke up. "Alex, could you take a pic of her contacts while I get these business cards squared away?"

"No can do," he held up his flip phone and waved it at her. "I don't have a camera."

"No problem, T-rex. I'm finished with the cards now. Sharon, it looks like we have similar phones. Can you just air drop those contacts to me?" she asked. She sure loved to criticize his technology skills or lack thereof.

"You're lucky I know how to do this. My sister-in-law showed me last night when we were taking photos at the party," she said as she tapped away at her phone screen. "I'll air drop the link to the party invite too. It has the whole guest list on it."

"Got it. Thank you, Sharon. We need you and the rest of Ms. Smith's siblings to stay in the area for the next few days while we sort this out," Genevieve told her.

"Sort this out?! What does that even mean?" Sharon reeled at her.

Alex cleared his throat and stood up. "Ma'am, your sister's death is currently classified as suspicious. It's going to take some time to look into what happened last night."

Sharon huffed. "Doug doesn't *do anything*, so he won't care if you make him stay. My twin brothers have real jobs and lives, though. This could be very disruptive."

Alex wondered if Genevieve also noticed Sharon's attitude about her brothers' potential job disruption. She almost appeared pleased by it.

Alex tilted his head. "Did all of the people on the electronic list attend the party?"

Sharon rolled her eyes. "How should I know? Are we almost finished? When can I see my sister?"

"I'm sorry, Sharon, but you're going to have to wait until after the medical examiner is finished with her. You'll be able to view her at the station, possibly later today," Genevieve said gently, hoping not to spark another outburst.

Sharon frowned and crossed her arms over her chest. "Did you have any other questions, or can I leave?"

"Just a few more questions," Alex responded. "How long had your sister lived in the Brenington area?"

"Hmmm…maybe twenty years? I didn't really keep track." She sat down on a recliner.

Finally.

"Where did she live before that?" Genevieve asked, looking relieved the woman had stopped pacing.

"Um, I don't really remember. Penny will know."

"You mentioned you have children, but said they didn't come to the party. Did anyone else accompany you to the party?" Genevieve asked.

Sharon glared at her. "No, I went alone."

"Okay. I think that's all for now, Sharon. Here's my card. Please give me a call if you think of anything else," Genevieve told her.

"So, you guys think she was murdered? That's why you're asking all these questions, right? Getting all her history and everything?" Sharon stood up and put her hands on her hips.

"We don't know anything at this time. As we said, her death is suspicious. Your sister seemed to be in decent health and was under seventy years old," Alex told her pointedly.

Sharon bent down and scooped up the business cards she'd dumped on the table. She shoved the cards into her bag and stomped over to the front door. Before she opened it, she turned back to the two detectives.

"I see the news stations are here already. I wonder what I can tell them." She glared at the two detectives.

"Ms., uh, Sharon, it would really be better if you could limit your interactions with the media—" Alex began.

"Oh, I've already talked to the newspaper woman. I can talk to whomever I want." She flipped her hair over her shoulder and lifted her chin as she marched outside. Alex scratched his head and sat back.

"I'm not sure I could like her less than I do," he grumbled.

Genevieve laughed. "She was pretty hard to get along with."

"Hard to believe she's divorced," he said sarcastically.

"Stop. You're terrible," she laughed. "What's our next step?"

He shrugged. "On the one hand, if she was murdered, we need to start tracking down everyone from the party. On the other hand, if she died of natural causes, then our work here is done."

Chapter 3

Cari sat down in her desk chair and waited for her computer to boot up. She wanted to speak with Sharon's sister, Penelope, next. From what the woman had said, Penelope seemed like the family member who would know the most about Gayle. After logging in and opening a browser window, she found Sharon Chiddy on Facebook and went to her friends list. Sharon hadn't mentioned her sister's last name, so Cari was hoping to find her on social media. Sure enough, Sharon had a friend named Penny Holbein. She opened Penny's page and scrolled through it a bit. Penny had just changed her profile photo to one with two small children and a woman with a very strong resemblance to the author. Another quick search gave her Penny's address.

Cari logged into LexisNexis to verify the woman's identity and hopefully find a cell phone number. She typed the name into the search bar, then selected the result with the matching address. She pumped her fist in the air when she spotted the cell phone number on the screen. Most people either blocked unknown numbers or let them ring to voicemail because of all the spam callers, so she was prepared to leave a voicemail if necessary. She punched the number into her cell phone and waited for it to ring. In the middle of the third ring, the woman's voicemail picked up.

"Hi, it's Penny. Leave me a message. Bye."

"Hi, Penny. My name is Cari Turnlyle. I'm looking into your sister Gayle's unfortunate death. I'm very sorry for your loss. Please give me a call back on this number or my work line when you have a chance."

She recited her work number and hung up the receiver. She drummed her fingers on her desk. Part of her wanted to send Penny a text, but part of her felt guilty about bothering a grieving family member. She decided to hold off texting her and spend time researching the other three siblings instead. She pulled out her notebook and looked at the list of names: Gary, Michael, and Douglas. All three had Facebook accounts and were friends with Sharon. She drew a line across the page and started with Gary.

Gary Smith was a dentist in upstate New York. He practiced at an office called Dendrite, Waller, and Smith, which sounded more like a law office than a dental office to Cari. She clicked over to the website to confirm Gary was one of the owners. The business was founded more than fifty years ago, so he was brought in as a partner much later. She went back to his profile and saw he was married with three adult children.

Cari tapped her pen on the desk. It felt pointless to research the victim's family when she didn't even know how the woman died. It could have been from natural causes. If it was, she only needed a cursory amount of information about the author's family. She opened a new tab and sighed. It was taking her a lot longer to get back in the swing of things since she returned from vacation. She felt like her thoughts were jumbled and unorganized. She ran her fingers through her brown curls and rolled her head around a few times.

She wanted to look up the books *Natasha Gillespie* had written before she looked into the siblings more. She typed in the author's name and the word books. Gillespie had a simple website that didn't include a photo. Cari figured that was because she wanted to remain anonymous until just recently. She wondered if the publicist would be updating the site at some point to reflect the change. One of the tabs in the menu across the top was 'BOOKS' so Cari clicked it and scrolled through the images of book covers. It looked like Gayle had churned out over fifteen books in her twenty years as an author. The most recent one, 'All-in Murder', had come out a few weeks ago. She clicked on the book cover to see what it was about. She'd only read two sentences of the description when she felt a hand on her chair. She jumped.

"Whoa, sorry, Turnlyle. Didn't mean to startle you. Have you found out anything more about the dead author?" Ollaman asked after removing his hand from her chair.

"I spoke with one of her sisters over at her home. She was fairly forthcoming with information, though it sounds like her family didn't know her very well. She promised to call me with any updates she learns from the police."

Ollaman raised his eyebrows. "Well done. Sounds like a good source of information for you. What else?"

"I was looking through her mystery series to get an idea of what kind of writing she did. Looks like she wrote thrillers. I've also left a message with her other sister. She was apparently closer with the middle sister than the youngest," Cari told him.

"What about the other story you mentioned earlier?" he asked.

"It turned out to be nothing…just a grieving family member," Cari told him.

Before Ollaman could respond, Cari's cell phone buzzed with an incoming call. She looked at the screen and saw it was Sharon Chiddy.

"This is the sister I've already spoken to. I need to take this," she told him as she answered the call.

Ollaman nodded and walked back toward his office. Cari noticed he stopped short and turned to watch from the doorway rather than go inside.

"Cari Turnlyle speaking," she answered.

"The newspaper chick, right?" Sharon's irritating voice sounded in her ear.

Cari grimaced. "That's me. How can I help you, Sharon?"

"Even though I told those idiot detectives I didn't know Gayle *at all*, they called to ask me if she regularly took melatonin or anything stronger to sleep," she paused. "I asked what they meant by anything stronger even though I have no idea what she took at all…ever. Anyway, they said there was an empty bottle of melatonin pills on her nightstand as well as an empty martini glass in the drawer of the nightstand—what a slob, right? They want to know if she drank a lot of alcohol at the party. How should I know that? I'm not her mother. They're going to test for it on the tox screen. I thought you'd want to know."

Cari started to respond, then realized Sharon had hung up. She wondered why the woman couldn't have sent a simple text but shrugged it off. She wrote down 'martini' and 'melatonin' on a fresh page in her notebook just as Ollaman waltzed back over.

"Get anything good?" he asked, rubbing his hands together.

Cari wondered if this was like a soap opera for him or where the extra interest stemmed from. He didn't usually micromanage her this much.

"Sharon said they found an empty bottle of melatonin and a martini glass. They're going to do a tox screen. I'm sure they were going to do one anyway."

"Hmm…I have no idea what that tells us," He cleared his throat and looked a little sheepish. "I'll let you get back to it."

* * * * *

Genevieve sat in Lieutenant Grusky's office waiting for Alex to return from the men's room. They had gotten a preliminary finding from CSU regarding one of the pill bottles at the victim's house. Initially, she didn't understand the implications of what Chris told them over the phone. He mentioned the melatonin again, along with the discovery of a martini glass in the drawer of her nightstand.

"Do you have any experience with melatonin, Viacorte?" Grusky asked her, bringing her back to the present.

"Sir?" she asked, confused.

"I'm not asking if you take it, Viacorte. Have you worked a case where it was involved before? Or do you know people who take it?"

She shook her head. "No, sir. It's new to me. Chris also mentioned a martini glass inside the nightstand."

"Right. That does seem like an odd place to put it."

"The medical examiner said combining the two could result in death, right?" she asked him.

"Yes. Dr. Green said it's very dangerous to combine the two, but we don't know that she had the melatonin last night. Just that it was near her bed." He looked up at the door and saw Alex starting to knock. "Runimoss, come on in."

"What's up, LT?" Alex asked as he sat down.

"This case with the deceased author needs a little more attention. I don't think we're ready to classify it as a homicide yet, but things get more and more suspicious by the minute."

Alex nodded. "Did the ME finish the tox screen yet?"

"Not yet. He's going to check for alcohol and melatonin, but it will be at least tomorrow before we hear back on that." He cleared his throat. "I was just telling Viacorte you need to find out what she drank at the party and if she regularly took melatonin. Maybe it was something she did every night and she didn't realize how it would interact with the martini."

"Did CSU dust for prints on the bottle?" Genevieve asked as she jotted down Grusky's requests.

"I don't know. Add that to the list. This case is starting to attract a lot of interest in the reading world. It's trending, as they say, on a lot of platforms. I already heard from the chief about how we need to get it sorted out yesterday. There will be a lot of people looking for leads and trying to get you to leak info. We cannot turn this into a circus. Do you understand? Keep a tight lid on it for now."

Genevieve felt her cheeks redden and noticed Grusky was looking at her when he said the last sentence. "Understood, sir."

"Dismissed." He nodded at the door.

Alex opened the door for her and she stood up to exit with him. He loved playing the gentleman with doors, mostly because he knew it got under her skin so much.

"Viacorte, hold up one second. Runimoss, get back to work," Grusky said before she reached the door.

Alex gave her a quizzical look, then shrugged and walked away. Genevieve pulled the door closed behind him and looked at her boss.

Genevieve cleared her throat. "Um, sir?"

Grusky was rearranging the stacks of papers and files on his desk. He cleared his throat. "Sit down."

She grimaced and sat in the chair nearest the door. She felt like a kid awaiting punishment in the principal's office. Grusky stood up and perched on the edge of his desk, rumpling several papers in the process.

"The chief is serious about not speaking with the press or anyone outside of this office," he began. "I know you have a, uh, working relationship with the journalist from the local newspaper, but until the chief lifts the restrictions, you need to keep your findings to yourself."

Genevieve knew it was risky to argue with a superior, but Cari's help had been invaluable to them in the past. "Sorry, sir. I think you can agree my friend at the newspaper is trustworthy. She's never leaked a case or published a story before I gave her the all-clear. I think she's a valuable asset to our team."

"Well, the chief doesn't see it that way," he responded.

She felt her cheeks heat up. "I understand, but I'm not going to give her evidence or reports. She is capable of finding out information that we aren't in some situations. Some people are more comfortable talking to a reporter than they are talking to a cop."

He nodded slowly. "I agree. Your friend has been critical in solving some of our cases in the last two years, but you need to be careful. The chief is pretty hot about this already. You're going to be the first person he thinks of if something gets leaked."

Genevieve gulped. "You would report me?"

"Don't give me reason to, Viacorte. Your actions reflect on this precinct whether you want them to or not." He nodded at the door again.

"Got it. Understood, sir." She stood up and started to open the door, but turned back when he inhaled sharply.

He looked at her pointedly. "And, Viacorte?"

"Yes, sir?" she asked timidly.

"I got the evaluation back from your time with the FBI today," he said as he squared a few papers in their various stacks on his desk. "They gave you high marks. Don't ruin your chances there by crossing the department on this case."

"Yes, sir."

She walked out of his office and closed the door behind her. Alex watched her walk back to their desks. His head was turned at an angle like he was trying to gauge if he should ask what she was up to. She walked past him like she hadn't noticed and started to sit at her desk when her phone buzzed with an incoming call. She pulled it out and glanced at the screen. It was Dureski, her contact with the FBI.

"I need to take this. I'll be right back," she said to Alex. His frown deepened as she passed his desk.

She slipped outside to take the call. "Hey, Dureski."

"I've been hoping to hear about some progress about the case we discussed when you were here," the older man said.

She pinched the bridge of her nose. "I haven't figured out a way in, yet. It's a bit complicated."

"You insinuated you were friends with these people," Dureski remarked.

She grimaced. "I am. It's just. I'm sorry. We caught another case here and I've had to put this on the back burner. I'll get it sorted out soon."

"We really need that contact, Viacorte," he grumbled. "Make it a priority."

The call ended. Genevieve shoved the phone into her pocket. She thought she had her foot in the door of the FBI, but this felt like she was sneaking inside through a window. She shook her head. She needed to focus on the case. She'd worry about Dureski later. She went back inside.

"Are you finally ready to get some work done?" Alex questioned her.

She didn't want to get into it with him, so she pretended not to notice his irritation. "Okay, if we assume she knowingly took the sleep aid, then this is an accidental OD, not a homicide," she proposed.

Genevieve typed it into a search engine and read aloud from the screen to Alex. "Both the medication and alcohol depress the central nervous system. No safe amount of melatonin can be combined with alcohol."

"We need to find out if there were prints on the bottle and the glass. Let's call down to CSU and see what they can tell us," Alex told her.

Genevieve frowned. "Maybe they've tested the martini glass for alcohol residue or something already. I guess we still don't know when the glass got there. It might not have been from the party."

"Just call down there and ask," he instructed her. "Ask for a list of contacts too. We only got the guest list and the siblings from the sister."

She looked at him. "What am I, your secretary?"

He shrugged. "Chris likes you more than me."

"Fine."

She picked up the phone receiver and punched in the extension for the CSU. Alex smirked at her while she waited for someone to answer. She returned the expression when Bob answered the call. Genevieve hit the speaker button and replaced the receiver.

"Hi, Bob. It's Genevieve. Alex and I were hoping you had a list of contacts from one of Gayle Smith's devices."

"Hey, Gen. Let me transfer you to Chris. He's working on that right now. Just a sec."

Alex's grin widened upon hearing Bob's words. "Told you it would be Chris."

She ignored him and waited for Chris to pick up.

"This is Chris."

"Chris! Great. Bob said you might have been able to pull a list of contacts for us from the victim's phone or laptop?" she asked nicely.

"Oh, hey Genevieve. Yeah, I have some stuff. Do you want to come down and look through it or…?"

"We're kind of in the middle of a few things. Could you just email it to me?" Genevieve requested.

"Oh, sure. I'll send it over now. Anything else?"

"I think we're okay. Oh, wait!" she clapped her hands together.

"What's up?" he asked.

"Did you dust the melatonin bottle for prints by any chance?"

"Let me send you back over to Bob," he said with a bit of disappointment.

"Thanks, Chris," Genevieve responded.

"Bob Hursley, CSU."

"It's Genevieve again. We're wondering about prints found on the bottle of melatonin now."

"One smudged print," Bob said quickly.

"What? Only one?" she asked dumbfoundedly.

"Yeah, only one and it was probably the vic's. The bedroom and bathroom were nearly devoid of prints," Bob responded.

Alex leaned forward in his chair and blinked. "Devoid? As in absent?"

"One and the same, Alex," Bob responded. "Any other questions for me?"

"What about the martini glass? Did it have prints?" she asked hopefully.

"The victim's prints were all over the martini glass. It had a lot of partials and smudges, so we can't be certain it's just her prints on there," Bob responded.

Genevieve had another idea. "What about other martini glasses?"

"Only one was found in the bedroom," Bob said in a confused tone.

"Right, but what about in the kitchen? Don't people usually buy more than one martini glass at a time? Was it from a set? Or was it from the catering company?"

"That's a good question. We didn't do a full inventory of the house since it isn't necessarily a homicide at this point. Can I help you with anything else?"

"That's all for now. Thanks, Bob," Genevieve said. She picked up the receiver to take it off speaker, then replaced it to end the call.

"Well, that's interesting. I would have guessed the pill bottle would have several prints, right?" Genevieve asked her partner.

"Right. It is pretty suspicious to have just the one print and so few prints in the bedroom and bathroom in general. It makes me think someone tried to clean up after themselves." Alex agreed. "Let's check with the alarm company and see if they can tell us about entries and exits."

Genevieve shook her head. "The housekeeper said the alarm was off, remember? She was expecting Ms. Smith to already be out of bed when she arrived and found the alarm off."

Alex rolled his eyes. "So, she either forgot to set it before getting in bed the night before…or someone else was in the house and left without setting it because they didn't know how."

"I would put money on sister Sharon, except she seemed completely indifferent when we called earlier to ask about Gayle taking sleeping aids. I got the impression she likes to tell people what she knows and show off about it somewhat," Genevieve observed.

"I don't know. She's mean and judgmental. I'm not ruling her out for anything." Alex disagreed. "Like I said, someone either didn't leave the party and was in the house after it ended, or they came back later."

Genevieve checked her email. "We have the contact list from her phone now. Chris sent it over as we asked. Let's check in with her agent or publicist. The guest list Sharon gave me didn't have contact information, just names, so we can grab the numbers from this list from Chris. It's going to be a lot of phone time, Alex. Will you be okay?" she asked sarcastically.

He narrowed his eyes at her. "I've been using phones longer than you've been breathing. Pull up the guest list. Better yet, print it out so I can write on it."

"That's more like it," she laughed. "One paper copy for the dinosaur coming right up."

"You're not funny."

* * * * *

Cari walked over to the break room to get some coffee. She needed to reset the day and get her thoughts organized. So far, she'd talked with one sibling, left a message with another, looked up some background on a third, and perused the author's website. She filled her tumbler with coffee and walked over to the refrigerator to see if there was any unexpired milk inside. She found some vanilla creamer and decided it would suffice. After stirring it into her coffee, she put the lid back on and returned to her desk.

She flipped the notebook to another new page and wrote 'timeline' across the top. She did a quick internet search to see when Gayle Smith was a guest on the Today Show. The woman had revealed her identity to America last Monday, had a party to celebrate on Sunday, and was found dead in her home this morning. Her death could be accidental, but it was equally likely her revelation triggered something that resulted in her death. *But what?* The woman wrote fiction, not biographies. It wasn't like she had shared someone's darkest secret. She drummed her fingers on her notebook trying to see a connection. Before one could surface, her cell phone rang with another incoming call.

"Cari Turnlyle speaking," she answered.

"Hi, Ms. Turnlyle. It's Penny Holbein. I got your message about Gayle. I'm just returning your call. Would you like to meet me somewhere instead of talking on the phone?"

The woman was soft-spoken and her words came out slowly, almost deliberately, as if she were reading them.

"Certainly. Thank you for calling me. Let me start by saying how sorry I am for your loss."

"Thank you. It's been…quite a shock," Penny said quietly.

I'm not sure where you're located," she glanced at her recently mixed coffee. "If you're nearby, we could meet at a coffee shop."

"I'm north of Brenington, just a spell. Close enough that I can get to anything near you within half an hour. Name a place and I'll meet you there."

"Okay, there's a local place I like to go to sometimes. I'll text you the address and see you there at 11:15?" she asked.

"That works. See you there."

Cari texted the address of the coffee shop and put her phone away. Before she could get back to researching Gayle Smith, her desk phone rang. The number wasn't familiar to her, so she hesitated before answering.

"This is Cari Turnlyle," she said cautiously.

"Oh! Ms. Turnlyle! I'm so glad you answered," a breathless Dahlia spoke into the phone.

"Dahlia? Did you find something?" Cari asked.

"Yes! I found this group on social media called 'False Suicides' so I joined it and there are other people in it with stories similar to mine and my great aunt's. I can email you a link to join and then you can see for yourself. All sorts of deaths are being written off as suicides because the police don't want to pursue the cases. Or they don't have time. Or whatever. But they aren't suicides!" Dahlia exclaimed.

Cari bit her lip as she composed her thoughts. Dahlia sounded so hopeful and she hated to disappoint her again. However, it seemed more likely that this group was full of people in the denial stage of grief.

"You have to see it from their perspective, Dahlia. If the police found a suicide note—"

"I told you! She didn't *write* that. She wouldn't!" Dahlia exclaimed.

Cari swallowed. The pain in Dahlia's voice cut deep. Cari felt torn; Ollaman wanted her investigating the author's death, but Dahlia earnestly believed someone had killed her great-aunt. She knew she should tell her no, but she also knew what it was like to feel like no one believed you.

"Go ahead and send it to me, Dahlia. I can't promise you I'll be able to look at it today. I have a different assignment which is going to require most of my time and attention," Cari told her, trying not to get her hopes up.

"But this is *big*! It's right up your alley. All these people have been killed and no one is investigating!" Dahlia's voice went up an octave.

Cari cringed. "I'm sorry, Dahlia. I wish I could do more, but I have to stick with my assignment. I'll keep you posted, okay?"

"Okay, bye."

The call ended. Cari felt guilty for not being able to do more for Dahlia, but it seemed like the woman was not ready to accept her aunt's death. She wasn't a therapist or a counselor; she couldn't help her in the way she needed it. She checked her watch and saw it was time to leave for the coffee shop. She locked her computer and gathered up her things. Sharon had told her Gayle was closer to Penny than she was to the other siblings. She hoped Penny could give her a better idea of the life Gayle led. It seemed like a mystery so far.

Chapter 4

Genevieve rubbed her temples. Going through the list of contacts and matching them up with Sharon's guest list was tedious work. She dialed the next number on the list and waited for someone to answer. She'd already left several messages and knew Alex had too. She heard the line click and hoped it wasn't another voicemail message.

"H-hello?" The stuttering voice sounded like an older woman, but she couldn't be certain.

"Is this Celeste Katarin?" Genevieve asked her.

"Uh, who's calling, p-please?"

"This is Detective Genevieve Viacorte with the Brenington police department. I'm calling about a friend of yours; her name is Gayle Smith."

"G-Gayle…oh, you mean Natasha. Yes, Gayle. D-d-did something happen?" she stuttered some more.

Genevieve took a breath before delivering the sad news to yet another friend of the victim. "I'm sorry to be the one to tell you, Ms. Katarin, but Ms. Smith died sometime late last night," Genevieve said gently.

"L-l-l-late…" she cleared her throat and started again. "Late last night? B-b-but her party was last night. She was fine. I saw her. It was a l-l-lovely party. I'm sorry about my stuttering. It's hard to control when I'm upset or nervous."

"No need to apologize. I can understand you just fine. You said you attended the party. How late did you stay?"

The woman took a breath and released it before speaking. "Let's see. I stayed through her toast around sunset. I gave her a hug and congratulated her. I always knew her as Natasha Gillespie, not Gayle. That was n-n-news to me last week too."

"You'd met her in person before?" Genevieve asked, surprised. None of the other authors admitted to meeting her before the party.

"Oh no, dear, uh, d-detective," she cleared her throat again and swallowed a bit loudly. "We were in a forum together for authors. Her books were more successful than mine. I wasn't j-j-jealous, but I was always surprised she did so well without ever holding a b-b-book signing or meet and greet."

"That does seem…different from what you'd expect," Genevieve responded. "You were saying you stayed at the party at least through the congratulatory toast. Did you leave right after that?"

"Yes, most of us did. It was starting to get dark and most of us are old or older, in my case. I don't like to d-drive in the dark," she explained.

Genevieve jotted down the woman's estimated departure from the party. "You said 'most of us' left at the same time. Do you mean the other authors at the party?"

"Yes, there were about twenty of us there, I think. We took up three tables and talked writing and b-b-books for a few hours. Natasha, uh, Gayle joined us off and on. I think some of her siblings stayed on after the toast. At least, it s-seemed like they were going to," she answered.

"You said earlier that Gayle seemed fine at the party. Nothing seemed off about her in any way?" Genevieve asked.

"Well…" the woman paused. "I don't really know how to answer that. Like I said, I only knew her from the forum and hadn't met her face-to-face before."

"Right. Uh, let's see. How would you describe Gayle's behavior or mannerisms during the party? Happy? Easy-going? Stand-off-ish? Sober? Drunk?" Genevieve tried a different angle.

"Um, happy, I guess. She was very business-like, for the most p-p-part. She seemed, well, grateful people had come to celebrate with her, but she wasn't very engaging with any of us," the woman responded slowly.

"Okay, did you notice if she was drinking a lot or more than others at the party?" Genevieve asked.

Ms. Katarin gasped. "D-d-did she die of alcohol poisoning?"

"We don't have an official cause of death yet, ma'am," Genevieve said quickly.

"Oh, I see. Well, I noticed she had a martini during the t-t-toast, but I can't say I noticed anything else. I'm sorry. I wish I could be more helpful," she apologized.

"Not a problem. That's all I need from you for now. Please don't hesitate to call if you remember anything else," Genevieve told her.

She hung up the phone and put an 'x' in the document next to the woman's name. She felt like she was having the same conversation over and over again. Maybe Alex was having more luck, but she doubted it. Their victim had kept to herself so much, no one really knew anything about her. Maybe her agent or publicist could tell them more. She rotated her chair to face Alex.

"I think we need to talk to the agent before we get too much further," she suggested.

"The agent or the publicist?" Alex asked.

"Both, I guess? Maybe they're the same person. I don't know a lot about publishing books," Genevieve admitted.

"I'm not sure either. It looks like she had an editor as well as a publicist," he responded as he leafed through the list of names.

"Then I think the publicist should be first. She will at least know whose idea it was to have the party, who took care of the guest list, and hopefully, who was there and for how long," Genevieve told him.

"Where is the publicist located?" he asked her.

"We only have a phone number. I'll call her and ask."

Genevieve picked up the desk phone receiver and punched in the number from the contact list. It rang three times before a woman answered.

"Janice Gummill speaking," a high-pitched, nasally voice rang in her ear.

"Hi, Ms. Gummill. This is Detective Viacorte with the Brenington PD. I'm calling in regards to one of your clients, Gayle Smith, a.k.a. Natasha Gillespie. Could my partner and I come by to speak with you?"

"My phone has been ringing nonstop about Gayle. I'm just devastated. I took a personal day because I just cannot handle the office, you know? Of course, I'll meet with you. I've heard rumors she was murdered. Is that true?"

"Uh, Ms. Gummill, if you could give me your address, we'll be on our way and answer any questions we can," Genevieve dodged her question.

"Oh, gawd. She was killed, wasn't she? Oh, the horror. What am I going to tell people?" Gummill moaned into the phone.

"Your address, ma'am?" Genevieve prodded.

"Oh, right. It's 2727 Stonybrook Trail. Uh, in Grand Oaks, just outside Brenington."

"We'll be there shortly. Thank you," Genevieve said and hung up the phone.

"She sounds dramatic," Alex commented.

Genevieve rubbed her ear. "This could be rough. I have her address. Ready to go?"

He grabbed the keys off the hook with a sly grin. "One step ahead of you."

She rolled her eyes and followed him out of the detective bay. He stopped to hold the door for her again. She glared at him and walked into the lobby. She hurried ahead to the exit and grabbed the door handle before he could.

"Age before beauty," she told him as he walked outside.

"Clever."

She had to jog to catch up to him as his long stride left her quickly behind. They reached the cruiser and he unlocked it.

"Maybe you should enter the 5k next week. You can probably walk faster than most people run," she encouraged him.

"Nah, I have no desire. I signed up to hand out water at the finish line and that's all I'm doing. It comes with a chair, which is even better."

Alex steered the cruiser away from the station and toward the highway. Genevieve pulled out her pocket notebook and a pen. She flipped through her notes from their conversation with Ms. McIlvain and Sharon Chiddy. So far, no one they'd spoken with knew much about Gayle Smith.

"Our victim really kept to herself. No one seems to know how she spent her time, other than writing, of course. Maybe her publicist will know a little more about her."

"She sounds like a mess. I could hear her voice screeching through the receiver. It will be a miracle if she's coherent at all," Alex commented.

"I'm guessing she has known the author for at least twenty years. Even if they only communicated over the phone, you get attached to people," Genevieve told him.

"She's also probably her most successful author. I bet she wasn't too excited to hear she was retiring," Alex responded.

"True, but killing her best client wasn't going to make that better," she countered.

"Think about it, though. When someone is killed, especially someone with some notoriety or fame, people take an interest. I bet she sold some books today. Her publicist probably gets a commission of some sort or a royalty from her sales."

She couldn't argue with his logic. "True, but we still can't say with certainty that she was killed. Hopefully, we can learn about some of her habits, though. All we know right now is she wrote books, drank coffee, and wasn't really a family person."

"She said Grand Oaks, right?" Alex asked, making a turn into the neighborhood. "What was the address again?"

"I have it pulled up on my phone. It's 2727 Stonybrook Trail—turn right here," she instructed as Alex almost blew past the woman's street.

"Screeee!" he laughed as they nearly two-wheeled the turn. "Made it…so 2727. We're in the fifteen hundreds. She must be way in the back."

Each home in Grand Oaks sat on at least half an acre of land. Genevieve had visited the neighborhood before, most recently when she spent an afternoon with Cari's sister and her kids. She was surprised their young family could afford a home in Grand Oaks; the houses all looked over 2500 square feet.

"Ms. Gummill must be very successful. This neighborhood is *posh*," Alex said, echoing her thoughts.

She laughed. "Did you just say posh?"

"What? Is that word not in the cool lingo anymore? Should I just say bruh, it's, uh, lit?" he shrugged.

"I think posh suits you better," she said, laughing again.

"Going back to what you said earlier, you're right; we don't know if this is a homicide. I think we'll get more out of the publicist if we don't treat her like a suspect," Alex remarked.

"Agreed. How soon until we get the tox screen results again?" she asked even though she knew the answer.

"I know…tomorrow feels like forever away. We could be wasting our time with all of this," Alex commiserated.

"But if she was murdered and we didn't do anything for 24 or more hours, we might never solve it," she countered.

They reached the address and Alex pulled the vehicle along the edge of the yard. There were no sidewalks or curbs and the posted speed limit ranged from fifteen to twenty miles an hour. Alex broke that law. Genevieve looked at the house and saw the curtains move back. Gummill must have been watching for them to arrive. The house sat back from the street at least one hundred feet. It had three white, wooden pillars along the front porch and an upstairs balcony with white railings. The front door was also painted white which contrasted nicely with the dark-colored bricks. A stone walkway led from the street to the porch. When they were halfway to the house, the front door opened, revealing a short, stocky woman with shiny black hair. She was wearing a white muumuu, which flapped in the breeze.

"Hello, hello! Hurry on inside," she called out, waving at them with a white handkerchief in one hand. "I don't want the neighbors to talk. Hurry on in."

Alex raised his eyebrows at Genevieve as they walked a little faster toward the house. Genevieve felt like the woman wanted the exact opposite as she was making a bit of a spectacle by shouting at them from the front door. She glanced down the street and didn't see evidence of any of Gummill's neighbors being home, let alone outside to eavesdrop. When they reached the house, she saw a band of silver hair accenting the woman's dark locks. Genevieve wondered if it was dyed or natural.

"Can I get you something to drink? Coffee, tea, water…mimosa?" she asked, picking up a champagne flute filled with something faintly yellow.

"I'm fine, thank you," Genevieve responded as Alex shook his head.

"What a lovely couple you make," the woman cooed. "You with your dark, brooding eyes…and you, the sweet, petite woman with such mysterious eyes. Goodness! It's like you can see right into my soul with those hazel orbs in your head."

Alex coughed into his hand, making Genevieve wonder if he had tried to keep from laughing or if he was caught off-guard by the woman's ridiculous statements. Genevieve was starting to think Alex had been spot-on when he said she might not be coherent. Her demeanor now was completely different than the one Genevieve heard on the phone just twenty minutes ago.

"We aren't a couple, ma'am. We're detectives," Alex told her pointedly.

"Yes, yes, of course. Have a seat. I'm sure you have lots of questions for me," she said as she perched on the arm of a white leather chair.

They sat across from her on a matching white leather sofa. The interior of the house was stark: only a single black and white painting was displayed on the opposite wall. The other walls were bare and the house hardly looked lived in.

"Ms. Gummill—" Alex began.

"Please, call me Janice. All my friends do," she interrupted coyly.

Alex tightened his jaw before continuing. "Janice, then. How well did you know Gayle Smith, a.k.a., Natasha Gillespie?"

"Oh, it's just like a real police show!" she exclaimed, causing Alex's eyes to widen. "Forgive me. This is my first murder."

"Ms. Smith's death has not been ruled to be a homicide yet, ma'am," Alex told her.

"Please, don't call me ma'am. It makes me sound so old," she whined. Genevieve resisted the urge to roll her eyes at the woman. She was easily over sixty years old.

"Janice, we're trying to get a better idea of how Gayle spent her time. Do you know if she had any hobbies?"

"Besides writing?" she laughed, then cleared her throat when they didn't respond. "Of course, that was her job, I suppose. I don't know. I think she just wrote all day, every day. She churned out more books than any of my other authors. Her books are still at the top of the charts too. Everyone loved her."

Genevieve hesitated. She wanted to ask about the author's drinking habits, but revealing the discovery of the martini glass could backfire. The woman did not seem like a cold-blooded killer, so she decided to go for it.

"Was Ms. Smith a martini drinker?"

Gummill's face clouded over. "Excuse me?"

"What was her drink of choice? Wine? Moscow Mule? Whiskey?" Alex prodded her.

"Oh, um, I have no idea. Maybe I saw her with wine last night. Or was it a martini glass? Hmmm…maybe she was an equal opportunity consumer, like me!" she exclaimed, tipping her mimosa glass back and taking a gulp.

"We understand she had a retirement party last night at her home. Did you plan that for her or with her?" Genevieve asked.

"Oh, that was all Gayle. Trust me, if I'd been in charge, the wine would have been *much* better and the guest list would have been much larger. I did manage to gain five new clients, thanks to Natasha, God rest her soul. I mean, thanks to Gayle."

"Were you there the whole time?" Genevieve asked her.

"Oh, of course! I tried to get Gayle to sign some books for people and set up a table with her books, and she did it reluctantly. She said it was just a casual get together commemorating the end of a successful writing career. I left just after ten, I think, when the catering crew was cleaning up—whoop!" Janice tried uncrossing and recrossing her legs from her perch. She lost her balance and slid onto the chair haphazardly. Somehow, the mimosa didn't spill.

"Are you okay?" Alex asked, rising from his seat.

"Oh, I'm fine. Just a bit tipsy, uh, clumsy," she corrected herself with a giggle.

"How many others stayed until the end?" Genevieve asked once Janice was settled into the chair.

"Hmm…maybe five or six, though some of those might have been servers from the catering crew. Let me look at my photos. I was constantly taking photos and videos…" she trailed off as she pulled out her cell phone. "Hmm…it looks like her brothers and their wives were around at the end—that is, the twin brothers. The youngest one left much earlier after he'd eaten way more than his share of the food. I guess that's it. Just the four of them." She tilted her head up and to the right. "Yeah, I remember now. They came to the party together and left just before me."

"Can you share your photos and videos with us?" Alex requested.

"Oh, honey! It's all on social media. Everywhere. Pick a platform. Janice is there," she winked at him.

Genevieve cleared her throat. "How well did you know Ms. Smith?"

Janice swung her head over to look at her. She shrugged. "As well as I know any of my clients."

"And that is…" Genevieve prodded.

"She wrote good books. We weren't, uh, besties or anything."

Alex sighed. "Could we get the name of the catering company? We would like to speak with them too."

"Of course, let me fetch my handbag. I grabbed one of their cards last night. I mean, I probably won't use them because they were a bit *average*, but in the right setting, it might work." She stood up a bit wobblily and walked down the hall, her bare feet slapping the hardwood.

Genevieve looked at Alex. He raised his eyebrows again. If nothing else, at least they could get in touch with the catering crew. She looked up when she heard the woman's footsteps returning. She waved a card in front of her as she walked down the hallway. Genevieve didn't see any signs of the aforementioned handbag.

"Here it is!" she handed the card to Genevieve. "Now, what other questions do you have?"

"How did you first connect with Ms. Smith? I assume you've been her publicist since her first book?" Alex asked.

"Yes, from the very beginning. I work alongside her publishing company, so once they accepted her manuscript, she was assigned to me. I got lucky with her. They just go down the list and assign new authors as they're received. You never know if you're going to get a one and done, but Gayle was the real deal. She's been my workhorse all these years. Her books practically sell themselves!"

"So, she has a separate person who's her publisher?" Genevieve asked.

"Oh, no. Not really. The 'publisher' is just the company. I represent them as a publicist. They accepted the book then assigned her to me. She happened to use an editor who has connections within the company, which helped her get her foot in the door. But Gayle was a natural. She could have gotten in on her own." Janice remarked.

Genevieve considered her last comment. "You've read her books too?"

Janice snorted. "Oh, I don't have time to *read* books. I just market them."

Alex spoke up again. "Can we get the name and contact info for her editor too?"

Janice gave him a mischievous grin. "I thought you might want that, so I grabbed her card too."

She pulled a second business card from somewhere within all the white, flowing fabric and handed it to Alex. He gave Genevieve a slight nod and then stood up.

"I think that's all we need for today," he told Janice.

Genevieve pulled out her card and reached toward the other woman. "This is my card; it has my direct line on it and my cell on the back. Give us a call if you think of anything else."

Chapter 5

Cari pulled into the coffee shop parking lot. She saw a middle-aged woman in a light pink top and khaki capri pants walking toward the entrance and wondered if it was Penny. She seemed to be about the right age. Her straight, sand-colored hair was streaked with grey and pulled back into a clasp at the base of her head. Her oversized purse thumped against her hip as she strode to the front door. Cari hurried to catch up to her.

"Ms. Holbein?" Cari called out to her.

The woman turned from the door and looked her way. "Cari? Oh good. I wasn't sure if I was keeping you waiting. Let's go inside and find a table…and please, call me Penny."

Cari reached out and pulled the door open for the older woman. "I'm truly sorry for your loss. Your sister Sharon said you and Gayle were close?"

Penny's eyes flashed in surprise. "Well, I guess I was probably the closest to her. I wouldn't say we were close. Uh, do they make good lattes here?"

Cari glanced at the menu. "I usually get regular coffee and add stuff to it, but it's never been bad."

"I love a good latte," Penny remarked as she stepped up to order. "Hi, yes. I'd like a large latte please. For here."

A male barista in a peach-colored polo keyed in her order. "That will be $7.04. Cash or card?"

Penny dug into her bag. "Uh, card. Here it is." She tapped a credit card against the payment screen and then signed it.

"Your order will be ready at the end of the counter," the barista told her.

"I'll get a large latte as well, hot and with honey, please," Cari said when it was her turn to order.

"Coming right up," the barista said as he flipped the screen toward her for her to pay.

"Thank you," the two women said in unison.

Cari spied an empty table off to the side and nodded her head at it. "I'll get our lattes if you'll get the table."

"It's a deal," she said enthusiastically.

The barista squeezed the honey container over one of the lattes and then slid the two mugs over to Cari. She adjusted her messenger bag and then picked them up.

"Here you go," she said, placing one mug in front of Penny.

"Thank you," Penny said, taking a sip. "Mmm, that's really good. Now, you have questions about Gayle. What can I tell you?"

Cari pulled out her digital recorder and held it up. "Is it okay if I record our conversation? I'm going to take notes, but don't want to miss anything."

Penny smiled. "Certainly."

"Thank you. Your sister Sharon called me earlier and mentioned a bottle of melatonin was found near Gayle's bed. Did your sister use sleep aids?"

Penny grimaced. "Sharon texted the family about that too. The truth is, none of us knew Gayle very well. She was a fairly private person, even before she became an author."

Cari raised her eyebrows. "You knew she was an author before her announcement?"

She shook her head. "Oh, no. I had no idea, just like everyone else. I now know when she started writing. I knew her just as well then as I do now, which is to say, I didn't really know her at all."

"What about your parents? Sharon mentioned they've been gone for a while, but was Gayle close with them?"

"Maybe at one time, but with six kids…the older ones are just expected to not only take care of themselves but keep the rest of us in line too. Our parents worked long hours; my mom shelved books at the library twelve hours a day and my dad was a car mechanic."

Cari made a note about the parents. "How much older was Gayle?"

"She was just thirteen months older than the twins, but six years older than me. I think the twins really wore my parents down. I'm two years older than Sharon, who is three years older than Doug."

Cari jotted down the age gaps. "It's like a math problem from high school."

Penny laughed. "It really is. Gayle was the leader of the pack, but she went to college and that was kind of the end of our interaction with her."

"Were you surprised to learn she'd become a famous author?" Cari asked. "I mean, was she a strong student in high school?"

"Um, well, I don't know about her grades in high school. I don't remember our parents getting onto her about grades or school, so I suppose she did well. They definitely got onto Sharon and me, but not Doug. I think they gave up on Doug. Anyway, no, I guess I wasn't surprised to find out she was an author. She did sometimes tell us bedtime stories. I'm pretty sure she just made them up on the fly."

"What about a journal or a diary? Did she keep one of those?" Cari asked hopefully.

Penny's eyes gleamed. "Well, as the younger sister, I did my fair share of snooping in her room. I did find a diary once, but it was locked and she caught me with it before I could force it open."

Cari laughed. "I did something similar to my older sister once; it was her cell phone, though, and I got in a lot of trouble for it."

Penny smiled. "I'm not sure I got in trouble at all. I never found it again, so she must have done a better job hiding it after that."

"I know you said you hadn't realized your sister was an author, but did you happen to read any of her books?" Cari asked.

Penny beamed. "I did! They're fantastic books. I'm a little behind in the series; I actually saw Donna, uh, that's Mike's wife, anyway. I saw Donna reading one when we were with them one time and she was raving about how good it was. Neither of us knew the books were written by our family member."

"I haven't read any of them, but I might have to add the series to my to-be-read list. They're mysteries, right?" Cari asked her.

Penny bobbed her head up and down. "Yes, suspense novels. She did such a great job of tucking little morsels into the dialogues or descriptions to help you figure out who-done-it before it was completely obvious."

Penny's phone jingled a short melody. "Oh, that's my cell phone. I got a text from someone. Just a sec. We're all scrambling to figure out about the funeral, but the police haven't released the body…" she trailed off and frowned as she looked at her phone screen.

"Is everything okay?" Cari asked her.

"You asked earlier about sleep aids. Sharon says she thinks Gayle overdosed. Combining melatonin and alcohol can result in a coma or death."

"Mind if I see the text?" Cari requested.

Penny turned the phone screen toward her. "Sure. Here it is."

Sounds like an overdose between the alcohol and the melatonin. Google says those should not be combined

Cari wrote "alcohol" in her notebook along with "sleep aid" and then looked up at Penny when the other woman started talking again. "I didn't realize you could overdose from a simple sleep aid and a martini. I hear of people taking melatonin for sleep a lot, but didn't realize it had an interaction risk like that."

"Was Gayle drinking a martini last night?"

Penny tilted her head as she considered Cari's question. "Hmm…I'm not sure now that you ask. I did see people with alcoholic drinks—I'm not a drinker myself, so I didn't really make note of what others were having."

Cari tried another angle. "Speaking of the party, Sharon told me most of the siblings were at the party last night. Did you happen to get any photos or videos?"

"Oh, yes! Actually, we're all tagged in them on Facebook. Why don't I friend you and you can see everything? Her publicist can operate Gayle's Facebook—well, her author Facebook page, I don't think she really had a personal one, so the publicist tagged all of us in a whole slew of photos and videos. Are you on Facebook? I know it isn't very popular with the younger crowd."

Cari nodded. "I am. If you type in Cari Turnlyle, I should pop up."

Penny ran her thumb over her screen and found the app. Cari waited while she typed her name into the search bar. The older woman looked up from her screen and scrutinized Cari's face.

"Is this you?" she asked, holding the phone out for Cari to see again.

The photo was of Cari and Bob from their recent trip to Wisconsin. Cari had the remains of a black eye from an unfortunate encounter with a kayak. She blushed.

"Uh, yes. That's me," she said choosing not to elaborate on her injury. "Let me get my phone out and I'll accept your request. I really appreciate this. Looking through the photos from the party will be a big help."

Cari's phone buzzed with an incoming call just as she pulled it from her bag. She recognized Dahlia's number on the screen and hit the decline option. She wondered how the young woman had gotten ahold of her cell phone number. Penny either didn't hear the vibration or was being polite.

Cari accepted the friend request and opened Penny's profile. Sure enough, Penny and several others were tagged in hundreds of photos. It said they were posted by Natasha Gillespie, just as expected. Cari scrolled through the tagged names again, but didn't see the publicist's name. Her phone buzzed again, alerting her to a new voicemail.

"Thank you again. Um, you said her book publicist actually posted these rather than Gayle. I don't see her name though. Do you know her? Or him?" she asked hopefully.

"Yes! We got to meet *her* last night. Her name is Janice Gummill. I think she gave me her card, though, why I can't say for sure. I have no literary aspirations," Penny said as she pulled her wallet from her purse. "Here it is. Janice Gummill. Go ahead and keep it. I have no need for it."

Cari accepted the card and glanced at it before tucking it into her pocket. "Thank you. I'm hoping her publicist can tell me a little bit more about Gayle, the person, rather than Natasha, the author."

"That could be a hard thing to discover," Penny said knowingly.

"Is the rest of your family close? I mean, do you get together for holidays and things? It seems like everyone lives in New York, right?" Cari asked her.

"We don't get together every year. Sharon is, well, you met her…and all of us except Doug have families of our own now. I'm sure it seems odd, us being so separate," Penny admitted.

"Did you used to have family holiday celebrations? Before people were married and had kids and so on?" Cari asked.

Penny thought about it a moment before answering. "Yeah, we still gathered for Thanksgiving and Christmas while I was in college, but Gayle didn't always come, or if she did, she only came for the meal or to give mom and dad a gift. Once mom and dad were gone, she never came again. It didn't take too many years of her being absent for everyone else to make other plans too. I send them all a Christmas card every year."

Cari nodded. "That's a nice tradition. My parents send out a bunch of cards every year too."

Penny looked at her watch. "Can I answer any more questions? I can stay a few more minutes, but I was hoping to have lunch with my grandkids today."

Cari raised her hands in an act of surrender. "Oh, and you should! I don't think there's anything else. I have your information if something comes up. Thank you so much for meeting with me."

"Happy to help. It was nice to meet you."

They got up and placed their mugs on the return shelf. Cari followed Penny to the door and waved goodbye as she turned to get back in her car. She should probably listen to the voicemail from Dahlia, but wanted to get back to her office and look into the author's publicist some more first. Dahlia would just have to wait.

* * * * *

Alex slowly keyed in his notes for their interview with the publicist. Janice Gummill was a bit odd in his opinion. He felt like she'd been putting on a show for them and wondered why. He could hear Genevieve rapidly typing on her keyboard and wondered if he could talk her into doing both reports. Probably not. He heard something vibrate and glanced her way.

"I need to take this. I'll be right back," she told him, rising from her seat.

He expected her to go to the break room, but she walked the opposite way and exited the building. He could see her through the openings in the blinds and wondered who was calling. He really hoped it wasn't the woman from the newspaper. Grusky had been pretty clear about where the department stood with this case. No media. Period. Genevieve was a rising star in the department, but her desire to operate outside the defined constraints bothered him.

It wasn't that he agreed with everything the department required. The new chief was a micromanager and would do everyone some good if he'd stay in his lane. If Alex was being honest, Cari Turnlyle *was* an asset to their investigations, but admitting that felt like a betrayal to his training. The press was never on the side of the police force, nor did they have the victims' best interests at heart. They just wanted the scoop and they wanted it first.

He watched Viacorte slip her phone back into her pocket and turned away before she caught him staring. Alex wasn't sure she could see through the windows with the sun shining off of them, but he didn't want to be accused of being nosy. What she did was not his problem. He heard the door open and looked up to see her walking back to their desks.

"Is everything okay?" he asked.

She shrugged. "Yeah, it's fine. Are you finished with that report yet?"

He sighed. "I just need to fill in two more sections of it. What did you think of the publicist?"

She smirked at him. "Are you sure you can type and listen at the same time?"

He made a show of forcefully punching the various keys. "I can do this all day."

"At that rate, it's going to take you all day. Hurry up, Grandpa."

* * * * *

The newspaper office was quieter than usual when Cari got back to her desk. She wondered where everyone was. As she logged into her computer, she remembered seeing an email about a ribbon cutting ceremony for a new business. Bryson Millar, the Beagle's newest journalist, had volunteered to cover it while Cari got caught up from her vacation.

She wanted to make a summary of her interview with Penny while it was still fresh in her mind. It sounded like Gayle had possibly caused her own death by combining a martini and melatonin, but she needed to look through the party photos to verify Gayle actually drank a martini last night. She also had no way of knowing if Gayle took any of the sleep aid. She drummed her fingers on her desk wondering who might know. *The housekeeper!* She found the woman's card in her bag and punched in the number on her cell phone.

"This is Myra McIlvain. Are you looking for a cleaning lady?" the woman's quiet voice spoke into the phone.

"Hi, Ms. McIlvain. It's Cari Turnlyle from earlier today," Cari said quickly, eager to ask about the martini glass. "I'm sorry to bother you again."

"Oh, right. You had said you were going to contact me about getting lunch or coffee tomorrow."

Cari cringed, having forgotten she'd said she'd call or text. "Yes, I had another question first, if you have a minute?"

"Certainly. What is it?"

"Do you know if Ms. Smith was in the habit of taking melatonin before bed?" Cari asked her.

"Melatonin? For sleeping?"

"Yes, you don't need a prescription for it," Cari responded.

"Hmmm. I never had to clean up after Gayle. I mean, I cleaned her house, of course, but it was always very tidy when I arrived," McIlvain told her.

"And you never snuck a peek into the medicine cabinet?" Cari asked hopefully.

The woman cleared her throat. "I wasn't nosy, but it would open on occasion when I was cleaning the mirror of the cabinet. It was one of those pressure-release type things. You pushed on it to get it to open."

"And?" Cari encouraged her.

"I think it had, uh, like Tylenol and toothpaste…a toothbrush. It was sparse, like most of her life."

Cari made a note. "What about martinis?"

"I'm sorry?" McIlvain sounded confused.

"Was she a martini drinker?" Cari clarified.

"Oh, I'm not sure; I always cleaned her home in the mornings," she said slowly.

"What about in the dishwasher? Did you ever empty that for her?" Cari prodded.

"Oh, of course! Only wine glasses or water glasses. I guess you could make a martini in another glass, right?"

"She didn't have a set of martini glasses?" Cari pressed her further.

"I never saw any. Is that important?" the older woman sounded concerned.

"It sounds like a martini glass was found in her bedside table—" Cari began to explain.

"Oh, she would *never*!" McIlvain exclaimed. "It's like I told you already. She was very tidy. Everything was kept in its place."

"I get the idea. Now, about getting coffee or lunch. Are you free tomorrow morning?"

"I'm cleaning a home until about one, but I could meet after that," she answered.

"How about 1:30 in downtown Brenington? I can text you the address," Cari offered.

"That should work. I'll see you then," she responded.

"Okay, thank you again, Ms. McIlvain."

"I'm not sure I helped, but you're welcome."

* * * * *

Cari kicked her shoes off in the direction of her bedroom and dropped her messenger bag onto the sofa. Yawning, she walked into the kitchen for some water. Her head had started hurting while she was researching death caused by alcohol and sleep aids like melatonin. She filled a glass with water and took a drink. She hadn't had a headache in almost a week and hoped this wasn't some lingering effect of getting a concussion. The doctor in Wisconsin had encouraged her to follow up with her local doctor, but she didn't have time for that. She was already behind at work.

She set the glass down and went to the bathroom to get some ibuprofen. Her watch pinged with an incoming text from Bob before she got there. He was running a few minutes late and wondered if he should grab some Chinese food for dinner. She responded in the affirmative and continued to the bathroom for the medication. As she started to pop the little tablets into her mouth, she wondered if Gayle Smith had done the same thing the previous night, not realizing what would happen. Cari returned to her glass of water and swallowed the pills.

She didn't want to look at any more screens until the headache was gone, so she sat down on the sofa and found her notebook inside the messenger bag. She made a note to look up what a bottle of melatonin looked like and what kind of warnings might be on it. She rubbed her eyes and yawned. It would be nice to just relax with Bob after a long workday. She had barely snuggled into her seat on the sofa when her cell phone buzzed with an incoming call. Glancing at her watch, she saw it was from her mom.

"Hi, Mom. How are you doing today?" Cari asked cautiously. She had a pretty good idea why her mom was calling.

"Oh, I'm doing just lovely, honey. How are you? Did you and Bob go running today?" she asked.

Cari tapped her foot impatiently. Her mom hadn't called to talk about running and she knew it. "We did. The 5k is on Saturday. I think it's—"

"That's great, honey. Hey, I was just wondering…" her mother began.

*Here it comes…*Cari thought.

"Have you set a date yet for the wedding? Your dad and I were looking at flights up to New York earlier and the prices are really good. I mean, we could always drive, of course. It might be better if we had another car there to help with errands and such. I guess Bea and Robby have vehicles too. What do you think?" her mother asked, reeling off statement after statement in rapid fire.

"Uh, what do I think about driving versus flying?" Cari asked, unsure which thing needed her opinion.

"About a date, sweetheart. Have you even talked about a date, yet? A lot of our friends have been asking and I don't know what to tell them," her mom protested.

"I'm sorry, Mom. We've barely been engaged three weeks. We both have a lot going on right now at work and—"

"Oh! Are you working on the story about the author who was murdered?!" her mom asked excitedly.

"I'm not sure her death has been ruled to be a homicide as of yet, Mom," Cari said calmly.

"Suspicious deaths are always ruled to be murders. Criminology 101. Trust me, I watch a lot of true crime podcasts." Her mom spoke matter-of-factly.

"More often than not. But, yes, I am looking into her death. Did you read her books, by any chance?" Cari asked with interest.

"Every single one. I'm basically a super fan. My book club down here reads every new book she writes. She is a fantastic writer. Those of us who know her books well know how to look for the little hidden clues she stows away within the text. I can't believe she's lived down the road from you this whole time and I never got to meet her," her mom said incredulously.

"Yeah, pretty crazy. Well, Mom, I'm still working on a few things here, so I need to let you go. Tell Dad I said hi. Love you."

"Love you too. Talk to Bob about dates!!" she called out as the call ended.

Cari sighed. She looked down at her notebook and flipped back a few pages. She had met with Ollaman and Bryson Millar on her first day back from vacation so they could divide up the various stories the newspaper was covering. Bryson preferred the political and business events while Cari usually covered local festivals and anything that allowed her to join forces with law enforcement. The Fourth of July was rapidly approaching and the Beagle was providing weekly coverage leading up to several community events. Brenington held an annual "Flame-Out Five-k" along with a parade, a barbecue, and, of course, fireworks at the end of the day. The Beagle was one of the big sponsors of the barbecue and supported all of the events by providing ad space at half the usual cost.

Cari ran her finger down the list of tasks and groaned. She had forgotten to send over the updated timeline for the 5k race and the parade to the copy editors before she left for the day. She also needed to write a quick summary of what people could expect from various vendors at the barbecue. All the information was in her inbox on her laptop, but it meant sitting in front of a screen again. She frowned and pulled out her laptop. She almost dropped it when a knock at the door startled her.

"Hey, it's Bob with dinner! Can you let me in?" he called out.

She set the computer on the coffee table and went to the door to let Bob in. He had two large bags of Chinese takeout in his hands. He had a little spot on the front of his grey polo shirt and a matching one on the knee of his khaki pants.

"Did you have something with ketchup for lunch today?" she asked with a smile.

He blushed. "I tried to wash it out with a paper towel in the men's room, but wasn't very successful. And it was barbecue sauce, thank you very much."

She laughed and stepped back to let him inside. "How was your day, other than the wayward barbecue sauce?"

He set the two bags on either side of her laptop. "Stressful. I can't talk about the case. The author's case. I'm sorry. I know we usually discuss some things, but they've put a tight lid on everyone for now. From what I've heard, the victim's sister leaks more information than a sieve, so the gag order could be short-lived."

She gave him a quick hug and a kiss on his cheek. "I understand. I guess I won't get to have any pow-wows with Genevieve either. You're definitely right about the sister. I think she put me on speed dial already."

"She's pretty fired up," he agreed. "I see your laptop is out. Did you have more work to do, or can we eat first?"

"We can definitely eat first. Well, you can. I've got to send a couple things to the copy editor really quick."

Cari picked up her laptop while Bob grabbed two plates from the kitchen. She logged into her email account and found the information from the various vendors. She still had her article about the barbecue saved from last year and could just tweak it a bit. She located the document and made the necessary changes. Then she opened the updated timeline from the race director and looked it over. She wrote up a quick summary about the race and how it benefitted the local fire department. She quickly scanned it for typos even though the copy editors should clean up any errors for her. Then she attached it to an email along with the article for the barbecue and sent it over just ahead of the deadline.

"Almost finished?" Bob asked between bites of fried rice.

"I just hit send. What did you order for me this time?" she asked as she slipped her laptop back into the messenger bag and moved it out of the way.

"I got some orange chicken and General Tsao's this time," he told her.

"Any edamame?" she asked with her eyebrows raised.

"Of course. It's in there somewhere. I got two orders of fried rice, which was overkill. We could have split one and still had some left over."

Just as Cari started to dig into one of the bags to find the edamame, her watch pinged. She glanced at her wrist and saw a reminder about the voicemail Dahlia left earlier in the day. Bob gave her a quizzical look.

"Who left you a voicemail?" he asked.

"Oh, I almost forgot to tell you about Dahlia," Cari answered reluctantly. "She called the newspaper this morning and asked to be transferred to me. Michelle obliged, of course. I mean, it *could* have been a great lead for a story."

"But?" Bob asked as she freed a few edamame beans from their pod and popped them into her mouth.

She covered her mouth and quickly swallowed the bite before responding. "Dahlia is a young woman—younger than us, in fact, who recently lost her great-aunt. She's really grief-stricken and I think possibly in a state of denial. She wanted me to go to her aunt's home to listen to her story, but I don't think there's anything I can do."

"Denial?" Bob asked in confusion.

Cari nodded. "Yes, when the police came to investigate her great-aunt's death, they found a suicide note *and* the woman had signed it. Dahlia does not accept this as a possibility. She thinks her great-aunt was murdered and she wanted me to investigate."

"Oh, wow!" Bob exclaimed. "She knows you aren't in law enforcement or even a private investigator, right?"

She bobbed her head up and down. "She does, but she's read some of my articles and I guess she hoped I would believe her…"

"And you would investigate what *really* happened." Bob finished for her. "That's nice of you to give her your cell phone number."

"I didn't. I think she weaseled it out of Michelle at some point today, but yes. She wants me to investigate. She called again while I was meeting with one of the deceased author's sisters…" she trailed off, unsure if Bob would stop her from finishing.

"You can tell me about your meeting. I just can't tell you anything we found out," Bob reassured her.

"Okay, I was meeting with Penny, who is child number three of five of Gayle Smith's siblings. She doesn't know the woman any better than anyone else I've talked to so far. She did give me a business card for Smith's, or maybe I should say Gillespie's publicist. Maybe that person knew her better."

"Are you going to listen to the voicemail?" he asked.

Cari noted his subtle job of changing the subject but kept it to herself. "I suppose I should. Just a sec."

She grabbed her messenger bag and fished out her cell phone so she could put the message on speaker. She unlocked it and pulled up the notification about the voicemail.

"Hi Cari. I hope it's okay I call you Cari. Um, anyway. Did you join the group yet? Some of the stories are so similar to Great-Aunt Vivian's. I told you her name is Vivian, right? Oh, yes, I did when we first spoke. Anyway, I made a big realization today. I went back to her house today to use her printer. I don't have one at my apartment, so I always print things at her place. Anyway, when I tried to print my document, the printer was out of ink. When I opened the printer to replace the cartridge, there was no—"

The message ended mid-sentence. Cari looked at Bob with her eyebrows raised. He had stopped eating and had a bite raised halfway to his mouth.

"Do you think she realizes her message got cut off?" Bob asked her.

"I have no idea. She was really rambling there," Cari commented.

"I think you're right. She is in denial and maybe somewhat lonely. I wonder if there's a grief support group that might be better for her to join," Bob mused and then put the fork in his mouth.

"I've thought about that too. I offered to help find her a grief counselor, but she wasn't interested. I'm not sure what to do. I'm hesitant to call her back because I don't want to encourage her to continue down this road, but I also don't want her to feel like she's being ignored."

Bob reached over to Cari's hand and squeezed it. "I'm not sure what the right answer is, Cari. I don't think it would hurt to give it another twelve hours before making a decision. She obviously isn't afraid to contact you."

She leaned in and gave him a hug. "Thanks for listening. I'll sleep on it and see how I feel about responding in the morning."

They ate the take-out food in silence for a few minutes. Cari wished she could talk to him about her thoughts regarding Gayle

Smith's death. It helped to bounce ideas off of people. She didn't want to get him into trouble at work. She took a drink of water and mulled over her discoveries from the day. Smith's house cleaner didn't think she was a martini drinker, yet a martini glass was found in the drawer of her nightstand. *Did she know she'd been poisoned and was trying to leave it as a clue or was she too delirious at that point to realize what she was doing?*

Cari's phone buzzed with an incoming call and startled her from her thoughts. *Dahlia again.*

"Are you going to answer it?" Bob asked her between bites.

She hesitated. "Ugh. I guess I should." She slid the green phone icon over to the right. "Hi, Dahlia. It's Cari. Is everything okay?"

"Cari! I'm glad I caught you this time. I hope I'm not being a nuisance. Would it be better if I sent texts? I mean, most people my age only text, but I wasn't sure if you were into that or not and—"

"Dahlia?" Cari asked, trying to get the young woman to focus.

"Sorry. Um. I called because, well, I mean, did you get my voicemail? I think I'm really on to something here."

Cari ran a hand through her curls and let out a breath. "I just listened to it. Dahlia, I—"

"I know what you're going to say. You think I'm searching for answers that aren't there. That I'm in denial. My mom told me the same thing, but she's wrong. I've been chatting outside of the group with six others who have a very similar story to Aunt Vivian's. Loved ones with trips scheduled, full calendars of activities, *happy people*, just gone and their deaths ruled to be suicide."

Cari absentmindedly rubbed her locket as she composed her thoughts. She didn't want to hurt the young woman any more than she was already hurting, but no one wanted to believe their loved one died in that way. Bob squeezed her leg and got up from the couch. She smiled at him and took a deep breath.

"Dahlia," she began slowly. "I understand it's hard to accept your great-aunt's death. It's hard to find closure, but I don't think this is the way. I'm sorry."

"Wait. Don't hang up. Can you at least look at the posts in the group? I can add you to it if you accept my friend request." Dahlia begged.

Cari bit her lip. She knew the young woman needed a friend, but she didn't know if she was really cut out for the job. She was almost thirty and Dahlia was still in college. "Okay, let me put you on speaker so I can pull up the app."

"Thank you so much! I know when you see these stories, you'll believe me," Dahlia exclaimed.

Cari pulled up Facebook and saw the pending friend request from Dahlia Roust. She didn't think the Gen Z crowd was into Facebook, but whatever. "Okay, I've accepted your friend request, but I'm kind of in the middle of dinner right now, so—"

"Oh my goodness. I am *so* sorry. I didn't pay attention to the time. I'll let you go. Thanks for looking into this for me. I know you can help us find the answers we need."

The call ended. Cari sighed and set her phone on the coffee table. She heard Bob in the kitchen and hoped he wasn't too mortified by her stack of dishes. She heard the water running and figured he was cleaning up for her. Again.

"Bob, you don't need to do my dishes!" she called out as she got off the sofa.

"Well, someone needs to!" he laughed. "How was your young friend? You said she's a young woman. How young?"

"She's a junior in college, so twenty, maybe twenty-one? She's very, uh, passionate about disproving her aunt's cause of death," Cari responded. "Here, let me finish these dishes. Then we can watch a few episodes of a show before we call it a night."

Bob tilted his head sideways and ran a hand over his scalp before responding. "I'm pretty beat after today. I'm probably going to head out. I know you're dying to talk about *the case* and have been on your best behavior."

Her shoulders slumped. "So, we're going to limit our time together because of the case?"

Bob frowned. "No, I just…I'm tired after processing the woman's bedroom and bathroom. It sounds like…never mind. I can't talk about it. We have more work ahead of us though. It seems like the victim's sister is sharing everything with you anyway, so maybe they'll ease up on the restrictions soon."

Cari put the dish she'd been rinsing into the dishwasher and turned the water off. "I'll finish these later. Let me walk you to the door."

Bob blocked her exit from the kitchen. "We've always known there would be a chance we would be involved with a case or a story where we couldn't collaborate, right?"

Her shoulders drooped. "Yes, but we've never really talked about it. I know I'm bad with boundaries, but I have gotten better. I don't want to jeopardize your job; I'm not going to try to weasel information out of you. You can trust me, Bob."

He pulled her into a hug and she rested her head on his chest for a moment. "I do trust you, Cari. I know you can be an asset to investigations like these and it frustrates me that we can't discuss it. How about for now, unless the chief lifts the restriction, we leave work at work?"

She pulled back and considered his idea. "I've always kind of worked wherever I am, but I can agree to set this investigation aside while we're together. Is that good enough?"

Bob blinked and let out a breath before responding. "I'm going to be the first one they suspect…well, me or Genevieve, I guess, if something gets leaked. We have to be really strict about it, okay?"

She mimed crossing an x over her chest. "Cross my heart, Bob. Are you sure you can't stay a little longer?"

He gave her a half smile. "I wasn't kidding when I said I was tired. Why don't we go somewhere for dinner tomorrow evening?"

She grabbed his hand and walked back into the living room. "It's a date. Do you want the fried rice for leftovers?"

He picked up the bag with the remaining box of rice. "Sure. I'll check in with you tomorrow at some point, okay?"

"Okay. I love you, Bob Hursley. We're going to figure out how to coincide with cases like this one, right?"

He put the bag back down and pulled her into an embrace. "Of course. I love you too, Cari."

They shared a quick kiss and then Bob picked up the rice again. "Talk to you tomorrow."

"Don't forget. We're running again tomorrow too. Six a.m. at the park," she reminded him.

He looked at the ceiling and then gave her a sheepish smile. "I still don't know why I agreed to this. Only five more days. Then, it's only walking for me."

"Just wait until you finish the race. You might never give this up," she said encouragingly before pecking him on the cheek again. "Goodnight. Thanks for dinner," Cari said as she closed the door and locked it behind him.

She really wanted to call Genevieve but figured her friend was under the same restrictions. At least her headache was gone. She pulled out her notebook and a pen. She wanted to organize her thoughts regarding Gayle Smith's death.

She didn't know why the police wanted to keep the investigation so tightly under wraps, but maybe it was because the victim was something of a celebrity. She still hadn't learned much about Gayle, the person, and wondered if the woman had any friends. Sharon had called Gayle a slob for leaving the martini glass in her bedside table, but the housekeeper was shocked to learn of it. Cari hoped Sharon would continue to feed her information from the police department. Her other sources were relegated to silence for now.

Chapter 6

Genevieve grabbed her coffee mug and started to walk toward the break room when Alex stopped her. He placed a hand on her arm and gestured with his head at their lieutenant's office. She looked through the gaps in the blinds and saw he was on the phone. He was definitely shouting into the phone and she wasn't sure when the last time his face had been that particular shade of red. They both flinched when the receiver slammed down. The door flew open and he marched over to their desks with a tablet in his hand. Genevieve quickly took a seat.

"Was I in some way unclear about not talking to the media about this case?" he growled at them.

"No, sir," they said in unison.

"Then why is there a tabloid headline announcing the author was *murdered* in her own home?!" he shouted, making other officers turn to look their way.

Genevieve looked at the screen he was holding up. She felt her hands get sweaty and her stomach flip-flopped. She never read the tabloids, so she didn't recognize the byline, though she was relieved it wasn't a post from the Beagle where Cari worked, not that she'd talked to her either. She leaned in to get a closer look and saw an image of a social media post along with the name 'Sharon Chiddy'.

"Um, sir? It looks like the tabloid is sharing information from a social media post by the author's sister. We spoke with Ms. Chiddy yesterday morning. When she left the interview, she mentioned speaking with the news vans she saw pulling up."

Grusky flipped the tablet back around and zoomed in on the post. She watched as his face relaxed and his color got closer to its normal hue. He grimaced and looked at them again.

"So it is. I guess the chief didn't see that either. I'll give him a call back. I'm sorry for overreacting. I take it you told her about the martini glass?"

"We called to ask if her sister was a martini drinker as a glass had been found in her nightstand. She didn't have a clue and called her sister a slob for leaving it there," Alex informed him.

"Well, let's try to limit the information we share with her from now on. We don't even know if she drank out of that glass recently."

Alex nodded. "Understood, sir. We'll keep things on a need-to-know basis as much as we can."

"Hopefully, they'll get the tox screen results back from the body and the glass this morning," he said as he ran his hand over his bald head. "Keep me updated on your progress."

He turned to walk back to his office. Genevieve gave him a moment to get settled, then raised her empty coffee mug at Alex. He lifted his already-filled mug.

"I'll be right back. Need a refill or anything?" she asked him.

"I'm good," he told her. "I'm going to start looking through the photos and videos from the party again, see if I can find that martini glass. Say, Gen?"

"What's up?" she asked hesitantly. Her heart rate was just returning to normal after the lieutenant's outburst.

"You aren't meeting with your reporter friend on this case, are you?" he asked, his brows furrowed.

She flinched. "Really? Now you're accusing me of being a leak too?"

He raised his hands in surrender. "No, I just…I know you and the reporter chick—"

"Her name is Cari and she's a journalist, not a reporter," Genevieve said icily.

"Hey, relax. I'm not pointing fingers, yet. I just don't want you to get in trouble. I know you two like to bounce ideas off each other…*and* I'm not saying it hasn't been productive or beneficial. I'm just saying you need to be careful right now."

"I haven't even talked to her this week. I'm sure she knows about the restriction. She's engaged to one of the CSU guys, remember?"

Alex looked down at his feet before responding. "Right. Hey, don't be mad. I've got your back, one hundred percent. I'm trying to look out for you, okay?"

Genevieve mumbled her appreciation and headed over to the breakroom. She quickly filled her mug and then made her way back to their desks. That had been an adrenaline-filled start to the morning. She brushed aside the grumpiness she felt at Alex's earlier questions. Hopefully, they could get a handle on the flow of information. Genevieve took a sip of coffee and looked at her computer screen again. She scrolled through the thumbnails of photos, looking for any with the author in them.

"Alex, look at this one," she said, pointing at the screen as she enlarged the photo.

"Okay, so we have her with a martini glass. Are these photos time-stamped somehow?" he asked her.

"Let me see what's listed. It depends on how the photo was uploaded. It might not be the original file, in which case the time-stamp would be meaningless."

She scrolled down a bit to see what details were included in the uploaded file. It only listed when the image was uploaded to the album, not when it was originally taken.

"We're going to need to ask for the originals on these," she told him. "I'll call Janice and tell her we're sending a CSU tech over to get the original images from her. You call down to CSU and see if one of them can go get them."

Alex nodded and picked up the receiver of his desk phone. She found the publicist's number and called her again.

"It's Janice," the woman's nasally voice said into Genevieve's ear.

She exhaled before speaking. "Hi, Janice. It's Detective Viacorte from the Brenington PD. We met yesterday regarding the death of Gayle Smith."

"Of course, of course. The lovely, petite detective woman with the tall, dark, and handsome partner. How are you?" she cooed into the phone.

Genevieve cringed. "Just fine, thank you. We have been looking through the photos you shared on social media and need to get the original files from you."

"Oh, huh. You're not going to take my phone, are you? Is that even legal?" she whined.

"We'll be sending a crime scene technician to your house. They can assist you with transferring the files to another device," Genevieve informed her. "Are you home right now? Or at the office?"

"I'm working from home today," Janice responded.

Alex wrote a name on a sheet of paper and held it up to her. She read it and then spoke again. "Our tech's name is Chris Luvenon. He'll have identification with him to verify who he is."

Genevieve heard Janice click her tongue. "Fine. I guess I'll just wait here until he arrives."

"Thank you so much, Janice. We appreciate it." She ended the call before the woman could complain further.

"CSU sent a team back to the victim's house to inventory glassware and dust the whole place for fingerprints," Alex told her. "Chris was one of the ones who stayed behind with Dr. Green."

"I hope they find something useful," she commented. "If someone had been in the author's house without permission, they knew a bit about cleaning up after themselves."

Alex's desk phone rang. He grabbed a pen and jotted something down in his notebook while he listened to the caller. Genevieve wondered if it was CSU calling about the tox screen or possibly the contents of the martini glass. She drummed her fingers on the desk while she waited for him to finish. He finally hung up the receiver and looked her way.

"That was CSU calling back. They got the results from the martini glass. The glass had barbiturates in it," he said grimly.

"So, someone spiked her drink somehow?" Genevieve asked.

"Maybe. We need to talk to Dr. Green about it. It's a prescription med…called methohexital. No idea if I'm saying that correctly."

"Lead the way, sir," she said as she stood up.

They took the stairs down to Dr. Green's office and the morgue. The medical examiner split his time between conducting autopsies and analyzing results from crime scene samples. They found him at his desk typing up a report on his computer.

"Hey, Dr. Green. Got a minute?" Alex asked as he knocked on the door they had just entered through.

The older man flinched and then rotated his chair around to face them. "Oh, detectives. I didn't hear you come in. Certainly. I'm guessing you're down here to talk about the methohexital?"

Genevieve smiled. "You guessed it. I've never heard of it."

Dr. Green spun his chair back to the computer and opened a web browser. He typed the drug name into a search bar and then selected one of the results. "Before we talk about the drug, I have an official time of death for you: twenty-three hundred hours on Sunday evening, give or take half an hour. Now then, on to the drug. Methohexital is used frequently in outpatient dental procedures as it is very fast-acting. It's typically administered via IV, but there are other formulations."

Alex rubbed his chin. "IV, does that mean it comes as a powder?"

"No. It usually comes in a vial. The medication is pulled from the vial with a syringe," Dr. Green explained.

"You said it's fast-acting. How fast is fast?" Genevieve asked.

"I'm going to have to do a little reading in that regard. When it's administered by injection, either IV or IM, it can reach the brain in minutes. This medication doesn't have an oral formulation. If it was swallowed, that changes things. I need to read about it some more and see if I can come up with a good estimate. Of course, the speed of delivery to the brain doesn't matter if it doesn't show up in our victim."

Genevieve jotted down the doctor's answers in her small notebook. "Who would have access to this type of med?"

Dr. Green turned to face her. "Let's see. Pharmacists, hospital physicians and nurses, dental professionals."

"Regular dentists or only oral surgeons?" she asked for clarification.

"Probably both. It depends on the office," he told her.

"Anything else we should know?" Alex asked raising and lowering himself on his toes.

"I'm still waiting on the tox screen results. I should have those for you later today. If your victim has barbiturates in her system, this death goes from suspicious to homicide."

They nodded their understanding. "Thanks, Dr. Green. Keep us posted."

"I always do," he said, turning back to his computer screen.

They pushed through the double doors and made their way back to the stairwell. Genevieve remembered seeing that one of Gayle Smith's siblings was a doctor of some sort. They knew so little about the victim it was hard to determine a motive for her death. A jealous sibling was just as likely as anyone.

"Let's talk to the five siblings," Alex suggested as he opened the door to their floor of the building.

"All at once?" she asked hesitantly. "One of the brothers is a doctor of some sort. Dr. Gary Smith, remember? Why don't we look up his practice first and talk to his office? Maybe they've had some of this stuff go missing."

They sat down at their desks and Genevieve pulled up the contact list again. She found Gary's name and ran a search to see what type of doctor he was. *A dentist.*

"He's a dentist. He's part owner of a dental practice south of here. I'm guessing he won't be at work today. Let's call over there and then we can talk to the other siblings," Genevieve suggested.

"Ring them up," Alex agreed.

She picked up the receiver and dialed the number for the dentist's office. It rang twice before an automated voice listed options for her. When it finally said, 'press nine to speak to the receptionist', she punched the number in relief.

"Robot?" Alex asked her.

She nodded. The line rang twice and she almost groaned before she heard a woman's voice come on the line. She thought she was about to get elevator music.

"This is Mandy with Dendrite, Waller, and Smith. How can I help you today?" she asked cheerfully.

"Hi, Mandy. I'm Detective Genevieve Viacorte with the Brenington police department. We're investigating the death of Dr. Smith's older sister—"

"Oh no! The one who just announced she's that famous author? How terrible!" Mandy exclaimed.

"Yes, I have a couple of questions for you, if you have a minute."

"Oooh! Are you calling for an alibi? Dr. Smith has been out, but I guess you probably know that," Mandy offered.

Genevieve resisted the urge to roll her eyes. "Uh, no. I need to know if your office uses a medication called methohexital."

"Oh, you mean Brevitol?" Mandy asked. "I think that's the generic you're referring to. People get them confused a lot. They're basically the same thing though."

Genevieve paused, unsure if the woman was confirming they used the med or not. "Does that mean your office uses it?"

"Oh, for sure. It's fairly common in dental practices," Mandy responded.

"Have you had any go missing?"

"Missing? Like, stolen?" she asked confusedly.

"I suppose it would be theft," Genevieve remarked.

She heard what sounded like typing for a few seconds before Mandy spoke again. "I'm going to have to put you on hold and see what we have in the med locker. I'll be right back!"

Genevieve covered the mouthpiece and turned to Alex. "The receptionist is checking their stock of methohexital to see if their records match their inventory."

She drummed her fingers on the desk while she waited. She figured it was a long shot for the brother to be responsible. He was most likely familiar with how the drug worked. The murder, if it was in fact a homicide they were dealing with, was well-shrouded and not sloppy. Their victim didn't show signs of a struggle. If they hadn't discovered the martini glass, they would have assumed she had an accidental overdose with the sleep aid and alcohol. She heard the line click and waited for Mandy to speak.

"Detective?" Mandy asked cheerfully.

"Yes, I'm here," Genevieve told her.

"All of our meds are present and accounted for. Did you have any other questions?"

Alex put his hand up to get her attention. He had written something on a notepad and was holding it up for her to read. She leaned in to get a better look.

Ask if the dentists have written prescriptions for the med recently.

"Can you tell me if any of your dentists have written prescriptions for, uh, Brevitol or methohexital recently?" she asked, double-checking she had the name correct.

"Oh, they wouldn't write a prescription for that. It would be administered in the office. You don't pick that up at the pharmacy and bring it to your oral surgery or something. They would only write prescriptions for pain meds or antibiotics or things like that," Mandy informed her.

Genevieve nodded. "Okay, that makes sense. Thanks for your help, Mandy."

"Oh, for sure. Bye!"

She hung up the receiver and made a note of the dental office practices regarding the med. It seemed like the dentist angle was a dead end for now. Alex cleared his throat.

"And? What did she say?" he asked her.

"They don't write prescriptions for it. I'm sure it shows up on the bill or claim summary, but it isn't something you'd pick up for yourself."

"Bummer. I thought we might have solved this thing just like that," he said, snapping his fingers.

"So, back to the siblings. Did you want to bring them in and talk to them all at once?"

He put his hands behind his head and leaned back in his chair. "No. Individually. I don't want them influencing each other. We especially need to talk to the twin brothers and their wives. They were some of the last people at the party."

"Besides the catering team," Genevieve remarked.

Alex opened his mouth to respond, then sat up. "You're right. We shouldn't eliminate anyone yet. Someone saw what she was drinking. Surely, one of them remembers. Remember, no leading questions. They already know about the martini glass. In hindsight, we probably should have asked the housekeeper about the victim's alcohol preferences rather than the sister."

Genevieve nodded. "Grusky told us to keep a tight lid on the investigation, but the victim's sister is basically the town gossip."

Alex sighed in agreement. "I think the chief is worried about the investigation turning into a media circus and making the department look incompetent. We can ask *Sharon* to stop sharing everything with the media, but we can't really make her do it."

"True. Honestly, I don't know what else we'll gain from speaking with her again at this point. Let's call the other four and let them know we need to meet with them."

"Works for me," he agreed. "You call the younger two; I'll call the twins."

"Wait, are we asking them to come here or are we going to them?" she asked as she lifted the receiver of her desk phone.

"Let's go to them. They're a bunch of gossipers, so it might be better to bring them all here, but we don't have enough rooms to keep them apart. I bet several of them are in the same hotel. I got the impression the two sisters live in the area, but the brothers might not."

"It's going to take some time to drive around to each of them, even if the brothers are at the same hotel. Should we go to Penelope's home first?" she asked.

Alex furrowed his brow and frowned. "How about you call the sister and find out where her brothers are staying? Then we can make a plan about who we see first."

"Works for me," she told him. "We also need to get in touch with the catering company so we can interview the servers from the party. Our suspect pool is still too large."

"One thing at a time," Alex said knowingly.

* * * * *

Cari opened her notebook and stared at her notes from the night before. While it wasn't exactly a smoking gun, the presence of the martini glass in the author's nightstand shifted the balance in favor of her being murdered. The house cleaner seemed certain Ms. Smith wouldn't have left a glass out of place. She also said she didn't remember the author owning a set of martini glasses. Perhaps it came from the catering company, which would boost its significance in the investigation. She needed to speak with the catering company, but didn't know which company that was. *But I do have the publicist's phone number. She'll know.*

Cari dug through her messenger bag and found the business card for the literary publicist, Janice Gummill. She quickly entered the number into her cell phone and pressed talk. The woman answered immediately.

"It's Janice."

Cari cringed at the grating sound of the woman's high-pitched, nasally voice. "Hi, Ms. Gummill, uh, Janice. I'm Cari Turnlyle with the Brenington Beagle," she paused. "How are you today?"

Cari heard the woman blow her nose, making a honking sound. "I'm hanging in there. I can't believe we lost Natasha, I mean, Gayle. It just doesn't seem real."

"I'm very sorry for your loss. Were you and Ms. Smith close?" Cari asked gently.

Another honk. "I mean, not really. Business associates would be more accurate."

"I understand. Janice, I was hoping you could give me the name or phone number for the catering company from the party Sunday night," Cari requested.

"Oh! Well, you know, I gave their business card to the two detectives who came by yesterday. Cute couple, do you know them?"

Cari's heart sank at the woman's words. Maybe she could at least remember the company's name. She hesitated before responding. *Had she called Gen and Alex a couple?*

"I wasn't aware they were a couple, but I'm familiar with Detectives Viacorte and Runimoss. Janice, do you happen to remember the name of the catering company? Was it local?" she asked, trying to keep the woman on track.

"Oh, I can do you one better. I snapped a pic of their card before I gave it away. Is this a cell phone you're calling me from? I can just send it on over!" Janice exclaimed proudly. "Luckily, the crime scene guy didn't delete all the photos from my phone when he came by to download the images to his little drive."

"That is a relief. Yes, this is my cell phone. I really appreciate this, Janice," Cari told her as she waited for the image to load. "There it is. Thank you again."

"Janice is always available to help," she responded.

Cari mentally debated asking the woman more questions. She could probably find out more about any party details from Sharon or Penny, but the woman seemed to be a bit of a busy-body and might know things others didn't. "Janice, was Gayle a martini drinker?"

"Isn't everyone?" Janice cackled.

Cari cleared her throat and swallowed, unsure how to respond. Thankfully, the awkward silence propelled Janice into actually answering her question. She blew her nose a third time, extra loud before speaking.

"Now that you mention it, I think I saw her with a martini glass toward the end of the party. The catering company was cleaning up and most of the guests had already left."

Cari leaned forward with interest. "Who was still around?"

"Well, some servers, of course…and her twin brothers and their wives. What are their names? Mark and Grant? Mmm…I think that's right."

Cari raised her eyebrows. Maybe the woman wasn't a busy-body, but a self-absorbed fool. "Were any of them drinking martinis?"

"The servers? They can't drink alcohol while they're working," Janice told her in a condescending tone.

"Oh, I meant the brothers or their wives," Cari clarified.

Janice giggled. "Oh, of course. I didn't pay attention. Maybe? You could check the party photos. Are you on social media?"

"Gayle's sister Penny helped get me connected to the photos from the party. Thank you."

"Wonderful. Any other questions for Janice?" she purred.

"I think that's it for now. Thank you for your time," Cari told her.

She ended the call and pulled up the photo Janice sent of the catering business. It had a website and a phone number. Cari wasn't sure if the rest of Janice's information was reliable, but at least she could reach out to the catering company and find out if they were missing any glasses.

Chapter 7

Genevieve sat at her desk as she looked up the other sister's name and phone number. Penelope, or Penny Holbein had been Gayle Smith's emergency contact according to Ms. McIlvain, the housekeeper. Genevieve punched her number into the corded phone on her desk and waited for her to pick up.

"This is Penny—careful! Sorry, I have family in the house. Who's calling?" a gentle voice spoke into the phone.

"This is Detective Genevieve Viacorte with Brenington PD. We were hoping we could come by and ask you a few questions," Genevieve tried to speak a little louder than normal. She could hear a bit of a raucous on the other end of the line.

"Oh! Sorry for the noise in the background. My children and grandchildren are just about to head home. They wanted to stay longer because…well, because of Gayle, but I assured them I would call if I needed anything. When did you want to come by? I live about twenty minutes from your station," she said, a bit frazzled.

"We could be there in about half an hour, if that works?" Genevieve asked hopefully.

"That will be just fine. Oh! Careful there. That's breakable," Ms. Holbein spoke in a diminutive voice, making Genevieve think it must be a child. "What was your name again?"

"Viacorte," Genevieve finished for her. "Just out of curiosity, are your brothers located nearby?"

"Oh, no, but they're still in town. They all got rooms at some swanky hotel in the city," she said jovially.

"Perfect. Thanks, Ms. Holbein," Genevieve cringed as she ended the call. Going into the city meant traffic and parking nightmares. Maybe they could take the metro in.

She ended the call and looked over at Alex. He raised his eyebrows.

"Bad news?" he asked.

"I mean, not exactly. The three brothers haven't left the area yet..." she trailed off.

"But?" Alex prodded.

"But they're staying at a hotel in the city," she finished. "The other sister, Ms. Holbein, is free to meet us in about half an hour. We can go from there to the hotel. I think we should call ahead in case they have sightseeing planned."

"I wish there was a way we could talk to them individually without one of them speaking to another while they wait. I guess that's inevitable."

"Honestly, they've probably already discussed and rehashed the evening. We can always bring someone in separately later if we need to isolate them for some reason," Genevieve suggested.

"Works for me," Alex agreed.

Genevieve stood up. "Why don't you grab your contact list and give each of them a call while I drive us to the Holbein house," she said as she grabbed the keys to the cruiser off the back wall.

"Oh, you're driving, huh?"

"Snooze, you lose, Alex," she told him as she moved past his desk toward the exit.

*****

Cari logged into Facebook to search for the catering company Opulent Eatery. Even though Facebook wasn't necessarily everyone's first choice in social media, most businesses seemed to still have a page. As she moved the mouse to the search bar, she saw she had several notifications. Normally, she only had one or two, but the little red circle displayed a six. She clicked on it and saw Dahlia had added her to the group rather than waiting for her to request to join. She started to move the mouse back over to the search bar but hesitated. The group seemed to be rather active; she was curious about what they might be sharing. She shrugged. It couldn't hurt to look for a minute. Then she could get back to researching the catering company. She selected the oldest notification.

Before reading the post, she decided to change the settings for the group so she wasn't notified every time someone posted. She scrolled back to the post. It was made by an anonymous member and needed to be expanded for her to see all of it. She clicked the 'see more' option and started to read:

Two weeks ago, I went to visit my uncle who lives nearby. He is a widower and gets rather lonely these days. I pick up groceries for him sometimes and do some light housework when it's needed. Occasionally, he'll join my husband and me for a baseball game or the symphony...we actually had symphony tickets for tomorrow. Anyway, when I knocked on the door, no one answered. He's getting older, so I thought he might be asleep. I have my own key, but only use it if he isn't home or doesn't answer the door in a timely manner. I let myself in and called out to him, but still got no response. At this point, I was a little worried he might have fallen and hit his head or something. I rushed through his home, calling out his name. I found him in his bed. It looked like he was asleep, but he was so, so very pale...almost grey really. I almost collapsed right then and there, but I somehow held it together. His chest wasn't moving; I knew he was gone. I called my husband and he told me I should call the authorities—who really knows what to do in a situation like this? Two police officers showed up and insisted on clearing the house even though I told them I was the only living soul there. In the process, we discovered a note on the kitchen table. It was from my uncle. He apologized and said something like 'it's better this way' and that was it. It was signed by him, so the police ruled it a suicide, but I know it's not—

"TURNLYLE!!!"

Cari jumped at the sound of her name. Ollaman was standing next to her chair and looking over her shoulder. She felt her cheeks flush.

"Yes, sir?" she asked timidly.

"What is this trash you're reading? What does it have to do with the dead author?" he asked, almost shouting.

She bit her lip and moved the mouse over to the search bar. "My apologies, sir. I was, uh…remember the other story I mentioned to you?"

He glared at her in response.

"Uh, never mind. I'll look into it later. I got a name for the catering company and was going to check out their social media to get a feel for their business before I give them a call. Did you need something from me?"

"I was coming by for an update. What do we know about the author's death so far?" he asked sternly.

Cari took a breath and let it out before responding. She couldn't figure out why Ollaman kept trying to micromanage her with this story. He usually let her run with things for the most part.

"I'm following up on the martini glass. Her house cleaner said she didn't own martini glasses, so this seems like a pretty big lead. I thought it might have come from the catering company, so my next step is to call them and see what they can tell me."

He pursed his lips and glowered at her. "Well, keep at it. And do your social media browsing on your own time!"

He turned on his heel and stomped back to his office. She bit down on her lip and tried not to be annoyed. The man was acting extra strange lately. In an effort to appease him, she minimized the window and unlocked her phone to look at the image of the business card again. The phone number was printed in a script font at the bottom, but Janice must not have the steadiest hands and some of the numbers were a bit blurry. She groaned and went back to the computer screen. She pulled up the window again and typed the catering company's name into the search bar.

Cari scrolled through the 'about' section to find their phone number. Opulent Eatery was based out of a neighboring town, but served most of the suburb area, including Brenington. It had opened about a decade ago and seemed to be doing well, if you believed the reviews people left. She found the phone number and punched it into her cell phone. It rang twice before a recorded message played in her ear.

You've reached Opulent Eatery. Thank you for choosing us for your catering needs. Press one to reserve a party. Press two to make changes to an already scheduled party. Press three for cancellations, but please keep in mind that your deposit is non-refundable...

"Get on with it," she mumbled under her breath as the recording continued with its options.

...for all other needs, press zero to speak to a representative.

Cari pressed zero and wondered if they really had a different receptionist for each option or if they were trying to minimize the number of questions he or she had to ask before speaking to someone. The line rang three more times and then clicked.

"Hello?" Cari asked uncertainly.

"Sorry about that. Hello! This is Ted with Opulent Eatery. How can I help you today?" The man's voice was upbeat and friendly.

"Hi, Ted. This is Cari Turnlyle with the Brenington Beagle. I'm looking into the death of Gayle Smith. I understand your company catered her party on Sunday evening and I had a few questions for you," she informed him.

"Oh wow, Ms. Turnlyle," he paused. "Can I call you Cari?"

"Of course!" she responded cheerfully.

"Yes, O-E did cater her party. I hadn't heard about her death. How terrible! I actually wasn't at the party. My staff of servers took care of serving the food and drinks for the event. What questions do you have?"

"Did any of your glassware go missing?" she asked pointedly.

"Glassware? Um, I haven't looked through the party notes. Let me pull it up and see what I can tell you."

She listened and heard typing and clicking through the phone's speaker. "Do you keep a tight inventory of glassware?"

The noises continued as he responded. "Tight? Well, I ask each of our servers to make a note if something gets broken, but we don't charge clients for breaks. It happens. Okay, I found the party from Sunday evening. It looks like Ms. Smith paid for an open bar and they went through several bottles of wine and two bottles of champagne…maybe there was a toast? Anyway, what else is on the list here? Ah, yes, our bartender made numerous cocktails over the course of the evening…let's see, glassware. Hmm…it looks like someone may have broken a martini glass, but other than that, everything is accounted for. Does that help?"

Cari frowned. "Can you be certain it was broken? Or could it just be missing?"

"We wash all the stemware and glassware once we return from the party; plates and silverware too, if that was part of the package. In this case, they used plastic disposable plates and plasticware, so it was all tossed on site and we only had to wash the glasses. As far as broken versus missing, I wouldn't be able to say one way or the other. One of our servers might remember."

"Could I get a list of names and phone numbers for your staff that evening?" Cari asked hopefully.

He hesitated. "I need to check with each of them before I hand over their contact information. Is there a number I can call once I do a little investigating for you? Or maybe an email?"

Cari recited her number and email to him. "Email would be my first choice, but I'll take a phone call too."

"Perfect. Any other questions?" he asked.

"I think that's all for now. Thank you for your time…and for your help with the staff. I appreciate it."

"You're most welcome. I'll be in touch. Have a good day!"

The call ended and Cari sighed. She wasn't sure if she'd learned anything from the rather long conversation. She could understand why Opulent Eatery was staying in business if the owner hired people with personalities like his. He was extremely friendly and patient.

*****

Genevieve drummed her fingers on the steering wheel as she drove toward the Holbein residence. Alex was on the phone with one of the victim's brothers. He didn't have the call on speaker, so she couldn't hear the other side of the conversation. His dinosaur phone probably didn't even have a speakerphone option. They were only a few minutes from their destination and she wanted to discuss a strategy with him before they arrived. She saw him close his phone and waited for him to speak.

"The brothers agreed to stay put for another day, possibly longer, if need be," Alex told her. "As much as I'd like to speak with each of them separately, it might be easier to just talk to them all in one room. We can watch them for any cues or hesitations and decide if we want to speak to anyone on their own later."

She bobbed her head. "That works. What about the sister? It seems like she might have been closest to our victim since she was her emergency contact."

"True. This family seems weird, though. I guess the brothers have some sort of relationship since they're all in the same hotel, but everyone seems to have these completely separate lives," he mused.

"Or maybe Gayle was a hermit and didn't interact with them at all," Genevieve proposed.

"That's entirely possible. I guess we'll see what Ms. Holbein can tell us. Are we almost there?" he asked.

She looked at the GPS display on her phone on the dashboard mount before responding. "Looks like two more turns. It's right there on the screen, Alex."

He shrugged. "Whatever. Did she say her family would be out of the house by the time we got there?"

"They should be. It sounded like they were on their way out the door when I spoke to her," Genevieve told him.

She pulled the cruiser along the curb and put it in park. The driveway was free of vehicles, making her hopeful that the woman wouldn't be distracted by small children. Alex unfolded his tall frame from the passenger seat and closed the door.

"Let's hope this sister is easier to talk to than the other one," he said to her as they walked up the sidewalk to the front door.

Genevieve saw someone quickly moving around the home and wondered if Penny was trying to straighten up before they got inside. She remembered her own mother doing that when she was growing up. The front door opened before they reached it and a middle-aged woman waved at them.

"Hello, detectives! I'm Penny. Come on in. I was just rearranging the furniture after our guests left," she stepped back to let them inside.

"Thank you for meeting with us, Ms. Holbein. I'm Detective Runimoss, and you spoke to my partner, Detective Viacorte on the phone," Alex said as he paused to let Genevieve enter first.

"Yes, yes, nice to meet you both. Please, call me Penny," she said kindly. "Can I get you something to drink? Coffee? Water?"

Genevieve and Alex both shook their heads no. "Penny, is your husband home too?"

"Coming!" A raspy man's voice called out from the interior of the home.

"Why don't you have a seat? Nelson will be right with us," Penny explained, gesturing to a large, dark green sofa positioned across the room from two recliner chairs. A well-loved coffee table sat in the middle of the room with coasters and a few stray marks, which Genevieve thought might have been left by some rogue crayons.

They took a seat on the sofa while Penny settled into the recliner on their left. Genevieve heard footsteps in the hallway and watched as a broad-chested man with a rather large gut ambled into the room. His thinning hair was combed over from one ear to the other, with a few wisps sliding out of place. He put a hand up to smooth them back over.

"Detectives. I'm Nelson Holbein. How can we help you today? Crazy thing, Gayle winding up dead," he said as he lowered himself into the other recliner.

Alex nodded at Genevieve to go ahead with questions. "We are very sorry for your loss and appreciate you taking the time to speak with us today. We understand you were both at the party she held on Sunday evening. What was it like? Did you notice anything out of the ordinary?"

Penny looked at Nelson, and they exchanged glances. "Well, you see, detectives, we'd never been to Gayle's home before this. She'd never invited us, so that in and of itself was out of the ordinary."

Genevieve's jaw dropped for a moment before she could recover. "You lived this close to one another and never went to her home?"

Nelson spoke up. "You would have had to have known Gayle, Detective. She didn't invite anyone over. She never married. Heck, we didn't even know she was an author!"

"As for the party, it was very nice. She said a few words, thanked people for coming—" Penny began.

"Had an open bar!" Nelson exclaimed. "That was my favorite part."

Alex chuckled. "Sounds like a fun evening. Did anyone at the party seem out of place?"

They both shrugged simultaneously. "It's hard to answer that. Like we said, everyone was out of place there. I'm guessing it was everyone's first time there besides for Gayle herself," Penny responded.

Genevieve tried the question a different way. "Did you see anyone bothering your sister, or did she seem uncomfortable around anyone?"

Their faces were blank. Nelson spoke first. "I didn't pay attention or see anything like that. I've only met Gayle a few times. I'm not sure I'd know if she was uncomfortable."

Penny nodded in agreement. "It wasn't a long party and we left a bit earlier than some of the other guests. Our grandchildren are pretty young and needed to get to bed. The party started around 6:30 and we left before 8:15."

"You mentioned an open bar. Did you see anyone drinking a martini?" Alex asked them.

The couple exchanged another glance. "Is this about the glass you found in her room?" Nelson asked.

Alex's eyes darkened. "We can't really get into the details of the case right now. We've had some leaks…you understand. So, martinis?"

Penny shook her head no. "For the life of me, I can't remember. Have you looked through the photos from the party? You might see something there. Nelson, do you remember who was drinking a martini?"

He frowned. "That book lady was. What was her name? Janice? And Sharon, of course."

"Sharon, your sister?" Genevieve clarified.

Penny nodded. "Oh, that's right. It seems like both Sharon and Gayle like martinis; I saw a photo of her with one in her hand, anyway. And, yes, Janice is the publicist's name. She gave me her card, but I, uh…" her face reddened.

"What is it?" Genevieve asked, leaning forward some.

The woman swallowed. "I hope I didn't do anything wrong. I met with a journalist the other morning; I guess it was yesterday—"

"The Turnlyle woman?" Alex barked.

Penny leaned back. "Oh, was that a mistake?"

Alex crossed his arms and frowned. Genevieve put a hand on his arm before he could say something rude. "It's completely fine, ma'am. Like my partner said, we are trying to keep the details of this case to ourselves while we sort out what happened. Sometimes, with the media, things can get away from us and muddy the waters a bit."

"Of course. I understand. If it helps, I didn't have anything to tell her either. I just didn't really know my sister. I know it sounds terrible, especially considering how close we are geographically. Gayle just wasn't built for family, I guess."

"We know Gayle moved back here about two decades ago. Where was she living before?" Genevieve asked.

Penny scrunched up her face. "Did we get a Christmas card from Gayle while she was gone? Or a postcard from somewhere?

Nelson shrugged. "Maybe? I can't remember."

Alex uncrossed his arms and leaned forward. "What about phone calls? Did you at least talk to her on occasion?"

The older woman winced. "She did call every now and then. I had a phone number for her, but she got a local number when she moved back. I've long since forgotten her old phone number."

Genevieve tried a different angle. "Where did Gayle go to college?"

Penny's face relaxed into a smile. "It was in Arizona. Um…it was Northern Arizona University."

"Do you know what she studied in college or when she graduated?" Alex asked.

Penny's smile faded. "I'm sorry. I have no idea. I was a self-absorbed pre-teen when she left."

"Just one more question, for my own curiosity," Genevieve said. "Did either of you read any of her books?"

Penny smiled proudly. "I've read every single one. I had no idea it was my sister writing them. They're really good mysteries. She writes, uh, wrote very well."

Alex stood up first and pulled a card from his pocket. "I think that about covers it. If you think of anything else, please give us a call."

Penny stood and walked them to the door. "We sure will, though I can't imagine there's anything else to tell you. I wish we could have been more helpful."

They shook hands with Penny and nodded their goodbyes to Nelson. Genevieve could tell Alex was brooding about something before they reached the cruiser. He yanked the passenger door open and squeezed into the seat.

"That felt like a waste of time," he grumbled. "How can no one know this woman?!"

Genevieve raised her eyebrows. "Someone knew her."

"And your journalist friend has her nose in this already too!" Alex growled without acknowledging her statement.

"Hey now, when are you going to let that go? I thought you were playing nice with Cari ever since she went to Wisconsin. You even told me your old mentor liked her," Genevieve challenged.

Alex crossed his arms. "Whatever. I'm sorry. I'm just frustrated. This person is like an enigma. You're right. Someone did know her and decided what they knew was worth killing her."

"We just need to figure out what that is. Maybe that will help us figure out who it is."

Alex frowned and rolled his eyes. "Thank you, Captain Obvious. I think we should take the metro into the city. Trying to drive in the city is a huge pain. We won't find anywhere to park and people will constantly be honking at us."

"One step ahead of you, Chief," Genevieve told him. "The nearest park-n-ride is just a few minutes from here. We can take the red or green line; I'm just trying to see which one gets us closer to their hotel. Okay, I found the hotel on the map. Let me see where that falls on the metro map…"

"Whoa! You can read a map?" Alex teased.

"Found it. We want the green line. Do you have a metro pass or should I buy you one from my phone?" she asked, ignoring his earlier question.

He pulled out his wallet and opened it. "I've got my own pass."

"Oh, a paper card. Why am I not surprised? If you ever joined the rest of the world and got a smartphone, you could just use your phone to ride," she jabbed back.

"No one is stealing my credit card information this way," he told her. "I'm guessing it will take us fifteen to twenty minutes to get into the city from here. I'll call Dr. Smith back and let him know we'll be ready to meet with them in half an hour."

"Perfect," she said as she started the car. "Penny seemed pretty normal, right?"

"Minus the fact she didn't visit her sister once in twenty years?" Alex asked.

"Well, obviously. She was much easier to talk to, and I got the feeling she told us everything she knew."

"Nelson was a little different. I felt like he was quick to throw out Janice's name when we mentioned martinis."

"True, but anyone who drank from the martini glass we found was going to really be struggling because of the barbiturate in it. I don't think the killer left it behind," she hypothesized as she steered them toward the park-n-ride.

"Well, not intentionally," Alex agreed.

"I'm trying to decide if I think the killer snuck inside her house and drugged her without her realizing it…"

"Or if they slipped something into her drink and then left the party?" Alex finished. "I can see it either way. We don't really know the timing of it yet. We know she died around eleven Sunday night, but was she drugged right before that or several hours earlier?"

"If we haven't heard from Dr. Green by the time we get back from speaking to the other siblings, we'll give him a call."

Chapter 8

Genevieve watched the walls of the underground tunnel whiz by the windows. Their stop was still three away, so they had a few minutes to spitball ideas before meeting with the brothers. She pulled out her cell phone and unlocked it.

"Do you even have service down here?" Alex asked, watching her.

She glanced at the screen. Zero bars. "Nope, but I'm connected to the wifi, so it doesn't matter."

Before he could respond, her screen lit up with an incoming call from Sharon Chiddy. She cringed and looked at Alex.

"You better answer it. Who knows what kind of rumors she'll sell to the press if you don't," he told her.

"Hi, Sharon. This is Detective Viacorte. How can I help you?"

"What's that sound in the background?" she asked snottily.

"It's the subway," Genevieve responded.

"Ugh. I hate that thing," she grumbled. "When are you getting off? Never mind. Why are you calling my brother's dental practice and harassing his staff about him being on drugs?!"

Genevieve's eyes popped open. "I'm sorry, what?"

"I was talking with my sister-in-law, Tonya, and she said his front office worker, I think her name is Mandy…anyway, she called to tell him *you* had called and implied he was mixed up with some kind of drug. Meth! You accused him of being a meth user or a meth dealer! That is not okay," Sharon screeched at her.

Genevieve's face reddened. She was glad the woman had called her rather than Alex, but still. It was hard to keep her emotions in check. "Sharon, let me explain what really happened. Let's both take a deep breath first."

"I'm breathing just fine," Sharon said icily.

"Okay, uh, great. I'd like to ask you to keep this to yourself as much as possible. Our chief of police and—"

"Just tell me already!" she growled.

Genevieve jumped at the woman's harsh tone. "Our crime scene unit found evidence of a barbiturate called meth-o-hex-i-tal, *not meth*, on a glass at your sister's home. We're trying to figure out the source of the drug. It is used in dentistry, so I'm sure you can understand why we needed to rule your brother's office out."

"Oh, for heaven's sake. That stupid, stupid woman. She's married to a dentist for crying out loud. She had better not be telling people *my brother* is a meth user. I will…"

The call ended. Genevieve looked at her screen to ensure it wasn't a dropped call, but Sharon had ended the connection. Satisfied that Sharon was finished yelling at her for now, she slipped the phone back into her pocket.

"Well? I could hear her yelling from over here." Alex said.

She rolled her head around to ease some of the tension in her neck. "Sharon accused us of telling Dr. Smith's office we thought he was selling meth."

Alex clamped a hand over his dropped jaw. "You're kidding, right?"

She shook her head. "No, not at all. I'm not sure where the miscommunication occurred, but at some point, when she heard *methohexital*, she thought it was the same thing as meth, or methamphetamines."

Alex clapped his hands together and giggled, drawing the attention of other passengers near them. He cleared his throat and lowered his voice. "Pretty comical. We're going to need to alert Grusky to this, though. It's possible she already lashed out on social media with this nonsense."

"Go for it. He already thinks I'm guilty of leaking our leads to the press," she told him matter-of-factly.

He flipped open his phone and showed her the screen. "No bars. You can make a wifi call though."

"How convenient for you," she grumbled as she dialed their lieutenant's number. "Hi, LT. It's Viacorte. We've had a, um, development of concern."

"What's that?" he asked.

"We just got a call from Sharon Chiddy, one of the victim's sisters—"

"I recognize the name, yes," he confirmed.

"Sharon was quite upset and thought we were accusing her brother Gary, the dentist, of being a meth dealer or maybe a meth user," she told him slowly.

"Viacorte, are you on the subway? What is all that noise?" he asked grumpily.

"Yes, sir, the subway. I tried to clarify what really happened and asked her not to share details, but she didn't really respond to that…" Genevieve trailed off a bit, unsure how her boss would respond.

He sighed. "Great. Well, there's not much else we can do. I'll let the chief know and see how he wants to handle it. Let me know what the brothers have to say."

"Will do. Thanks, LT."

She ended the call and shrugged in Alex's direction. They reached their stop and exited the subway car. Genevieve checked the map on her phone to see which direction they should go to get to the hotel. Alex jerked his head to the right.

"Come on. It's this way," he told her.

He pointed at the sun. "It's morning; the sun is still in the east. The hotel is east of the station, so we need to go right."

She looked at the phone screen. Sure enough, the hotel was east of their location. "Let's go see what the brothers can tell us."

* * * * *

Cari went back to Facebook and hoped Ollaman would realize she wasn't wasting time but looking at photos from the party. She took a quick peek at his office, but the door was closed. She didn't want to upset him again, but the party photos could help her get an idea of what happened without needing to speak to someone.

She typed Penny's name into the search bar and found her page. The party photos were the most recent thing shared. It said there were over two hundred images. She sighed and took a drink of water. This could take a while. She wished she had some sort of facial recognition software that could pull up all the photos the author was in. Unfortunately, she had to settle for her own eyes. She decided to look for any photos with martini glasses. She opened the album so each of the photos displayed as thumbnails. Only about fifteen were visible on her desktop screen at any one time, but she could still sift through them faster at this size. She scrolled through the photos and finally spied a tray of martini glasses in one. She enlarged the photo to get a better look.

A male server held a tray with five martinis on it. Someone in a green polo was pulling one off the tray, but their back was to the camera. She looked at the other faces in the image and saw Sharon was off to the side. She recognized the green shirt from other photos and scrolled back up to look for the man's face. Thankfully, the photos tagged people's faces if it recognized them, and the green-shirted man turned out to be Gayle's brother Gary. She made a note of it and scrolled back to the photo with the tray. In the next image, the server's tray only held one martini, but no one in the picture had one except for Gary. Cari scrolled down further and saw one photo was blurred a bit. When she enlarged it, she realized half of the image was skewed by a martini glass blocking part of the camera lens. She made a note that Janice must have had a martini too. She continued scrolling, but only saw a martini in one other person's hand: Sharon's. *Where is that other martini?!*

She went back to the first photo with the tray of five martinis and enlarged it. She had assumed the photos were posted in chronological order, but maybe they had been randomly jumbled for some reason. Sure enough, tucked between two photos of Gayle signing books, was a photo of the author with a full martini and a beautiful sunset in the background.

Cari looked at the three other names in her notebook: Gary, Janice, and Sharon. Did any of them have a motive to kill the author? She flipped back a page and read through her interview of Janice. The woman had mentioned Gayle having a martini at the end of the party. Surely, someone else had gotten other photos of it, but maybe the older crowd didn't take photos like her generation. She decided to look through one more time. She started at the end and scanned each one for Gayle. The last few photos only had her two brothers and their wives, Sharon and Gayle, in them. Sharon had mentioned the five of them were the last to leave. It seemed like Janice took most of the photos and only showed up in the ones in which she chose to take a selfie. She wanted to watch the videos to see if she could find Gayle drinking the martini at any point. The martini glass felt important, but she wasn't going to find anything else about it from the photos. As though on cue, her cell phone buzzed with an incoming call from Sharon.

"Hello, Sharon. This is Cari speaking,"

"I know. I called you," she said condescendingly. "I spoke to my brother Gary's wife earlier. He said someone from his dental office called to say the police were asking if his office used something called, just a sec, I wrote it down…it has the word meth in it—but before you freak out, it *is not* meth. Can you imagine? I mean, when Tonya first called me, she must have mispronounced it. I called his office and cleared that up before any rumors got spread. People can be downright *ruthless* with information, you know? Anyway, it's called methohexital and I think they must have found it in her system or maybe in that martini glass they were asking about yesterday. Thought you'd want to know!"

"Thanks, Shar—" Cari said to a dead line.

"She sure gets off the phone fast," she said to no one.

She looked at the cell phone screen and wished she could text Genevieve to ask about the drug and where it was found. She knew better than to bring it up with Bob; he already felt conspicuous just by being engaged to her. *Engaged!* She stole a glance at her left hand and relaxed. She'd remembered the ring today. The emerald cut diamond was in a channel setting in 18K yellow gold. It shimmered when the light caught it just right. It felt like just the right size for her hand. She admired it for half a minute longer before bringing her mind back to the author's death.

She opened a new tab so she could search for the drug Sharon mentioned. It took her a bit to get the spelling correct, but she finally found the information. It was a barbiturate and was sometimes used prior to dental procedures, amongst other things. She could easily connect the dots as to why Alex and Genevieve called the brother's dental practice. Sharon hadn't said what they found, so Cari thought it was likely they couldn't connect him to the medication. Still, Gary was one of the people with a martini glass. She underlined his name in her notebook and drew a line to where she'd written down the drug name.

On a whim, she typed the author's pen name into the search bar and filtered it for news articles. The most recent one was still from the gossip column and it didn't have an update. Cari had seen the article when she got back from running that morning and assumed Sharon was the source behind the gossip. She wondered if Sharon had decided sharing with tabloids wasn't in the best interest of the investigation after all. The newspaper hadn't gotten informed of a pending press conference, so that meant the brother most likely wasn't responsible for the author's death. She drummed her fingers on her desk. She needed more information and hoped the catering company would come through for her soon.

* * * * *

Alex knocked on the door of room 306 and took a step to the side. Genevieve hoped to avoid saying, "Brenington PD, please open the door," out of courtesy to the guests inside. She didn't want to frighten any other hotel guests with an announcement like that. She pulled out her detective shield and held it up to the peephole hoping they would realize who was outside and open the door. Thankfully, the hallway was clear. A few seconds later, 306 opened to reveal two middle-aged women and three men, one of whom had just opened the door in his bare feet. Alex pushed the door open further and held it ajar for her to walk through first. She gave him the side eye on her way by and ignored his smirk.

The room was part of a suite that connected to a second hotel room. It was complete with a TV, two easy chairs, a large sofa, a coffee table and a desk with a chair. The man who opened the door returned to his seat in the desk chair, facing away from the desk, while the other two squeezed onto the sofa with their wives. One of the women grabbed the remote and turned the TV off. Her hair was dyed platinum blonde and her makeup was done to perfection. She looked like she was less than forty years old, though Genevieve knew both wives were well into their fifties. She was dressed in a black pencil skirt and flowy red top along with red stiletto heels. Her attire stood in stark contrast to the other woman in the room, who wore jeans and a graphic tee. Her greying, mousy brown hair was pulled back in a low ponytail. The twin brothers were dressed identically, wearing khaki shorts, white polo shirts, and boat shoes without socks. The only difference she noticed was one wore wire-rimmed glasses. The third brother had on athletic shorts and a New York Knicks jersey.

The group of five eyed them cautiously. Genevieve slipped her badge back onto her belt and then pulled out her notebook. Rather than sit on either side of the sofa, both detectives chose to stand and face the family members.

"Thank you for meeting with us this morning. Let me start by saying how sorry we are for the loss of your loved one," she paused when the blonde woman snorted. "This shouldn't take too long; we'd like to go over some things from the party Sunday evening first," Genevieve said as she clicked her pen. "My name is Detective Viacorte and this is my partner, Detective Runimoss. If we could get your names first?"

The blonde woman spoke up first. "I'm Tonya Smith and this is my husband, Gary. He's a dentist." She gestured to the bespeckled twin.

"I'm Michael and this is my wife, Donna. Doug is the one on the chair looking at his phone," the other twin spoke up, earning a glare from his younger brother.

"I take it you two are identical twins?" she asked them as she wrote down their names.

The brothers nodded.

"Your sister's party ended at what time?" she asked them.

The women looked at their spouses before responding. "I think it was what, honey? 9:15, uh, 9:30 when we left?" Tonya proposed.

Donna shook her head. "No, it was after ten. We didn't get back here until almost eleven."

Tonya gave her an irritated glance. "Was it? I really think we made it back just in time to watch the news."

Doug mumbled something and they looked his way. "Did you want to add something, Mr. Smith?" Alex asked.

"I said the news comes on at eleven."

Tonya glared at him. "Whatever. We were vacationing in Chicago last week so we had to fly back here to come to this party. My sense of time is still off."

"You live in upstate New York, correct?" Genevieve asked.

"Yes. We wanted to do some sightseeing and see the fireworks here, so we'll be here for the rest of the week."

"You plan to drive home Sunday?" she asked for clarification.

"That's correct," Tonya responded.

"And everyone else?" Alex asked with a hint of frustration.

Donna looked at Michael, then back at Alex. "We drove too, so we don't really have a strict timetable."

"The hotel room is only booked through Saturday night, though," Tonya said with sass.

"Right, so I guess we're here until Sunday," Donna agreed.

"Doug, speak up already," Gary growled at him.

"I said I'm only staying as long as I have to," Doug grumbled. "I was barely at the party at all. I made an appearance, drank some free booze, and took an uber back here."

"Okay, back to the party. Should I estimate you left to come back here around 10:30?" Genevieve asked.

Their heads bobbed up and down in response.

"Tell me about the party. Did anyone feel out of place?"

"You mean, besides Doug in his Knicks gear?" Tonya giggled.

Genevieve coughed to avoid laughing at Donna's eyes rolling. "Yes, I mean, was anyone behaving oddly or maybe acting strangely around Miss Smith?"

"Just call her Gayle. It's too confusing otherwise," Tonya admonished her. "And none of us knew Gayle well. She was a complete recluse. We didn't even know she wrote all those books. Not that we'd read any of them anyway."

"I read them," Donna said quietly. "They're pretty good books."

"Clearly, you aren't the only one since she was invited onto the Today Show, but could it have hurt for her to be a little more forthcoming?" Tonya remarked.

"She left a good trail of breadcrumbs for her readers. Little clues along the way, you know? If you read the books carefully, you could usually figure out who the bad guy was before she out and out told you," Donna explained.

Michael ran a hand over his closely cropped hair. Genevieve had the impression he was about to raise his hand initially and tried to hide it after the fact. "Um, you asked about people out of place.

Everyone at the party seemed nice. The authors she invited were interesting to talk to as well. I thought it was a nice party."

"I can't remember, Michael. What do you do for a living?" Genevieve asked.

"I work for an architecture firm in the IT department," he told her.

"Doug is unemployed before you ask," Tonya said snottily.

"So is Tonya," Doug retorted audibly this time.

Genevieve grimaced. "How did the party end? Did Gayle declare it was over? Did the caterers pack up and that was your cue to leave?"

Alex interjected before anyone could answer. "Did Gayle go inside and leave you to take the hint?"

"I said she was a recluse, but even she wouldn't leave her own party before her guests did," Tonya rolled her eyes. Genevieve noticed Donna giving her sister-in-law a quizzical look before returning her eyes to the two detectives.

"Were people allowed in her home during the party?" Alex asked.

"Not really. She has a half-bath just inside her backdoor which was available for guests to use. She kept the French doors leading to the rest of the house closed, sort of implying you shouldn't pass that way," Michael responded.

"Pretty rude, if you ask me," Tonya muttered.

"Are you going to ask us about the martini glass or what?" Gary erupted, catching Genevieve off guard.

She gave him a slight smile. "That is on my list, yes. As you may have heard, our CSU techs found a used martini glass in Gayle's nightstand."

"In or *on*?" Tonya questioned her.

Alex stepped forward. "It was inside the top drawer of the nightstand."

"We're still looking through videos taken during the party, but did any of you see Gayle drinking a martini?"

The four heads on the couch bobbed up and down. Doug had gone back to his cell phone. "Doug! We're still talking to the detectives for crying out loud!" Tonya yelled at him.

He rolled his eyes and set his phone on his leg. "Yeah, I saw Gayle drinking a martini. Was she poisoned or something?"

"Or something," Alex mumbled. "We understand none of you knew Gayle well, even well enough to know whether or not she was a martini drinker. We were hoping maybe one of you saw something. Did she walk away from the drink at some point? Did she seem different after she started drinking it?"

"I told you she was poisoned," Doug responded.

"More like drugged, you idiot," Gary said quickly. "I saw her take a martini around the same time I had one. I think she had it when her publicist did a toast near the end of the evening."

Genevieve made a note. "Do you remember if she drank all of the martini?"

He looked up and to the right. "Hmmm, can't say that I do."

"Anyone else?" Alex encouraged.

"I didn't really pay attention. If I'd known she was going to die, maybe I would have been more attentive," Tonya shrugged and others nodded in agreement.

Genevieve scribbled another note. She could feel Alex growing frustrated and she had to admit, this family certainly had some weird dynamics. Oddest of all, none of their victim's siblings seemed upset or sad their sister had died.

Tonya sat up and smoothed her hair. "Did Gayle have, like, an estate or anything? I mean, did she have money?"

"We're still working through her financials. We can't really answer that right now," Alex responded curtly, causing Tonya to pout.

Genevieve cleared her throat. "We appreciate your time. Please do your best not to share our discussion with your peers or on social media. We're trying to keep the details of the case quiet while we figure out what happened."

"Did you tell Sharon? Because she never met a word she couldn't say twice," Tonya laughed bitterly.

"We have advised her in the same manner," Alex said through tight lips.

"I think that's all we need for now. Here's my card," she pulled out a business card and set it on the table. "Please give us a call if you think of anything, however irrelevant."

Alex beat her to the door and pulled it open for her. "After you, detective," he said overly sweetly.

"Cram it," she said under her breath.

They took the elevator back down to the lobby and exited the hotel. The wind had picked up since their arrival and blew Genevieve's hair into her face. She removed a hairband from her wrist and pulled her hair back into a low ponytail.

"Is that a female staple?" Alex asked, somewhat amused.

"Is what a staple?" she asked, looking around her.

"The hair thingy. Do women just grow up and have those on their wrists?"

She rolled her eyes. "The smart ones do. Now, where are we with this case? I've never met a family with a stranger dynamic. The sister-in-law, Tonya, was especially enjoyable. I bet she and Sharon get along smashingly."

"I'm getting a headache just imagining it," Alex remarked. "We do need to nail down her financials. Surely, Chris or someone with CSU has gotten into her computer by this point, right?"

"Seems reasonable. We can give them a call on our way back to the station."

"Our time of death was around eleven Sunday night. We need Dr. Green to get back to us with how long he thinks it would take for the drug to have an effect. If we assume the martini glass in her house was the same glass she was drinking from, then anyone still around while she has the glass in her hand is a suspect. That includes four of the people we just spoke to, as well as Janice and

Sharon," he speculated. "It's all still supposition until we find out if there was any of the drug in her system."

"And the catering crew," Genevieve reminded him as they walked down the steps to the subway station.

"What motive would anyone on the catering crew have to murder the author? This feels pre-meditated and planned. You don't just have a barbiturate in your back pocket."

"I'm just saying, we can't technically rule them out. None of the people we just spoke with struck me as having a guilty conscience. There was the one moment when Gary kind of erupted about the martini glass, but I think he was just set on edge because we spoke to his office, and they alerted him to it," she surmised.

"Agreed. He and his wife were a little off-putting. I noticed she tried to claim they left earlier than they did. It makes me wonder if he told his wife that if they could say they left earlier, all the better, in case we suspected them of spiking her drink."

"We ruled him out as the source of the methohexital, though. It didn't come from his office," she challenged.

"I know, but he strikes me as someone who wants to be above reproach. Not just not guilty, but not even suspected," Alex told her.

"One thing I want to follow up on is when we asked about Gayle turning in for the night before they left, Tonya scoffed at the idea."

"But Donna gave her a funny look, just briefly, I saw it," Alex commented.

"Yeah, I don't know what to make of that. No one challenged the assertion that Gayle stayed with them until the end of the party, but maybe she did steal away at some point for longer than just a quick restroom break?" she proposed.

"For what reason? Make a phone call?" Alex asked.

"I don't know, but I would like to chat with Donna about it. I'll put it on the list," she said as they sat on a bench near the landing.

The digital sign indicated the next train would arrive in three minutes. Genevieve took out her phone.

"I'm going to call CSU and see where they are with her computer. When we get back to our desks, let's call the catering company too. We need to get a list of names from them. Maybe one of their servers saw something useful."

Chapter 9

Cari felt like the morning was dragging on and leaving her little to show in the way of progress. She checked her watch. She still had almost two hours until she was meeting Ms. McIlvain for a late lunch. She had watched a handful of the videos the publicist shared on Facebook, including one with a toast to Gayle's accomplishments. Janice had been a little tipsy when she led the toast and needed to steady herself on the chair next to her a few times. It was the only video that interested Cari, as the others were spontaneous interviews of various guests. In the toast video, Gayle was holding a martini. She took a drink of it in response to the toast in her honor, so it was still mostly full at that point, which was close to sunset. Cari opened a search engine to see what time the sun had set on the evening of the party.

The results showed daylight ended at 8:31 p.m., but it also said that night didn't start until 10:36. She read some more and saw something about civil twilight and nautical twilight, which only added to her confusion. *Guess I should have paid more attention in those science classes.*

She pulled out her phone to text Bob and then hesitated. Technically, this was just a question about when the sun set, not a question about the case. She hoped he wasn't irritated and sent a text asking him for clarification on the various terms. Before she could set her phone down, it buzzed with an incoming call from him.

"Hey, Bob! Thanks for giving me a call," she said happily.

"Answering your question was more than a text can handle. I'll be as brief as I can," he said quickly. She could hear the wind in the background and figured he'd stepped outside to call her. Either that or he had gone to get coffee or…

"Are you with me?" Bob asked, interrupting her thoughts.

"Sorry, let's start from the top. I'm listening," she said sheepishly.

"Okay, you asked about twilight. Civil twilight is when the sky is still light, but the sun isn't visible. Nautical twilight is when you can start to see very bright planets; it's more of a deep dusk."

"That makes sense. So, if daylight ended at 8:31 p.m., but civil twilight didn't start until 9:04 p.m., would that mean the sun started to set at 8:31 and was down fully by 9:04?" she asked.

"More or less. How is your day going other than learning some new astronomy terms?" he teased her.

"It's slow, but that's just how it is sometimes, right? Ollaman seems irritable lately, so I better get off the phone. Thanks for your help. Love you!"

"Love you too. Hey, we never decided where we wanted to go for dinner," he reminded her.

"Uh, pick a place and text me. Gotta run," she ended the call as she watched Ollaman's office door and willed it to stay closed.

Satisfied that he wasn't about to stomp out and tell her to stop wasting time again, she looked at her computer screen. It seemed like Gayle's glass was still full at the start of sunset, so 8:31 p.m. At some point, she must have drunk some of the martini, if not all of it. None of the photos showed her drinking the martini, but maybe if the catering owner ever called her back, she could ask some of the servers about it.

* * * * *

Genevieve saw the message light on her desk phone blinking when they returned to the station. She picked up the receiver and entered the code to have it play back any messages. She put it on speaker so Alex could hear too.

Hi, uh, Detective Viacorte, this is Chris with CSU. I got into your victim's laptop and…well, if you could return my call.

Alex chuckled. "That sounded awkward. Guess you turned him down for a date one too many times, Viacorte."

Genevieve felt her cheeks redden. "Let me call him back."

"How is it going with your fireman, anyway?" Alex needled her.

She pursed her lips in irritation as she disconnected from the answering service. "I don't have a fireman…anyway, he's moving away…it's complicated."

She dialed the extension for CSU and waited for it to connect. She tried not to let Alex's comments get under her skin, but she liked to keep her personal life to herself. She fiddled with the cord on her desk phone while she waited for someone to answer.

"Hey, sorry. I know you're a private person. My bad, Gen. Don't give me that hurt puppy look," Alex apologized.

She ignored him for the moment as Chris picked up. "Hey, Chris, you're on speaker, by the way. It's Genevieve. We got your call. You mentioned the laptop?"

"Yeah, we got it unlocked and found several interesting files I think you'll want to see. She has a will. It has to be validated through Surrogate's Court, but assuming it's legit, it gives us a lot of information. It lists her lawyer's name, bank account info…" he trailed off, clicking something in the background.

"That's fantastic. Thanks, Chris. Should we come down or is this something you can email?" she asked him.

"I put it on a thumb drive. I can run it up to you. I already e-faxed it over to Surrogate's Court for validation," he responded.

Alex's face darkened a bit at the word 'e-faxed'. "What the hell is an e-fax?" he mouthed to her.

Stifling a laugh, she cleared her throat. "Perfect. See you in a bit."

She ended the call and looked at Alex. "An e-fax is like a regular fax, but you email it. It comes out on their fax machine."

"Why wouldn't you just fax it like a regular fax?" Alex said, annoyed.

"Because then he would have had to print it out and feed it through the fax machine. This saves several steps, Mr. Dinosaur," she teased him.

They heard the door to the stairs open, and a few seconds later, Chris arrived out of breath. Alex gave him the side eye.

"You didn't need to literally run it up here, man. Save your energy for Saturday. I put my money on you and your long, skinny legs winning."

Chris shrugged and smiled. "Cardio is cardio, man. Anyway, here's the thumb drive. You probably know this, but it will help to have her lawyer reach out to Surrogate's Court with his copy of the will. It's most likely notarized and will speed the process."

Genevieve nodded. "Thanks. We appreciate it."

Chris turned to go but stopped when Alex spoke again. "Any word on the tox screen yet?"

He shook his head. "Not that I've heard. I know Green will call you the minute he knows something."

Alex put his fist out for a bump and Chris complied on his way past. Genevieve logged into her computer and plugged the thumb drive into the USB port. She clicked through a few screens and then got the files open.

"Okay, here's the will. Let's see what we have," she said as she scrolled through the document. "Her lawyer's name is Taylor Gomer."

"Man or woman?" Alex asked.

Genevieve shrugged. "It doesn't say, but now we have her bank information and medical information. Do you want to call the lawyer, the banker, or the doctor?"

"This has bad joke written all over it," Alex punned.

She rolled her eyes. "Okay, funny guy. You get the lawyer and the banker. I'm calling her doctor."

Alex opened his mouth to protest, but Genevieve was already punching the numbers into her desk phone keypad. She smirked at him as she held the receiver up to her ear. He glared before leaning over her shoulder to write down the other two names and numbers.

The doctor's office had a recorded greeting that played after the call connected. Genevieve listened to the options and selected "speak with a receptionist." The elevator music continued, so she put the call on speaker and continued to look at the files Chris had included on the thumb drive. She saw one labeled "tax information" and opened it. The author's tax returns from the previous ten years were in the folder as well as several other items saved with the year as the file name. She was surprised to see her annual income was less than $50,000. She opened one of the other files and saw it was a copy of her property taxes. The house was over 3,000 square feet, which meant it had to be worth close to a million dollars. She switched back to the tax return and saw the woman didn't have a mortgage interest payment listed as part of her itemized return. She started to wave Alex over, but saw he'd connected with the bank or the law firm already. She grabbed a pen and scribbled a note about the property value versus the woman's income. It seemed like she'd paid off the house already, but how? Before she could dig deeper, the phone clicked and rang. She picked up the receiver and waited for someone to speak.

"Brenington Medical, this is Pam. How can I help you today?" The woman had a raspy voice.

"Hi, Pam. This is Detective Genevieve Viacorte with the Brenington PD. We're investigating the death of one of your patients, a Ms. Gayle Smith."

Pam cleared her throat before speaking, which only slightly lessened the raspy sound. "Date of birth?"

Genevieve scanned the files still open on her screen. "Uh, it's 2-21-1964."

She could hear Pam typing on the other end of the line. "We're going to need you to send a death certificate before we can release any files about a patient."

She closed her eyes and pinched the bridge of her nose. "Of course. What are your hours? I'll try to get the medical examiner to send it over today."

"We're open until five," Pam told her.

"We'd like to meet with her doctor, if at all possible," Genevieve mentioned.

"I'll make a note. Is there anything else I can help you with?" Pam asked.

"No, thank you. That's all I needed." Genevieve returned the receiver to its cradle and looked over at Alex.

He appeared to be off the phone, so she decided to ask him a question. "Did you reach the bank and the lawyer?"

"Yeah, the bank said we need a—"

"Death certificate? Yeah, I got that from the doctor's office too," Genevieve said with frustration in her voice.

"You knew we would, right?"

"Yes, I just would rather get some information over the phone for once. Ugh," she groaned. "What did the lawyer say?"

"He, yes, Taylor is a guy. He said he just got back from a vacation and hadn't seen the news. He looked it up while I was on the phone with him, though. I asked if he could help coordinate the validation of the will, and he's going to get started on it. He has time to meet with us tomorrow morning at nine," Alex said, reading from his notes.

"Okay, let's get the death certificate from Dr. Green and get it sent over to each of these offices. I'm hoping we can meet with her doctor this afternoon. Their office closes at five," Genevieve informed him.

Alex looked at his watch. "Sounds like it's time for lunch, then."

"Hold up. I was just looking through these files. Her declared income is much lower than what you'd expect for a house like that. It looks like it's paid off too," she turned her screen toward him.

He leaned forward and watched as she flipped between the two documents. "That does seem off. Maybe her lawyer can enlighten us tomorrow. C'mon. I'm hungry. Let's go get some tacos."

* * * * *

Cari watched the other videos from the author's party at 2x speed, but didn't see anything of interest in any of them. Janice had taken short clips of herself interviewing the other authors in attendance. After watching the collection, Cari had the feeling Janice was more interested in landing some new clients than she was in celebrating Gayle's success. She wondered who stayed the longest at the party. Looking through the photos again, she could see Penny's family left before sunset, and Doug was gone well before the toast began. Sharon had told her she didn't stay long, but she was present for the video at dusk and in some photos with her twin brothers when it was almost dark. Cari wrote down their names and added 'plus spouse' to the list of people present when Gayle started drinking the martini. She tapped her pencil. Someone could have dosed the martini well before she started drinking it. She frowned, realizing she had no idea how long the drug might be active or effective after being added to alcohol. She wanted to call Bob and ask, but already felt like she'd toed a little too close to that line for the day. As though he could feel her thinking about him, her watch lit up with a text.

How about The Yellow Duckling for dinner at 6:30?

She smiled. She'd first eaten at the restaurant with a man who had lost his daughter and was demanding people give her death attention. He'd been angry, but once he saw Cari wasn't giving up on his daughter's story, he calmed down. She responded to Bob's text.

Sounds delicious. Pick me up at home?

It's a date!

She laughed and then looked at her notebook to remember what she'd been thinking about before his text. *The martini and the drug.* She tried to think of who else she knew who could explain the science behind the medication to her. Cari opened the file manager on her computer and searched for her document where she kept a list of sources from other articles she'd written. She opened it up and scrolled through the list of names. *Rick Sawyer* stirred something in her memory. She read the description she'd included next to his name: *compounding pharmacist, friendly.*

"Let's hope you're ready for round two, Mr. Sawyer," Cari said as she dialed his number.

The line rang once and then clicked in her ear. "Brenington Compounding, this is Rick. How can I help you?"

"Rick!" Cari tried to control her excitement, but still felt like she shouted his name into the phone.

"Uh, yes? Who's calling, please?" he asked uncertainly.

"Sorry, I'm just glad I got you on the phone. It's Cari Turnlyle with the Brenington Beagle," she explained.

"Ah, yes. The aspiring journalist. How can I help you, Miss Turnlyle?" he asked.

"I'm doing some research on a medication called methohexital and was hoping you could answer some questions I have," she began.

"Research on methohexital, huh?" he asked skeptically.

She pursed her lips, unsure how to read his tone. "Yes, I'm writing an article on dental procedures and the use of both local and general anesthetics. I've been reading about the use of methohexital by dentists and wondered—?"

"Hypothetically speaking?"

"Well…" she started to explain, but he spoke again quickly.

"Because last time, you spun me some tale about research you were doing for a story with potential scenarios regarding a possible overdose when really you were trying to figure out if Anerva could be used to kill someone," he stated matter-of-factly.

Cari cringed. "Yes, that's right. You got me. I'm wondering what happens if someone's drink is spiked with it."

Rick laughed. "I'm just teasing. So, ingested methohexital, huh? Let me look it up on my pharm app here. Let's see…yeah, it's usually injected and fast-acting, but if someone took it by mouth…hmm…we can compare it to other drugs in that class. How large of a person are we talking about?"

Cari imagined the author and tried to estimate her weight. The woman was on the tall side, maybe five-foot-eight, but slender. "Let's say 145 pounds."

"Male? Female?" he asked next.

"Female."

"What sort of volume do you think they ingested?" he asked.

"Volume?" Cari asked confusedly.

"Yeah, like how much did she drink?" Rick explained.

"Oh, I don't know how much was in her drink, but it was in a martini. What is that, like six ounces?" Cari estimated.

"Ah, alcohol *and* drugs. This was a bad combo to try," Rick mused.

Cari waited for him to say more.

"Let's see, based on the normal formulation of the drug and the fact that it sounds like this person *was drugged* with it…" Rick mumbled a few more things unintelligibly before speaking up again. "Okay, I think I have a decent estimate for you. Now, remember, we made a lot of assumptions here, the biggest being we don't know the concentration of the drug spiked into the drink. I'm assuming it couldn't have been a large volume added as the drink was already full and the concentration of what was added is probably the most commonly dispensed. Based on what you've told me, I think the person would start feeling the effects of the drug within about ninety minutes. If they drank all of it, they were probably dead no more than two hours later unless they were able to get some medical help first."

Cari wrote a note of his findings. "Two hours. Okay. Got it. One more question. How long would the drug be active once it was in the alcohol?"

"Hmm…that's a good question. Let's see. Methohexital is a barbiturate, much like phenobarbital. I can't say for certain, but I think methohexital is probably soluble in alcohol. It can stay active at room temperature in water for weeks, so I don't think the alcohol changed it chemically."

"That means it was still active?" Cari asked for clarification.

"Yes, it most likely did not react with the alcohol even though ingesting it along with alcohol greatly increased its effects on the central nervous system," he told her.

"Okay, that makes sense. I really appreciate your help, Rick. I owe you one."

"I think you owe me two now. Am I at least going to get my name in the paper this time?"

"Oh, uh, I'll do my best to give you a shout out, okay? I can't promise my editor will keep it, though," she told him.

"I get it. Glad I could help."

The line went dead and Cari replaced the receiver. She looked at her notes. She needed to figure out when Gayle got the martini. Anyone who had left the party before that point didn't spike her drink. She really needed to talk to the servers from the party. Hopefully, they could remember when the guest of honor first asked for a martini. She knew she was operating on the assumption Gayle drank the spiked martini. It was equally possible the author took the glass and hid it in hopes the police could figure out whose it was and therefore, who killed her. Until the police department decided to have a press conference and share what they knew, she'd just have to keep following her instincts.

A realization hit her like a ton of bricks. She pressed her palm into her forehead. While she knew approximately how long it would take someone Gayle's size to succumb to the drug and alcohol combo, she didn't know the official time of death. She groaned. She wondered if the police were as frustrated as she was with these constraints. She couldn't ask Genevieve for the time of death, but maybe Ms. McIlvain overheard it while she was still in the house. It was finally time to meet her for lunch.

* * * * *

Genevieve watched Alex lick the grease off his fingers. They'd brought their tacos back to the detective bay so they could eat and work. She wasn't sure Alex was really made for multitasking, but he had at least avoided dripping grease on his computer keyboard. His pants were another story.

"Stop judging me. You're worse than my wife," Alex grumbled, but his grin gave away his real feelings.

"You're worse than a child. Those pants are totally ruined," she told him.

"Like, so totally ruined," he said and pretended to flip long hair over his shoulder.

She laughed and then cleared her throat. "Okay, we sent over the death certificate to the three offices. Let's see if we've heard back from any of them yet."

There weren't any messages on her desk phone, so she checked her email. She didn't find anything new there either. Alex was still wiping grease off his fingers.

"Anything on your side?" she asked him.

He refreshed his email screen. "No. You call the doctor's office back and I'll call the bank."

Genevieve found the phone number for the doctor's office and punched it into her desk phone again. She navigated their automated system and heard the same music from her call earlier in the day, so she put it on speaker. She hadn't finished combing through the financial information in the victim's tax return, so she opened it again while she waited.

Gayle Smith was earning less than $50,000 a year from selling her books. Her home was paid off, otherwise, she would have an interest payment as part of her itemized deductions. Genevieve opened a search browser so she could estimate the value of the author's home. She typed in the address and selected one of the results. The home wasn't on the market, but was valued around $780,000. She wanted to find out when the home was paid off. Unless the author had earned more in previous years, it seemed like the house was way out of her price range. She heard the phone line click and quickly grabbed the receiver with her left hand while making a note about the house financials with her right.

"Brenington Medical. This is Pam. How can I help you today?" The woman's voice sounded weary.

"Hi, Pam. It's Detective Viacorte. We spoke earlier about Gayle Smith. I was able to send over her death certificate via e-fax. Did you receive it?" Genevieve asked hopefully.

"Just one moment. I need to look through the notifications from our e-fax," she said slowly. Genevieve could hear her clicking and typing in the background.

"Yes, here it is. Forgive me, but I can't remember what you needed from us," Pam apologized.

"We would like to meet with her physician and discuss any medications Ms. Smith was taking as well as get a feel for her medical history," Genevieve reminded her.

"Oh, right. Hmm..." Genevieve heard more clicking. "Dr. Janner has a very full schedule today. I'm not sure she can squeeze you in for a meeting."

Genevieve sighed. "We'd be happy to meet with Dr. Janner at the end of the work day. We really need to speak with her."

Pam clucked her tongue. "I need to check with her. I'm going to put you on hold."

The line clicked and Genevieve groaned as the music started up again. She looked over at Alex who was watching her with an amused expression. She moved the phone away from her mouth and covered it with her hand.

"Tell me you had more luck with the bank," she begged.

He held up a sticky note. "We've got an appointment for 11:00 tomorrow."

She started to respond when she heard the line click again.

"Ms. Viacorte?" Pam asked

Genevieve cringed. "This is Detective Viacorte, yes."

"Oh, detective, right. Dr. Janner will meet with you at our office at five this evening. Please don't be late. This is a big inconvenience for her."

"I understand. We'll be there," Genevieve responded.

"You'll need to check in with me at the front desk first. Bring a form of identification," Pam said curtly.

"Will do. Thanks, Pam," Genevieve said as kindly as she could.

The line clicked again. She held up the receiver and looked at it before replacing it into the cradle.

"And? Did the doctor agree to meet with us?" Alex asked her.

"Yeah, though they sound pretty reluctant about it," Genevieve responded. "Maybe the receptionist is just mad she has to stay late because of us."

He shrugged. "Oh well."

"Come look at our victim's tax return again. Something isn't adding up," Genevieve said, changing the subject.

Alex got up and came over to her desk. She pulled up the tax return on her computer.

"See, here's her income for the year," she pointed at the screen.

"I guess she isn't a millionaire like her family thought," Alex commented. "What's wrong with that?"

"It's not her income that bothers me. It's her income and the fact that her house, which seems to be worth just under a million dollars, is completely paid off. How does she pay off a house she should never have been able to afford?"

Alex scratched his head. "Maybe she had a more lucrative position before she started writing books. When did her first book get published?"

"I think it was two decades ago. Let me look."

She typed the author's name into a search window and found her website. "Here are all her books. It looks like the first one was published in 2006, so yeah, about twenty years ago."

"Okay, so she was in her early forties at that point. She must have had another job. The sister told us she was out of the house and on her own as soon as she could be, right?" Alex asked.

"Right. The parents weren't rich, so they probably didn't leave their kids a huge windfall. We need to dig deeper into her background. Maybe something from her past came back to haunt her," Genevieve hypothesized.

"Hey, not to change the subject, but did you ever call the sister-in-law, uh, Donna, and ask her if there was something she held back? You know, with the look she gave Tonya when we asked about Gayle abandoning the party early?" Alex asked her.

"Oh, it slipped my mind. Let's see if I can get her on the phone," she said, grabbing the receiver.

Genevieve found Donna's phone number and punched it into her desk phone. The call connected and rang three times before the older woman answered.

"Hello," Donna said quietly.

"Donna Smith? This is Detective Viacorte. I had a follow-up question if you have a minute," Genevieve told her.

"Okay, just one second." Donna's voice was barely above a whisper. "I'll go out in the hallway."

Genevieve listened and heard Donna mumbling to someone else in the room. A door opened and closed and then Donna spoke again.

"Okay, Detective. What is your question?" she asked timidly.

Genevieve could barely hear her. "When we spoke with you and your family members earlier, we discussed how the party ended. My partner floated the idea of Gayle just leaving the party as her signal to tell everyone it ended. The other Mrs. Smith, uh, Tonya, stated that even Gayle wouldn't leave her own party before her guests. You gave her a funny look. Why was that?"

Donna didn't respond right away. Genevieve strained to hear any words she might be saying, but the line was silent.

"Donna? Are you still there?" she asked gently.

"Yes. Um, it's just…well, I…I'm not sure what to say. Gayle did go inside for a bit longer than seemed normal. It was just starting to get dark, like really dark out. She went inside and didn't come back out for over fifteen minutes. I honestly thought she'd gone to bed and left the rest of us to figure it out," Donna replied.

"But she did come back out?" Genevieve asked for clarification.

"Oh, yes. She came out and not long after that…I guess it was around ten or so, the catering crew started cleaning up. We said our goodbyes and headed back here…to the hotel," Donna explained.

"How did Gayle seem when you were leaving?" Genevieve asked.

"She seemed like herself, I guess. You have to understand, Detective. We rarely saw Gayle. We almost never talked to her. I don't really know what *normal* is for her," Donna told her. "It's just…"

"It's just what?" Genevieve prodded.

"Well, it's probably nothing, but I noticed she was wearing a charm bracelet early on in the party. Several of the charms were danglers, so it made some noise as she moved around," Donna responded. "When she came back outside toward the end of the party, she wasn't wearing it anymore. At the time, I thought she might have started getting ready for bed, but decided she should say goodbye to her guests."

"You're saying she took off the charm bracelet while she was inside?" Genevieve clarified.

"I assume that's when she did it. I didn't see it again," Donna told her.

"I understand. Well, that's all for now. Thanks for your help," Genevieve said and hung up the receiver.

"So, she did leave the party for a bit," Alex commented. "How long was she inside?"

"Fifteen minutes, according to Donna. That's longer than your normal bathroom break. She said it was around ten o'clock. Maybe she was starting to feel the effects of the drug and…" Genevieve wasn't sure how to finish the sentence.

Her desk phone rang, interrupting their brainstorming session. It was Dr. Green. She grabbed the receiver and then put it on speaker phone.

"Detectives Viacorte and Runimoss," she answered. "You're on speaker."

"Detectives. I got the tox screen back from your victim. She had both alcohol and the barbiturate in her system," Dr. Green told them. "I estimate it would take one and a half to two hours for the drug to have an effect on her."

"What about the melatonin?" Alex asked.

"I didn't find any evidence of that. I can run it again, if you'd like," Dr. Green offered.

"No rush. If it wasn't there, it wasn't there," Alex told him.

"The levels of both the alcohol and barbiturate," Genevieve began, "were they high enough to incapacitate her?"

"More so, detective," Dr. Green responded. "They were high enough to kill her. And there's something else."

"We're all ears, Dr. Green," Alex told him.

"I've completed the autopsy. Her stomach contents included one small, metallic charm. I assume it's from a bracelet."

They looked at each other. "What was the charm?"

"It's the ace of hearts."

Chapter 10

The lunch crowd at Mae's Corner had mostly cleared out when Cari arrived. She scanned the room but didn't see Ms. McIlvain inside. She chose a table near the entrance so she could watch for her to arrive. She slipped the strap of her messenger bag over the back of the chair and sat down.

"Oh, Ms. Turnlyle! Great to see you here again," the waiter said.

Cari quickly glanced at the nametag pinned to his shirt and smiled. "Justin, it's good to see you too. I'm meeting a…friend for a late lunch today."

Justin smiled. "Can I bring you some water while you wait?"

"That would be great," Cari paused. "Hey, I heard you were taking college classes while working here. How is that going?"

"Two more semesters until I graduate. Gramma Mae is pretty excited," he proudly said as he handed her two menus.

"What are you studying?" Cari asked him.

"Hotel and Restaurant Management," Justin replied. "Gramma Mae says the business is mine once I have my degree."

The bell over the entrance rang. Cari looked over and saw Ms. McIlvain coming inside. Her hair was pulled back into a bun at the base of her head and her face looked flushed. Cari waved her over to the table.

"Sorry I'm late. I had a little extra to do for my client," she said as she pulled out the chair across from Cari.

"No problem. Ms. McIlvain, this is our waiter, Justin. His grandmother owns the business," Cari said, gesturing toward the young man.

"Hi, ma'am. Can I bring you something to drink while you look over our menu today?" Justin asked.

"I'll get a lemonade, please," she told him as she picked up the menu.

"I'll be right back with your drinks. Our lunch special today is the BLT, one of my faves," he said, grinning.

Cari nodded and watched him walk away. "Have you eaten here before, Ms. McIlvain?"

"Please, call me Myra. No need to be so formal," she said, waving her hand. "I used to come here all the time, but it's been years since I ate here. Just got out of the habit, I guess. I didn't realize it was still open."

"It's got great comfort food. I come more often in the winter," Cari said. "I think I'll get a chicken salad sandwich today."

"I can't pass up their BLT. It is delicious," Myra said as she set her menu aside. She placed her napkin in her lap and then fanned herself with her right hand. "Is it warm in here?"

Cari shook her head. "It feels fine to me."

Justin returned with their drinks. "Are we ready to order, ladies?"

Cari turned his way. "This is all on one ticket for me, Justin. I'll have your chicken salad sandwich."

She saw Myra frown briefly before smiling at Justin. "I'll get the lunch special, please."

"Sounds good. I'll get it out to you in just a few minutes," he said, smiling.

"You don't need to buy me lunch," Myra said as she handed her menu to Justin before he walked away.

"My treat," Cari said, waving her off. "I wanted to chat with you about Gayle Smith. It seems like she really kept to herself. I've had a hard time finding anyone who knew much about her at all.

Also, is it okay if I record our conversation? It makes it easier for me when I'm trying to go over things later."

Myra nodded and then smoothed her hair back with a slight tremble in her hand. "That's perfectly fine with me. Let's see. Gayle. She was a *very* private person. She didn't talk about herself a lot, but I did consider her a friend. I think I told you I've been cleaning her house every week for over twenty years."

Cari set her recorder to the side after switching it on. "The police haven't released an approximate time of death for Gayle yet. Did you happen to hear them say anything while you were there?"

Myra took a drink of her lemonade. "I heard them discussing it while I was downstairs. I think they said eleven o'clock, but I'm not sure if that was official."

"You said you considered her a friend, right? What can you tell me about her?"

Myra fussed with her hair again. "I, um, I…well, she was kind. She always seemed genuinely happy to see me when I arrived. She would ask about my family, how my vacation had gone…I never realized I did most of the talking. She was a great listener."

Cari tried another idea. "What about hobbies? Did she ever mention what she did for fun? Did she play games? Was there ever a book left on the nightstand?"

Myra arranged her silverware, then clasped her hands in her lap. "It was rare for things to be left out or out of place. I used to joke that my rags got cleaner after cleaning her house," she chuckled. "So, no books or games. She didn't talk about hobbies, not to me anyway…there was one thing…" she trailed off.

"Yes?" Cari asked leaning forward.

Before Myra could respond, Justin returned to the table with their sandwiches. Both plates had a serving of potato chips on them too. Seeing they were in the middle of a conversation, he quickly retreated from the table.

Cari took a bite and savored the sandwich before prodding Myra to finish her sentence. "You were saying there was something you noticed?"

Myra slowly chewed and slightly nodded her head. "Oh, that is such a good sandwich. My favorite."

Cari tried to mask her frustration. "Was there something else about Gayle you remembered? About her habits or something you saw?"

The older woman put a hand to her mouth and paused. "You know, it probably doesn't mean anything. It wasn't even *that* frequent."

"What wasn't?" Cari asked as gently as she could.

Myra bit her lip as though she was considering her words. "When I first started cleaning for Gayle, she used these euphemisms or phrases when she talked. It took me a bit to recognize some of them, but they were all related to the game of poker. I thought she just had some odd turns of phrase for the longest time, but one day, my husband was watching, uh…Texas Hold 'Em on TV. I heard some of the same kinds of phrases. Things about hoping for a draw or having cowboys in your pocket or float the river. I don't remember all of them, and maybe I was just imagining the connection."

Cari took a drink and thought about Myra's comments for a moment. "Poker, huh? That's interesting. You said you cleaned her house for over twenty years. Had she just moved to the area when you started or were you replacing a different house cleaner?"

"She had just moved into her home. When she invited me to interview for the position, there were still boxes in the garage," Myra responded.

"She gave you a tour of her house during the interview?" Cari asked, intrigued by the idea. She'd never had a house cleaner before. Maybe this was normal.

"Oh, that's pretty typical, especially in nicer homes. They want you to know what the space looks like and see your reaction to it before they hire you," Myra told her.

"Twenty years ago…social media was pretty new. How did you connect with her in the first place?"

Myra smiled. "Ah, the good ole days. I had an ad I used to run in your newspaper to find clients. I got a lot of business by word of mouth too. In Gayle's case, I would guess it was from the newspaper. She didn't have neighbors exactly as her home is kind of off on its own in the countryside."

Cari pictured the house and had to agree. "True. It's almost like a farm house, but without the farm."

Justin appeared at their table with a pitcher of water and lemonade to refill their beverages. "Can I get either of you ladies anything else?"

Cari was full and anxious to consider the idea of the author being a poker player. "Nothing for me."

Myra smiled at Justin. "I'm full. That was delicious. Please tell your grandmother Myra says hi."

Justin pulled the bill from his apron and handed it to Cari. "I'll be your cashier whenever you're ready." He turned to Myra, "I'll let her know you're here. Are you a friend of Gramma's?"

"I used to be a regular here. I came every Saturday for brunch with my girlfriends," Myra told him. "Your grandmother was just getting started with running everything on her own, but she always came over to chat with us gals."

Cari slipped her credit card into the folder with the bill and gave it back to Justin. "Thank you, Justin."

The young man walked away and Cari stood up. "Thank you for meeting me for lunch. I really appreciate your time. I'm very sorry for your loss. I can tell Gayle meant a great deal to you."

Myra's cheeks flushed. "Thank you and thank you for the meal. I'm going to wait around a moment and see if Mae comes out. Oh, there she is now!"

Cari looked toward the kitchen and saw a petite woman coming through the door. She had a hairnet over her bluish-grey curls and a streak of flour on her forehead. The full-figured woman was untying her apron straps as she walked toward their table. Cari didn't want to intrude, so she waved goodbye and walked to the exit. While the lunch had been informative, she couldn't shake the feeling Myra was hiding something. Talking about her employer made the woman nervous and Cari wanted to know why. She pulled out her notebook after getting into her car and wrote herself a note. *What else does Myra know?*

* * * * *

"Our victim swallowed a charm from her bracelet. It seems clear she was trying to tell us something," Genevieve observed.

"Agreed. No one has said anything about her being a card player though. Is there anything in her financials that suggests she was a gambler?"

Genevieve pulled up the author's tax records on her computer. "The file with her tax records only goes back ten years. She never filed a W2-G form while she was a resident of New York."

"To get older tax returns, we need to call the state department of revenue or taxation, but where did she live before she came back here?" Alex asked.

Genevieve scrolled through the files, but nothing mentioned a previous residence. "I can't find anything. Her sister told us she went to school in Arizona. Maybe she stayed after college?"

"It's as good of a guess as any," Alex remarked. "Her lawyer might know too. We can ask him tomorrow."

"Something in her past triggered her return to New York. She didn't come here with debt. She came here with enough money to buy a house," Genevieve mused.

"We can brainstorm scenarios all day, G. We need to find evidence of what happened back then. Speculating will get us nowhere." He checked his watch. "We've got some time before we need to be at the doctor's office. Let's go talk to the catering company," Alex suggested.

"We need to get a look at the charm bracelet," Genevieve argued. "I'm going to check the list of recovered items in the case file."

Alex stood behind her as she opened the digital case file on her computer. She found the evidence list and scrolled through it. No charm bracelet was on the list.

"That's weird. There's no bracelet on the list. I want to talk to CSU. Maybe they overlooked it."

She picked up the receiver and punched in the extension for CSU. "Hey, Bob. It's Genevieve. When you went back to inventory the house, did you find a jewelry box?"

"We did. It had a few pairs of earrings and some necklaces," he answered.

"No charm bracelet?" she asked.

"No, no charm bracelet. Is it missing?" Bob asked her.

"I think so. Could you do me a favor and look through the items from her bedroom again and see if it isn't hiding somewhere else?"

Bob clicked his tongue. "Uh, sure. I'll let you know if it turns up. Should we go back to the house if it doesn't?"

Genevieve mulled it over. "I hate to make you do that, but yes. Hopefully, you won't have to. Thanks, Bob."

"Before you hang up, we inventoried the kitchen. She didn't own a set of martini glasses," Bob told her.

"So, it was just the one? It must have been from the catering company," Genevieve surmised. "Thanks for letting me know." She replaced the receiver and turned to Alex.

"No bracelet, so either the killer took it or she hid it somewhere as another clue for us," she told him. "CSU is going to look through her belongings again and see if they can find it. They didn't find any other martini glasses in the house, so it seems like the one in her bedroom came from the party."

"We should confirm with the catering company. We have time to go talk to them now," Alex said.

"Let me find the card. I took a picture of it," Genevieve said as she scrolled through her photos. "Here it is. Opulent Eatery."

She stepped back to grab the keys to the cruiser, but they weren't on the hook. She swung around to look at Alex, holding the keys up in his right hand.

"Looking for these?" he asked with a smirk. "I'm driving. Let's go."

She slipped her phone into her pocket and followed him toward the exit. His long stride carried him there much faster and he reached the door first. Genevieve felt a bit childish for mentally trying to race him to it, but she really didn't want him to hold the door for her like she was incapable of taking care of it herself. He knew it bothered her and continued to do it, probably for that very reason. Much to her surprise, he opened the door and went through without stopping, letting the door slam in her face. She pulled it back open and found him laughing on the other side.

"Your face right now…that was *so* worth it," he laughed. "Isn't it better when I hold the door?"

She glared at him but mentally admitted it was a good prank. "Whatever. You just don't get it."

"Oh, I get it. You work hard at being independent. You want people to respect you for you, not because you're my partner. You want respect for being a good cop, not because you have a bigger, stronger, *male* partner who looks out for you," he said as they walked to the cruiser.

She felt her cheeks redden. "Fine, but if you know that, why do you continue to make me look like the diminutive female?"

He looked at her incredulously. "Look at yourself, Gen. You *are* a diminutive female. You can be a good detective and still get help from other people."

He unlocked the vehicle and they got in. She tapped her foot and looked out the window while she tried to get over the encounter. She knew she was being ridiculous.

"Okay, enough of that. The catering company. I counted five servers at the party. I suppose it's possible one of them completely avoided having their picture taken, though," she told him as he steered the car.

"True. We can ask the owner when we get there how many servers were at the party," Alex responded. "Their office is over in the warehouse district. We're almost there."

He turned left on the next street. Genevieve looked ahead and saw several warehouses lining the street, but the closest one had a parking lot next to it with large, white delivery vans in it. The vans all had the Opulent Eatery logo on them: the 'O' resembled a plate and the word 'Eatery' was scrawled on it like a chef might drizzle chocolate onto a dessert dish. Alex turned into the lot and parked in a visitor spot. They exited the vehicle and walked to the front entrance.

"Welcome to Opulent Eatery! We're here for all of your catering needs," the man behind the counter greeted them.

Genevieve looked around the space and saw two people in hairnets rolling silverware into cloth napkins and placing the rolls into a box on a table. Past the counter, she could see part of a kitchen, but it was dark. A small office space was walled off to the left of the counter. They both took out their shields to introduce themselves. "I'm Detective Viacorte and this is my partner Detective Runimoss. We have a few questions, Mr.?" Genevieve searched for a nametag, but didn't see one.

"Immihan. Ted Immihan," he said, extending his hand. "Just call me Ted."

She and Alex shook the man's hand. "Ted, we understand your company catered Ms. Gayle Smith's retirement party on Sunday evening."

"Yes, I heard she died. How awful!" he said sincerely.

Genevieve nodded in agreement. "Sir, we're trying to get a feel for the party as that was the last place anyone saw her alive. Were you at the party?"

Ted shook his head no. "I don't usually attend the events. I'm better at getting them organized, making sure they have the appropriate number of servers, the right kind of food, enough alcohol…I'm not a chef. I'm a business guy, so to answer your question, no, I wasn't there."

"We'd like to speak with the servers who worked the party. Can you connect us with them?" Genevieve asked.

"Two of them are here right now," he said, gesturing to the two young women rolling silverware. "Ainsley and Becky? Could you join us for a minute?"

The two women set the silverware on the table and walked over to the counter.

"Ladies, these detectives have some questions about the Smith party from Sunday," Ted told them, then turned to Genevieve and Alex. "Would you like to use my office? It's probably more comfortable."

"That would be great. Thanks," Alex replied quickly.

Ted led them to the office space and pulled out his keys. He unlocked the door, then walked around to the computer and pressed a few keys. "Make yourselves at home."

Alex motioned to the two chairs in front of the desk and the two women sat down. The only other chair in the room was the office chair behind the desk. Genevieve felt awkward using the owner's chair. She walked behind the desk to face the women while Alex perched on one corner of it. They both pulled out their pocket notebooks and pens.

"This is Detective Viacorte and I'm Detective Runimoss," Alex said. "We understand you both worked the retirement party for Gayle Smith?"

The women nodded in unison. The taller one with dark skin and dark hair with a hint of pink at the ends spoke first. "Nice to meet you. I'm Ainsley. Yes, we were both at the party. I was mostly at the food table, uh, it was like a buffet of finger food."

The small blonde-haired woman with a face full of freckles smiled. "I'm Becky. I refilled drinks, non-alcoholic ones. I haven't turned eighteen yet, so I can't serve alcohol."

"How many servers were at the party?" Genevieve asked.

"There were five of us," Ainsley responded.

"Who was in charge of the open bar?" Alex asked them.

They exchanged a glance, then Ainsley spoke up. "The others sort of took turns throughout the night."

Genevieve made a note to get the names of the other servers from the owner before they left. "Is that normal? To switch, uh, bartenders mid-party?"

Ainsley shrugged. "Several servers here are trained bartenders, so people swap out sometimes. I haven't done the training for that, so I stick with serving food and mingling with the guests."

Becky nodded. "I'm still pretty new to the company." She looked over her shoulder at the open door, then lowered her voice. "This is really just a summer job for me, so…"

"Got it," Genevieve said making a note. "You said five servers, so what did the other two do when they weren't serving alcohol?"

"They were runners. They made sure we always had plates, silverware, napkins, glasses…all of that. They cleared plates too," Ainsley said.

"What was the guest of honor drinking that night?" Alex asked.

"Uh, mostly water. Someone gave her a martini for the big toast toward the end of the party, though," Becky told him.

"Did she drink it?" Genevieve asked.

They looked at each other. "I think she took a drink for the toast. I didn't really pay attention. We were pretty busy refilling glasses there for a bit," Ainsley said.

"Yeah, I mean, I didn't do any alcoholic drinks, so I have no idea," Becky said.

"How did the party go?" Genevieve asked.

"What do you mean? It had an okay vibe, I guess. It was a lot of old people…" Becky trailed off and looked at Alex. "I mean, not that old is bad."

Genevieve saw his jaw clench and release. She spoke up before he could make a snide comment. "Everyone got along all night?"

Ainsley scratched at the hairnet, then shrugged. "It was pretty low-key."

"Well, there were those two women…" Becky started to say, drawing a look from Ainsley.

Alex leaned forward. "What two women?"

Ainsley turned to look at him. "It was nothing. We were refilling drinks at one of the tables and overheard two women talking about the guest of honor. She was an author, I guess, and I think they were too. It sounded like they were pretty jealous of her accomplishments."

"What did they say?" Genevieve asked.

"I don't think they were authors. That was the family table, Ains. Remember?" Becky responded.

"Oh, that's right. I guess they were sisters or something. One had like platinum blonde hair and this knock-off designer dress. The other one was plainer, but dressed up a lot. She had on a fancy dress, like a regular cocktail dress, you know, and they were talking about how Ms. Smith was holding out on them this whole time. Like she owed them or something," Ainsley said.

"It was meaner than that, though," Becky argued. "The blonde one was angry. It sounded like she hated Ms. Smith. Why would you come to someone's party if you didn't like them at all?"

"Bougie," Ainsley laughed.

"For real," Becky agreed.

Alex looked at Genevieve with his eyebrows raised. She gave him a confirming nod. "That was the only note of contention all night?"

They both shrugged. "Yeah, I mean, it was pretty chill besides that," Ainsley replied.

"Did you see the author wearing a charm bracelet?" Genevieve asked the young women.

Ainsley's eyes lit up. "Yes! It was so pretty and delicate. It jingled when she walked or lifted her hand."

Alex leaned in. "Was she wearing it the whole night?"

The two young women exchanged a glance and shrugged. "I think so? I didn't really pay attention. Is it important?"

Genevieve clipped her pen back into her notebook and pulled out a business card. "It's something we're looking into. Thanks for your time. If you think of anything else, please give me a call."

"For sure. Nice to meet you," Ainsley said as they got up from the chairs.

They exited the office and Alex nodded toward the owner. "Let's get a list of names from him."

Genevieve approached the counter again. "Hey, Ted. Thanks for letting us borrow your waitstaff for a few minutes. Can we get a list of all your workers from that night? We just want to be thorough."

"Sure, do you need contact information, though? I only got permission from four of the five workers for that and you just spoke with two of them," he responded.

"You anticipated us asking for that information?" Alex asked, confused.

"Oh, no. A reporter called about it earlier, so I had to call around to ask each of them. It isn't part of their contract. I mean, we've never had anyone die after a party before..." he whitened. "I never heard the cause of death. It wasn't food poisoning, was it?"

"We haven't released a cause of death, yet," Alex replied vaguely. "You said a reporter called?"

"From the paper...Turnlyle," Ted told him. "I was waiting for the fifth person to respond before sending it, but it's basically been a day, so..."

Alex looked at Genevieve but kept his mouth shut. She wondered what he was thinking. "We'll take the names and whatever contact info you can give us," she responded.

He typed something on the computer keyboard and she heard a printer start up. A few seconds later, he reached down and gave her a sheet of paper.

"That has the five names and four of their phone numbers. There's a chance I'll hear back from the other guy. If he's cool with it, I'll let you know," he explained. "Do you have more questions?"

"Yes, did a martini glass go missing from your party?" Alex asked him.

His eyes brightened. "The woman from the newspaper asked me the same thing. The servers marked down one martini glass as broken, but it could be missing. There's no difference from our perspective."

"Makes sense. Here's my card in case you think of something else, or if your other server reaches out. Thanks for your cooperation," Genevieve told him.

"Happy to help. If the station ever needs something catered…" he paused, reaching down for a business card. "I hope you'll give us a call."

She accepted the card and smiled. "It's probably not in the budget, but thanks."

They got back in the cruiser and Genevieve looked at the printout the owner had given her. She put a check next to Ainsley and Becky.

"We should call the other two servers. I bet we can find a number for the fifth guy on the list without too much effort," she said to Alex as he pulled out of the parking lot.

"Yeah, let's get them on the line and see what they know. They served the alcohol, so they will hopefully know more than the two young women we just interviewed." His grip on the steering wheel tightened. "I can't believe your friend is ahead of us on this catering group, but I guess it was a bonus for us. We didn't have to wait for most of the phone numbers."

Genevieve gave him a half-hearted grin and pulled out her phone to start making calls. She wondered if Cari was free later to fill in any gaps in their stories. Alex couldn't see what she was doing, so she thumbed off a quick text to Cari before entering the first phone number.

* * * * *

Cari's phone buzzed with notifications. She checked her watch and was surprised to see a text from Genevieve. She pulled out her phone to respond.

Free tonight? Text me a time to come to your place.

Cari started to ask about dinner, then remembered she was meeting Bob. They would probably be finished well before eight o'clock.

See you at 8

She closed the messaging screen and saw a little red number one on her email app. *Please be the catering guy. Please be the catering guy.* She opened the app and almost shouted with excitement. Ted had finally sent her a list. She opened it and frowned. Five names, but only four phone numbers. She read through the email again and saw he was unable to reach the fifth person, so he could only give her 'the young man's name' and not his phone number. Cari made a mental note of his reference to the server's gender and age. She could probably find him on her own. She highlighted the first phone number and hit the phone button to call it. A woman answered on the second ring.

"Hello?" a pleasant voice answered.

"Hello, uh, Deb? Deb Trowe?" Cari asked to confirm.

"This is Deb. Who's calling please?" Deb asked.

"Ms. Trowe, this is Cari Turnlyle. I'm with the Brenington Beagle—"

"Oh, right. Ted said you'd be calling. This is about the author lady?" Deb interrupted.

"That's correct. I understand you were one of the servers at her party on Sunday evening. Your boss mentioned someone marked down a broken martini glass. Were you the lead server? Did you fill out that paperwork?" she asked hopefully.

"I was the lead server," Deb said confidently. "Oh, right the glass. I don't know if it was broken or what the deal was with the glass, but we were short one at the end of the night. Broken or stolen, it's still gone, right?"

If you only knew, Cari thought. "Right. So, what was your role as lead server, besides filling out paperwork at the end of the night?"

"I assigned everyone a role. Three of us were old enough to serve alcohol, well, maybe four, but two of the female servers are friends and they stay on task better together than apart, so I put them on drink refills and mingling. I split time between being the bartender at the open bar and running to the van to get extra supplies like glasses, silverware, et cetera," Deb told her.

"Did you serve the guest of honor a martini?" Cari asked.

"What's with all the focus on the martini glass? Never mind, I don't actually care. Uh, did I serve her a martini? No. She only asked for water when I was tending," Deb said with certainty.

"So, you were the bartender first and the runner later?" Cari asked for clarification.

"That sounds right. It was a small party, but we were busy the whole time. I didn't get a break, except to use the restroom once or twice," Deb said thoughtfully.

"How did that work? Did the host give you access to her home?" Cari wondered aloud.

"She has, uh had? Uh, she *had* a half bath near the back of the house. It was just inside the back door. The rest of the house was closed off, so unless you were nosy, you only saw a little bit of hallway and the bathroom," Deb informed her.

"And were you?" Cari asked pointedly.

"Was I what?" Deb asked with confusion.

"Were you nosy? Did you check out the rest of her house?" Cari asked.

"Ha, no. It's possible those other doors were locked and if something ended up stolen later, I did not want my fingerprints to be part of the equation."

Cari's eyes widened. "Do things often go missing from parties with Opulent Eater as the caterer?"

Deb made a sound with her lips. "Not that I know of. I'm just careful, is what I'm saying."

Cari wondered if someone else had ventured into the house, but figured Deb didn't know. She decided to ask one more question about the martini. "I was given access to some video from the party. Ms. Smith was drinking a martini during the final toast of the night. Do you know if she finished it?"

"I can tell you I only cleaned up empty martini glasses, so if hers was one of those, then yes, she finished it. Otherwise, I didn't see her with the drink. It was kind of hectic for us at that moment. Trying to get some people champagne and others water, clearing off used plates and dinnerware. I wish I could tell you more, but I just couldn't pay attention to details like that," Deb said apologetically.

"That's totally fine. I just have one more question. How was the party overall? Did everything go smoothly? Any disagreements or issues with a guest?"

"It was a bunch of old people having heavy hors d'oeuvres and drinking mostly champagne, martinis, or wine. How out of control could it get?" Deb asked flippantly.

"True. What time did the party end?"

"Hmm, well there was that final toast, which cleared a lot of guests out after it ended. People mingled for a bit and gradually took off while we cleared plates and food. I think everyone was gone and we had the van loaded up by ten-thirty probably."

"Did you close out the tab or bill with Ms. Smith at that point?"

"We checked in with her, but it was all pre-paid. We have a flat fee for the open bar that includes different levels. She picked the max, so we didn't need to settle up any open tabs or anything at the end. We cleaned up and got out of there," Deb said matter-of-factly.

"Did she seem okay when you checked in with her?" Cari asked.

"She might have seemed tired, but I think she is close to my age, maybe even older. I'm not quite sixty. We're all tired by that time of day," Deb laughed harshly.

"Well, I appreciate your time. Feel free to call me on this number if you think of anything else."

The call ended and Cari went back to the list to highlight the next number. A young woman answered immediately.

"Is this the newspaper woman?" the young voice asked.

Cari wondered how Ted had instructed his staff to respond to her calls. "It is. I guess you were expecting my call. Is this Becky?"

"Mr. Immihan said you were going to contact each of us. I already talked to the police. They were literally just here," she said abruptly. "And we're still at work. Me and Ainsley."

Ainsley and me. Cari grimaced but tried to remain light-hearted. "That's great. I know they are looking into Ms. Smith's death too. I'm trying to get an understanding of how the party went as well as establish what the guest of honor was drinking."

The girl sighed loudly into the phone. "She was drinking water mostly. We don't know a lot about other drinks because we didn't serve any alcohol. We aren't certified…I mean, I'm not even old enough to be certified yet."

Cari scribbled a note to herself about Becky and Ainsley being the two young members of the service team. "What can you tell me about the party?"

"It was an old person's party. It was boring…just a sec. Ainsley wants to talk," Becky said. Cari heard a scraping sound and wondered if the phone was being slid across a table.

"Hi, Ms. Turnlyle. I'm sorry Becky is being grumpy. She was hoping to finish rolling all this silverware early so we could go see a show, but we keep getting interrupted. Do you need to interview us for your newspaper article?" Ainsley asked sweetly.

"It could come to that. Right now, I'm still trying to piece together what happened or what might have happened," Cari replied.

"Do you need to know how to spell our names? Or a photograph? I have a lot of selfies I could send you," Ainsley offered.

"Uh, I have your names from your employer. Thank you for offering. I don't know that I'll need any photos. What do you remember from the party? Did you see Ms. Smith with a martini by any chance?"

"Oh, yes! That was during the final toast. We were getting drink refills, but almost everyone was toasting with alcohol, of course, so we got to kind of stand and watch that part for a bit," Ainsley said in a hushed tone like she was keeping a secret.

"And? Did you see her with a martini? Did she drink it?" Cari asked with interest.

"She definitely took one drink…for the toast, you know? Uh, I assume she drank all of it. Why wouldn't you?" she laughed. "We started cleaning up after that. A bunch of people left after the toast. I think the last two couples left around ten or maybe ten-thirty. They were all drinking water at that point as we'd cleaned up the open bar already."

Cari made a note. The ending time was basically the same as what the lead server had reported too. "Did the host ask you to close down the bar? Is that typical?"

Ainsley didn't respond immediately. Cari almost asked the question again when she spoke up. "I asked Becky your question, but we don't know. I think people maybe choose a stop time for an open bar, but since we've never been on the alcohol team, we don't really know."

"Okay, well, I appreciate your time and candidness. Please call or text if you think of anything else," Cari said.

"Will do! I can't wait to see my name in the paperrrr!" she squealed, drawing the r out.

Cari skipped Ainsley's name on the list and called the last number instead. A woman answered on the first ring.

"You must be the newspaper lady we're supposed to talk to," the woman stated in a breathy voice. "I'm a bit out of breath as I've been out for a jog."

Cari glanced at her watch and wondered who chose to jog at the hottest time of day. "That's fine. Take a minute to catch your breath. I hope you didn't interrupt your run for me."

The woman choked out a cough. "Sorry, I just choked on my water. No, I'm more of a wogger. I know that's not a word. I walk and jog, but mostly walk. You caught me on a walk break. It's hot. I can be done for the day and not care a single bit. I missed a call earlier, but I think they left a message. I'll check it later."

"And you're Melia? I'm sorry if I mispronounced it. I haven't seen that name before," Cari said the name *meal-ya* like the end of Amelia.

"It's actually muh-lee-uh," Melia told her.

"Ah, that makes more sense," Cari replied. "About the party, I understand you tended the open bar for part of the evening?"

"Pfft. Barely. The new guy took over and I turned into a runner," Melia grumbled. "And I had to harp on our two young ones to stay off their phones. Deb thinks they're hard workers, but they need reminders."

Cari blinked. "So, you weren't the bartender during the toast?"

"Oh, no. At that point, I was again. He filled up some drinks and then told me to take over," Melia explained.

"Were you able to watch the toast?" Cari asked.

"Well, he was taking a round of martinis somewhere as well as a tray of champagne flutes and told me to distribute another tray of champagne, so I offered it to those nearest the bar," Melia told her. "We're not supposed to leave the bar unattended, so I got back behind it and filled a few more flutes with the bubbly, which he came back for a few minutes later."

"So, you didn't watch the toast?"

"Not really, I guess," Melia responded.

"Can you remember if the guest of honor finished her drink from the toast?" Cari asked hopefully.

"I did see her with a martini, but I didn't stick around to watch her drink it. The bar was off to the side from where they did the toasts, so she wasn't really in my line of sight," Melia stated.

"And the party was finished by ten or so?" Cari asked to confirm.

"I think it was closer to ten-thirty. I wish I could tell you more. It was a pretty quiet party," Melia told her.

"I appreciate you taking time to speak with me. If you think of anything else, please don't hesitate to call me back," Cari said.

The call ended and Cari sighed. Three phone calls and all she had learned was the author might have been tired at the end of the party. Was that really surprising? Maybe she could track the other server down and finally get something useful. It sounded like he served the martini to Gayle. Maybe he saw someone spike it.

She pulled up LexisNexis and typed 'Opulent Eatery' into the search bar. Once she found the correct business, she looked at their list of employees. She knew a lot of waitstaff were often paid in cash and might not be listed as employees for a business, but OE seemed to keep better, and probably more legal, records. She found the young man's name and selected it from the list. LexisNexis had his address and cell phone number. She copied both and then opened her email on her desktop computer. She navigated to the message from Ted Immihan and opened the attached document. Then, she pasted the young man's phone and address into the document. Before punching the number into her cell phone, she went back to the screen with all his information. James Dolling, age twenty-one. She smirked. He must be a really assertive young man to be telling the two older women what to do. Maybe he came off as older. Melia hadn't grouped him in with the young ones, and Ainsley had to be over eighteen. Becky had only said she herself wasn't old enough to be certified to serve alcohol, implying Ainsley was. Shrugging it off, she entered the number into her cell phone and touched the phone icon to call. The call connected straight to his voicemail. She decided to leave a message, but when the opportunity came, the recording informed her his inbox was already full.

"That's strange," she said to no one in particular. "People rarely leave messages anymore unless it's a spam call that just hangs up too late."

She checked her watch. She had just enough time to swing by Mr. Dolling's apartment before Bob would be picking her up for dinner. Luckily, he didn't live too far from her complex, so it wasn't exactly out of the way. She gathered up her things and shut down her computer for the evening. She noticed Ollaman was still in his office. Thankfully, the door was closed and the blinds were shut; he wouldn't be giving her the third degree about her progress before she could leave for the day.

Chapter 11

ari entered James Dolling's address into her maps app and waited for the directions to load. She was going to drive past her apartment complex to get to his, so at least she was heading in the same general direction. She synced her phone to her car's dashboard screen and then pulled out of her space in the parking garage. The screen said she would arrive in nine minutes.

It wasn't quite five o'clock; she wondered if Genevieve was off the clock yet. She drummed her fingers on the steering wheel as she navigated to the server's home. It couldn't hurt to try calling.

"Siri, call Genevieve," Cari instructed.

Her phone connected the call and the ringing sound reverberated through the car. After the fourth ring, her friend's voicemail picked up. Cari ended the call rather than leave a message. She could check in with her later. She called her grandmother instead.

"Hello, Cari!" her grandmother said in a sing-song voice. "How are you today?"

"I'm tracking down one of the servers from the author's party the other day," Cari told her.

"I thought you might be assigned to the story!" Grandmother exclaimed. "I've been a big fan of Natasha Gillespie for years. I was sad to hear she died and under mysterious circumstances too. Someone said she was murdered! Is that true?"

"It's looking that way. The police chief is worried about leaks to the press, so Bob hasn't been able to talk about it after work," Cari said disappointedly.

"Oh, well, I suppose cases like this will crop up from time to time for you two. How are you handling it?" Grandmother asked.

Cari sighed. "I'm okay…we're okay. I don't want to jeopardize his job in any way, of course. It's just hard to get information with these restrictions."

"I guess this means you can't chat with Genevieve either," her grandmother stated.

"I haven't tried. She texted me earlier asking if she could meet with me, so maybe she can collaborate some. I guess I'll find out later. Bob and I are going to The Yellow Duckling for dinner tonight and she's coming by my apartment afterward," Cari responded.

"Oh, that sounds like a nice evening. I read your articles in the paper today about the Fourth of July festival this weekend. It sounds like it will be a nice event. You know, Bea mentioned she and Robby were going to bring the kids over for it," Grandmother informed her.

"I haven't talked to her in several days. I'll have to touch base with her soon," Cari said. "Well, I made it to my destination, so I have to let you go. I love you, Grandmother."

"I love you more."

Cari put the car in park and ended the call. The complex wasn't gated, so she was able to drive up to the server's building without requesting entrance. He lived in building number six, in the back right corner. She hadn't realized the wind had picked up so much until she opened her car door. The force of the wind almost ripped the door from her grasp. She was barely able to keep it from swinging into the vehicle next to hers. She quickly pulled her hair back to keep it from turning into a tangled mess.

Mr. Dolling lived on the second floor in unit 612. Cari climbed the stairs quickly. She hoped he was home so she didn't have to try to track him down again tomorrow. She reached his doorstep and knocked assertively on the door. She pumped her fist in satisfaction when she heard someone moving inside the apartment.

She reached into her bag and clicked on her digital recorder. She could ask him if it was okay after he answered. The door swung open and revealed a young man with a scruffy beard. He was wearing black workout clothes and holding a bottle of water.

"Can I help you?" the man asked.

Cari pulled out her press ID and lifted it toward him. "James Dolling?"

The man's face dropped. "I'm sorry. He isn't home. He hasn't *been* home in over two days."

"You're his roommate?" Cari asked.

"Yeah, my name is Xander. We share the apartment, uh, just as friends," he said quickly.

Cari smiled. "I understand Mr. Dolling works as a server for Opulent Eatery. Do you work there too?"

Xander shook his head. "No, I do freelance graphic design. I work out of the apartment most days."

"You said you haven't seen James in over two days. Does he often take off without warning?" she asked.

"Not really, especially at the start of the week. We both basically live paycheck to paycheck, so it's not like he can go on vacation or something," Xander responded. "But…"

"But what?"

Xander scuffed his sneaker on the concrete floor. "I shouldn't spill…it's not my place."

"Xander, if your friend is missing or hurt or needs help, you need to tell me what you know!" Cari scolded him.

Xander grimaced. "I know. I hear you. I just…ugh," he groaned. "James has had some drug problems, but that was in the past. He hasn't used in over a year."

"Okay, are you trying to say he used to disappear when he was using?" Cari prodded.

Xander slowly nodded his head. "The first year we lived together, he would sometimes go to all-night parties and not come home for over twenty-four hours. Then, he'd show up, smelling like death and who knows what else, and act like it never happened. But I'm telling you, it's been weeks since he even smoked a cigarette! He's been working really hard to clean himself up. I really don't think he's using again. He has a job and he's been really responsible and reliable lately."

"Did he say where he was headed when he left on Sunday?" Cari asked him.

Xander ran a hand through his dark hair. "To be a server at some party. He was supposed to get there early to set up. He said he might get home late because he didn't know how long the party was scheduled to last."

"Sorry to ask obvious questions, but have you tried calling him?"

The man put his hands out, palms up. "Many, many times. It goes straight to voicemail. He usually turns his phone off when he's working an event. They get in trouble if they're caught on their phones, I guess."

Cari was starting to feel concerned. "Do you know his parents? Could he be with them?"

Xander nodded his head. "I had the same thought. I didn't want to worry his parents, but when he didn't come home last night again, I called them this morning. They haven't seen him or heard from him either."

"What about siblings or co-workers?" Cari felt her anxiety rising.

"I didn't reach out to his co-workers. I don't really have a way to do that besides just calling the main line. He's an only child," Xander explained.

"I think you should file a missing person report," Cari advised him.

"Like with the police?" Xander asked.

She nodded. "Yes. I mean, maybe check with the catering company first to see if he's missed any jobs."

"Oh, he doesn't have another job scheduled until this weekend, but he does sometimes take prep shifts. I'm not sure if he has any of those lined up or not. He's going to school part-time and working as a server part-time," Xander told her.

"Could he be studying with another classmate?" Cari asked hopefully.

"I don't know. Maybe? It would be pretty out of character. He's not what you would call a good student. He usually goes to class, but he's skating by with Cs for the most part."

"You should give all this information to the police. It will help them find him faster," Cari told Xander. "The sooner the better."

A cell phone rang from inside the apartment. "Excuse me one second. Maybe that's him now." He let go of the door and it swung shut. Seconds later, Xander opened it up again with the phone held away from him. His face was tight with worry.

"This is James' parents. They still haven't been able to reach him and are really worried. I need to talk to them. Do you have a card? Once we find James, I'll have him give you a call," Xander offered.

Cari fished a card out of her bag and handed it to Xander. "Text me so I have your number saved."

"Let me just minimize the call…" Xander said as he swiped across his phone screen. "Okay, that's me."

Her phone buzzed with a text. "Got it. Thanks for your help. I hope you find your friend."

As she walked back down the stairs to her car, she tried to remember what the servers looked like in the photos and videos she'd gone through. She had been so focused on finding the author with a martini glass, she hadn't paid much attention to the waitstaff at all. Is it possible that James never made it to the party?

* * * * *

The Brenington Medical facility was located near Brenington West hospital. Genevieve figured the doctors from the practice had privileges at the hospital too. The white-bricked building had a handicap accessible ramp next to the three-staired sidewalk. Both connected to a concrete porch. The building almost looked like it had originally been a house but was later converted into a clinic. A white wooden sign with blue letters hung over the front door. The glass doors were etched with the clinic's hours of operation and a phone number.

"We got here at just the right time," Alex pointed out. They could see someone turning off lights in the interior as they approached the entrance.

Genevieve tried the door and found it locked with the deadbolt. "Spoke too soon. We're locked out."

She pulled out her badge and gestured at the receptionist. The woman gave her an irritated glance before coming around the counter to unlock the door. She struggled to pull the door open and Alex grabbed the handle to help. The wind was blowing against the door making it seem heavier than normal. Genevieve stepped inside and kept a hand on the door to keep it open for Alex.

The receptionist was dressed in a light pink button up shirt and a black pencil skirt. She had short, grey hair and wore bifocals. The name plate on the counter showed her name to be Pam Maliddy. They pulled out their detective shields and showed them to her. Pam picked up the receiver of the phone on her desk and lifted it to her ear.

"The detectives are here. Should I send them back?" She spoke quietly into the phone. "Okay, thank you, doctor."

Pam looked their way. "Doctor Janning will be along shortly. You can have a seat."

Alex bumped his fist on the counter before he turned away to find a chair in the waiting area. Genevieve gave Pam an awkward smile and a light shrug. She took a seat next to Alex and he leaned over.

"This better not be like a typical visit to the doctor's office. Make you wait for forty-five minutes and then rush through all your questions," he grumbled in a whisper.

Genevieve cocked her head. "Sounds like you need a better office."

He shook his head. "Nah, I never go anyway."

She rolled her eyes. "Why am I not surprised?"

He shrugged and sank back into his seat. Genevieve scanned the room. It was like most medical offices she'd been in before: pamphlets about self-care on the end tables, fake potted plants in the corners, and non-descript art on the walls. Alex drummed his thumbs on the tops of his thighs. She wondered if it was a distraction technique or if he was trying to be annoying so they'd get the doctor out faster. She heard the door of the waiting room ease open and turned to see a rather tall woman of Indian descent. She had on a white medical coat and comfortable black shoes.

"Detectives? If you could please follow me," she paused and turned to the receptionist. "Pam, my patient is on her way out with the nurse. Can you help her make a follow-up appointment for three months down the road?"

"Certainly. Should I wait for you or clock out after updating the schedule?" she asked.

"You and Nurse Beth are free to go at any time. I'll be fine," Dr. Janner told her. "Right this way, detectives."

They followed Dr. Janner into the hallway. Genevieve saw two examination rooms on each side of the hallway. Three were dark and the fourth went dark as two women stepped into the hallway, one in scrubs and the other in a t-shirt and jeans. The doctor squeezed the patient's hand on her way by and then turned right at the end of the hallway. Genevieve glanced to the left before following and saw three other closed doors with nameplates on the wall next to each one. The doctor pulled a set of keys from her pocket and unlocked the only door on the right branch of the hallway.

"Have a seat. You can put those journals on the floor. I was doing some research earlier and didn't have a chance to tidy up yet," Dr. Janner told them.

Genevieve picked up a pile of journals and gently placed them on the floor next to the chair. She and Alex took a seat while the doctor logged into the computer on the desk. Genevieve pulled out her notebook and pen to signal to Alex she'd take notes for the both of them.

"Pam said you wanted to talk to me about Gayle Smith. I'm just pulling up her records now. What questions do you have for me?" Dr. Janner asked as she typed on the keyboard.

"What medications did you prescribe for Ms. Smith?" Genevieve asked.

"Let me see. Over the last twenty or so years, I've prescribed antibiotics twice and an anti-viral for the flu once," she replied.

"This includes over-the-counter meds?" Alex asked.

"She rarely had complaints," the doctor said as she rotated the monitor to face them. "In fact, I didn't even see her annually. She came if she was sick; otherwise, I didn't hear from her," Dr. Janner clarified.

Genevieve looked at the screen. Gayle Smith had only visited the doctor twice in the last decade.

"Was she generally in good health?" Genevieve asked.

Dr. Janner moved the monitor back and clicked her mouse a few times. "We did bloodwork for her once. Everything was normal. She reportedly exercised regularly, never smoked, and only had the occasional alcoholic beverage. So, yes, I would say she was in good health."

Alex rubbed his jaw. "What about mental health? Did she ever complain of difficulty sleeping?"

"Not to me. She didn't share a lot of details. I barely remember her visits. If you'd like a copy of her file, I can have it sent over to you," she offered. "Do you have other questions?"

Genevieve felt like they were just learning more of the same thing, which was nothing. "Did you receive her medical records from her previous doctor?"

Alex touched his nose and then pointed at her after the doctor went back to the computer screen. She smiled and then turned her attention to Dr. Janner.

"Let's see. We do request the name of your previous physician and-or clinic, but patients don't always comply. It's an optional portion of our intake paperwork." She paused while she entered some more information into the computer. "This would have been filled out before 2015 when we went totally digital with virtually all of our paperwork. We had our summer interns scan in all our old medical files a few years back. That was an undertaking. With all the HIPAA laws and everything…I digress. I found her documents. Let me just skim them and see if she filled out that part of the form."

Genevieve realized they hadn't found out where the author lived before moving to New York and embarking on her career as an author. She leaned forward in anticipation of real information about the woman.

"Here it is. She listed a medical practice in Dolan Springs, Arizona. There's a note here. Let me enlarge it," she paused and pursed her lips. "It says '*file was requested, but not received.*' I'm not sure if we followed up or not. Our practice was pretty new at that point, so it's possible we let that slide."

Alex cleared his throat. "The name of the practice is in the file, though? We could look them up?"

Dr. Janner nodded. "Yes, you should be able to. You'll need to give them a copy of the death certificate, of course."

Alex stood up. Genevieve pulled out a business card. "Here's my card. You can email me the file at that address."

Dr. Janner took the card. "I'll do it right now. I'm sorry I couldn't be more helpful. It sounds like you're hearing that about Ms. Smith a lot."

"It has felt like we're banging our heads against the wall a bit," Genevieve admitted. "Thank you for your time. I know you and your staff had to stay late for us."

"It's not a problem. Let me know if I can help with anything else," Dr. Janner responded as she took off her medical coat and hung it on the rack behind her desk. "Pam most likely locked the deadbolt on the front door. I'll follow you out."

Dr. Janner hit a few keys on her keyboard and the screen went dark. She grabbed an ergonomic backpack, swung it onto her back, and headed out of the office. Alex uncharacteristically followed behind her, leaving Genevieve to almost jog to keep up with the two taller adults. The doctor used her keys to unlock the glass door and Alex pushed it open. The wind howled and the bushes outside the office swayed in their direction.

"Is it supposed to storm?" Dr. Janner asked as she gazed to the east. "I never keep up with the weather."

Dark clouds loomed in the distance. Genevieve shrugged. "Could be. Thank you again for your help."

The doctor nodded in their direction and turned back to resecure the door. She entered a code on the digital panel next to the door which beeped in response. They walked back to the cruiser and got inside.

"Look up Dolan Springs, Arizona," Alex requested as he started the car. "I've never heard of it."

Genevieve pulled out her cell phone and turned it back on. She saw she'd missed a call from Cari and resisted the urge to look to see if Alex saw the notification. She unlocked the screen and pulled up her maps app.

"Dolan Springs, Arizona. Looks like it's southeast of Vegas in northwest Arizona. Pretty sparse out there. The internet says less than two thousand people live there," she told him.

"But she grew up somewhere out here, right?" Alex began.

"I assume so. That was the impression I got, especially since all of her siblings live in New York," Genevieve concurred.

"At some point, she moved to Arizona for college. She lived there for twenty or so years and then one day, she came back."

"What made her come back?" Genevieve wondered.

"First thing tomorrow, before we go to the lawyer's, let's dig into her past some more. Find where she went to college, if she was ever married—" he started.

"Married? She's still a Smith, though," Genevieve argued.

"She could have changed her name back," Alex challenged.

"True. I'm free tonight. I'll see if I can find any details on her background," Genevieve offered.

"One day, you're going to have a life outside of this job," Alex told her.

"Are you about to lecture me on healthy boundaries?" she asked him.

He briefly took his hands off the steering wheel and held them up in mock surrender. "I'm just making observations. What is it you young millennials like to say? You do you."

* * * * *

Cari hadn't stopped her digital recorder and pulled it out of her bag after she got into her car. "Rewatch party videos and pay attention to servers," she said aloud before hitting the stop button. She tossed the device back into the bag and glanced in the rearview mirror. Luckily, she was only a few minutes from her apartment. The wind had frizzed her curls quite a bit despite her efforts to keep them tied back.

She quickly navigated the turns to her complex and hurried up to her apartment. She kicked off her shoes near her bed and pulled the hair tie from her hair at the same time. She opened her closet and found a lightweight sundress that seemed suitable for the restaurant. She quickly swapped her blouse and jeans for the dress and slipped on her flats. They'd be more comfortable than heels.

She glanced at her watch; she only had fifteen minutes to tame her hair.

Cari had barely started detangling her curls when she heard a knock at her door. Bob was early as usual.

"Coming!" she called out as she teased the pick through her hair.

She quickly opened the door and found Bob waiting with a bouquet of sunflowers in his hand. "Ah, Bob, those are so pretty. Can you put them in water for me? I'm trying to force my hair into submission," she said as she turned back to the bathroom.

Bob grabbed her hand with his free hand and pulled her toward him. She swung around and kissed him lightly. "Okay, I've really got to get my hair under control."

He laughed and released her hand. "I'll try to find something that can masquerade as a vase."

"Not funny! I saved the vase from last time. It's probably under the sink," she yelled over her shoulder.

She heard him rustling around as she finally got her hair to settle down. "Did you find it?"

He grunted. "I found a lot of plastic lids and several grocery receipts."

Cari swapped her phone and wallet to her small clutch and joined him in the kitchen. "Um, you know, now that I think about it…" she turned and looked on top of the refrigerator. "I think I put it on top of the fridge."

She reached up and retrieved the dusty vase. "Here it is!"

"Wonder of wonders," he laughed. "Are you ready to go once I get these in water?"

"I am. I've only eaten lunch at The Yellow Duckling. I'm excited to see their dinner menu," she mused.

"I looked it up. It looks really good," he said as he slipped the sunflowers into the vase.

Cari's phone buzzed inside her bag. She looked at her watch and saw Dahlia's name flashing. "Oh, it's Dahlia. I'll let it go to voicemail. Let's go get some dinner."

"Got your keys?" Bob asked as he pulled the door closed behind them.

"Oh, I think I tossed them on the coffee table on my way inside earlier," she said as she reached for the knob.

He put a hand out to stop her. "I saw them and grabbed them for you."

She took the keys from him and locked her apartment. "Thanks," she said with a sheepish grin.

"No problem," he responded. "So, you said that was the young woman, Dahlia, on the phone? Have you been looking into her theory today?"

Cari shook her head no as she walked down the steps with him. She had to keep a hand on her dress to keep the wind from lifting it up. "No, not really. She added me to this conspiracy theory group and I started to read one of the posts, but then Ollaman came around. He thought I was wasting time scrolling through my personal news feed rather than working on the author story. I haven't looked at it again."

"Do you think her theory is plausible?" he asked her.

"I'm not sure. I haven't had a chance to think about it a lot. I've been all over today with this story and I still don't feel like I've learned much," she paused, thinking about Genevieve's request to meet. "Is the case still, uh…"

"It's still locked down as far as I know," Bob told her.

She nodded. "Enough shop talk, then. I'm glad the restaurant is so close; I'm starving."

"Did you eat lunch?" he asked as he drove down the road away from her complex.

"Yeah, I had a late lunch, but like I said, I've been running around quite a bit. Tell me about the menu while you drive," she requested.

"Well, it had a few pasta dishes, a couple cuts of steak, a chicken dish, but I think you'll be most excited about the sides," he said licking his lips.

"Brussel sprouts?" she asked in anticipation.

"Yes, and roasted asparagus wrapped in prosciutto!" he said with a big smile.

"Oh wow, those are two of my favorites. We should each get one and share…I mean, if you want to," she proposed.

He grinned as he parked the car in front of the restaurant. "It's a deal…unless, of course, I find something I like better."

She laughed and walked with him into the restaurant. The ambiance was much different than her experience at lunch. The lights were dimmed and each table had a small white candle as a centerpiece. Bob walked up to the hostess stand.

"Party of two for Hursley," he told the young woman.

She ran her finger down a screen and then looked up with a smile. "Right this way, Mr. Hursley."

They followed the hostess to a side table and took a seat. She handed them each a menu and set another smaller menu between them on the table. "Your server will be over shortly to get your drink order."

They nodded in understanding and opened the menus. Cari reached for the drink menu after glancing at the food options. "This was a good idea, Bob. It's fun to go out with you."

His cheeks reddened. "I'm glad you like spending time with me."

She laughed. "I *love* you, Bob. Of course, I enjoy spending time with you. Since we can't talk about the case, what should we talk about?"

He tilted his head and smirked. "Well…I'm guessing my mother isn't the only one who's been asking about a wedding date."

Cari felt her own cheeks redden. "And you'd be correct. I'm sort of enjoying being engaged still, you know? It feels pretty recent to me."

He reached across the table and grabbed her hand. "No rush at all. We can take all the time we need."

Chapter 12

Genevieve checked her watch for the fifteenth time. She hadn't realized Cari wouldn't be home until closer to eight o'clock. She was anxious to talk through the investigation, but she also didn't want to be seen lurking outside her friend's home. Rather than wait outside Cari's unit, she returned to her vehicle. She then moved it two units over and sunk low into the passenger seat. Headlights reflected off the side mirror and she slowly turned to look. Bob's car pulled past her toward Cari's guest parking spot. She looked away as her friend leaned across the console to kiss Bob goodbye. Even though she was small, she worried Bob might have noticed her large vehicle. The expedition was pretty easy to spot. She hoped he was too caught up paying attention to Cari to see her. Finally, Cari got out of the car and made her way up the steps of the apartment building. Genevieve waited until Bob exited the complex before getting out of her car. She went up the steps and knocked on Cari's door.

"Wow, you're right on time!" Cari exclaimed as she pulled the door open. "I'm just going to change into some shorts and a t-shirt. Help yourself to water. I probably don't have anything else…well, I might have some wine. It could go either way."

Genevieve laughed and went to the kitchen to get a glass of water. After filling it up from the tap, she sat down at the table. She set her laptop bag on the empty chair near the window and pulled her notebook out of her pocket to page through it while she waited for Cari.

"Ready for the race on Saturday?" Cari called out from the bedroom.

"More or less," she shrugged even though her friend couldn't see her.

"Is Quentin going to be there?" Cari asked her.

Genevieve clicked her tongue. "We broke up. Partly because I wasn't giving him the attention he wanted and mostly because he has to move to Virginia to be closer to his family. I'm over it…I mean it was only a thing for a few months."

Cari padded into the room in her bare feet. She stopped short after seeing Genevieve sitting at the table rather than in front of the TV. Genevieve saw her face go from confusion to understanding with one glance at the notebook. She bit her lip.

"Are we, um, working tonight?" Cari asked hesitantly. "I mean, it's fine, it's just…"

"I'm sure Bob told you the chief is worried about leaks to the media," Genevieve commented.

"I don't want to get you in trouble, but I could definitely use some insight," Cari admitted.

Genevieve ran a hand over her dark hair. "It's my choice to be here. If you could keep it to yourself, I would appreciate it. It's just…Alex and I can only chase down so many things. It feels like one of the siblings is actively working against us, and no one knew this woman at all. How can someone possibly have no friends?!" She took a breath and slowly let it out. "Okay, so tell me what you've discovered so far. I don't want to assume you know something and cause confusion."

"Time of death is around 11 in the evening?" Cari asked with her eyebrows raised.

Genevieve felt herself smirk. "How did you find that out?"

"Housekeeper overheard it the other day, but she wasn't positive it was true," Cari responded. "I know about the martini glass, the metho…hex…stuff, and I've looked through the social media posts from the party."

Cari crossed the room and picked up her messenger bag. "I've learned a few more things today." She walked over to the table. "The housekeeper told me Ms. Smith used to use some odd turns of phrase."

"Like what?" Genevieve asked as she turned to a blank page in her notebook.

"She said she used some poker language early on. She realized after some time that the phrases were used to describe events in Texas Hold 'Em," Cari explained. "Have you ever played?"

Genevieve shook her head. "No, I've never had the desire. Poker, huh? Now we might be getting somewhere. According to her doctor, she used to live in a small town called Dolan, Arizona."

Cari's face clouded. "I'm not following. Is that a popular place for gambling?"

She smiled. "It's not far from Las Vegas. Definitely within driving distance."

Cari nodded. "Okay, so maybe she used to go to Vegas a lot? I'm not sure what that tells us."

Genevieve hesitated. It was one thing to discuss some arbitrary facts, many of which Cari could most likely find on her own. It was another to tell her about specific evidence they'd uncovered. Cari was giving her a quizzical look.

"Cari, I, you see, um…" Genevieve began.

"What is it?" Cari asked her.

"I'm sorry. It's not that I don't trust you. Please believe me when I say that. It's just. Ugh," she groaned. "Forget it. The ME found something in the author's stomach contents."

Cari's eyes grew wide. She slowly nodded her head.

Genevieve plowed forward. "It was a charm from a bracelet: the ace of hearts."

"Oh my gosh! It's like she was leaving little clues behind!" Cari exclaimed. "Almost everyone I've talked to who read her books said that was her writing style."

Genevieve tilted her head in confusion. "Writing style? How else would you write a mystery?"

Cari shrugged. "I mean, I haven't read the books, but they say she leaves subtle clues within the text rather than stating something outright. I think it made her readers feel like they were helping the main character solve the case."

"Huh. Well, this definitely feels like a clue. She intentionally swallowed the charm hoping we would find it," Genevieve remarked.

"Wait. She probably left the rest of the bracelet somewhere relevant too," Cari remarked.

"One step ahead of you. I've already got the CSU guys tracking it down. Hopefully, that will help us connect the dots a little more easily."

"So, do you think she was a gambler? But what does that tell us?" Cari wondered aloud.

"Maybe? Her finances say she shouldn't be able to afford the house she lives in, but she owns it outright, no mortgage. We haven't been able to figure out how she was able to purchase it on her book royalties."

"But don't people usually lose money if they gamble a lot?" Cari argued.

"It's not always the case. Maybe she was a card counter or something," Genevieve suggested. "Her siblings said once she went to college, they hardly heard from her. She moved across the country for about two decades, then one day came back...and decided to be an author? Why?"

"It is odd," Cari agreed. "What else do you know about her background?"

"I spent the last two hours trying to find out her history. She went to college at Northern Arizona University and got a degree in mathematics. I have some of this saved on my laptop. Let me boot it up," she said, reaching for her bag.

"Did she teach math after that?" Cari asked.

Genevieve shook her head as she opened her laptop. "No, I didn't request a transcript, so I don't know if she had a specialty within that degree. She became an actuary for an insurance company. The company is no longer in business."

"Maybe that's why she moved back," Cari proposed.

Genevieve found her folder marked G-Smith and opened it. She selected the document entitled 'history' and double-clicked on it. "Let's see. No, they closed down in the last decade. It looks like it was a mom-and-pop type place. The owners must have wanted to retire. Their names are Molly and Oliver Duncan—"

"Molly and Ollie?" Cari laughed.

Genevieve chuckled. "I didn't even notice. Yeah, but their company was Duncanins." She flipped her screen so Cari could see it and write it down. "She didn't work for them for too long. I think she became self-employed after gaining experience with the small firm," Genevieve told her. "I need to dig further back into her tax records to figure that out."

Cari frowned and bit her lip. "I'm feeling a big ignorant. What is an actuary?"

Genevieve smiled. "They analyze risks and benefits using statistics and theory to help a business be more profitable."

"So, they're good with numbers," Cari replied.

"Yes, very good with numbers," Genevieve agreed.

"What about friends?" Cari asked as she tapped her pencil on the table. "Like you said, no one seems to have known Gayle Smith the person at all."

"We called the authors who attended her party. None of them knew much about her either," Genevieve responded. "It's hard to believe she was that reclusive, but maybe she really did live like a hermit."

"Wait. Did you get a copy of the guest list? Maybe there's a person on the list who wasn't able to come, but did consider her a friend," Cari proposed.

"I guess it's possible they were sick and had to cancel. Let me pull up the guest list. We called the authors who were there—at least the ones who gave Sharon a business card. I marked them off on the list already. Let me pull it up."

The list was numbered and had fifty-two names on it. She and Alex had eliminated twenty-three with their phone calls. Hopefully they could find one or two people who were unable to attend, but were actually the woman's friend.

"Looking at the list, some of these are Gayle's family members who didn't show up. Sharon's kids, Gary's kids, and Michael's kids. That's…three, five, eight people we can ignore," Genevieve told her. "That leaves us with six names. I can print it for you. Maybe you can chat with them tomorrow? Do you have a printer here?"

"Yes, it's wireless. I just changed the cartridge last week, so it should be good to go. Can you see it on the list?"

"I got it. It should be printing now," Genevieve told her. She could hear a printer making noise, but didn't see one in the room. "Where is your printer?"

"Oh, it's in my room. I'll go grab it," she said and paused.

"What is it?" Genevieve asked. "It's like a light bulb just went off in your head."

Cari bit her lip. "The cartridge," she paused and then shook her head. "It's not a big deal. I'll be right back."

Cari got up from the table. Genevieve wondered if one of the people on the list had known Gayle before she moved back to New York. Maybe they could explain Ms. Smith's history with poker or why she wanted someone to find that specific charm.

Cari's phone buzzed, interrupting Genevieve's thoughts. "Your phone is ringing…it's your sister."

Cari stepped back into the room with the printout. She glanced at her phone. "Just let it ring. I can call her later."

"No, go ahead and take it. I need to refill my water," she told her.

Genevieve grabbed the glass and pushed back from the table. She walked over to the sink and turned on the water. She couldn't help but eavesdrop on Cari's conversation.

"…this Friday evening? I don't know, Bea. I'll need to check with Bob. We usually catch a new movie on Friday night. And we have the race the next morning…" Cari turned around and mouthed, "She's looking for a babysitter."

"I can do it," Genevieve said quickly.

Cari raised her eyebrows in surprise. "Uh, Bea? Genevieve is here and…I'm not hanging up on you. Genevieve offered to babysit for you," Cari listened for a moment before speaking again. "Can you go to their house? They have a late dinner reservation with one of Robby's bosses."

"I can do that. No problem," Genevieve responded. "She has my number, right?"

"Do you have her number?" Cari asked in confusion. "Love you, Bea. Talk to you soon. Yeah, see you Saturday," she ended the call. "Okay, she said to call her tomorrow and work out the details. How do you have her number?"

Genevieve shrugged. "I think it was when you were texting the photos from your vacation. Yeah, she figured the other number on there was mine and called me a few times to see if your concussion was as mild as you were claiming it to be. She was worried about you. I brought her coffee Saturday or Sunday after your accident. We kind of bonded. They'd made plans to go to the lake that day, but it rained and Robby got called into the office. I hung out and played some games with Bea and the kids. We're all buddies now."

Cari smiled. "Not to change the subject, but I know you talked with the servers from the party. Were you able to speak with all five?"

Genevieve shook her head no. "We talked to two young women at their warehouse today. They weren't a lot of help. I wasn't able to connect with the other three yet. What did you learn?"

"I talked to four of the five. The fifth one didn't release his contact info, so I tracked it down on my own. I tried to pay him a visit before dinner tonight, but he wasn't home. His roommate said he's been missing for days," Cari told her.

"Days? Is this normal behavior for him?" Genevieve asked.

Cari bit the inside of her cheek. "Now that is a tricky question. His roommate admitted his friend has had a problem with drugs in the past and he used to occasionally disappear for a day or so while he was out getting high. He was pretty adamant that he was clean right now, so I don't think this falls under normal behavior any more. He tried calling the young man's parents and they hadn't heard from him either. He hasn't done much else to try to find him, but the young man isn't answering his phone at all."

Genevieve paged through her notebook, then remembered the names were on a printout on her desk at the precinct. "What's his name?"

"James Dolling," Cari responded. "He's twenty-one years old."

Genevieve stared at her. "Did you say twenty-one?"

Cari nodded. "That's what I found in the database."

"Then who was the older male server? All the others were female. Did you see a photo of him?" Genevieve asked.

"No, I told the roommate to go file a missing person report. I don't know if he listened to me. I've just barely started trying to find him, but I honestly wondered *if* he made it to the party on Sunday," Cari said as she pulled her laptop from her bag. "Let me see if I can find him on social media."

"I'll pull up the video from the party," Genevieve said as she opened her internet browser. "Janice made all of the photos and videos public."

Cari snorted. "That's funny. The author's sister, Penny? She added me as a friend so I could see them. I guess that was unnecessary…I found James Dolling. This has to be him. The photos have his roommate in them."

Genevieve leaned over to look at Cari's screen. "That's definitely not the server from the party. The James Dolling on your screen has thick black hair that he seems quite proud of. I'm surprised he would willingly put a hairnet over that as a server. Not that I'd know, but it seems like a lot of effort went into that 'do."

"Oh, agreed. He definitely uses product. Can I see the server at the party?" Cari requested.

Genevieve shifted her laptop toward Cari. "Here he is: old, balding, but rather fit for someone his age."

"I spoke with the head server for the party. Surely, she would have mentioned something about a change in staff, right?" Cari said in confusion.

Genevieve pulled out her phone and unlocked it. "I don't know. I mean, maybe she's just told how many servers to expect. I don't think they all ride to the events in the company van. We need to find out what happened to Mr. Dolling. It might be unrelated, but it feels like too big of a coincidence."

Cari put a hand on Genevieve's arm. "Should you wait to call from your own place? How are you going to explain finding this guy?"

Genevieve pulled her thumb away from the call button. "I have his name from the owner of the catering company. I'm following up on a hunch. But you're right. I should call from somewhere else. Just in case."

"I'll give the catering place a call tomorrow and see if they can tell me who this other guy is," Cari offered.

"No!" Genevieve almost startled herself with her outburst. "I'm sorry. I didn't mean to shout. Let us handle talking to the owner about the personnel change."

"What's the big deal? It's the obvious next step," Cari argued.

"I know and we should take it," Genevieve countered.

Cari flinched. "I thought you said you needed my help."

Genevieve put her hands up in surrender. "I don't want to argue. I'm concerned your questions might flush this guy out."

"Then you can bring him down," Cari said pointedly. "C'mon. This is my job too. You wouldn't even know he was missing if I hadn't told you."

Genevieve opened her mouth to argue again, but then quickly closed it. Cari was right. She didn't have a good reason for her friend to stay away from the owner of the company. She just didn't want Alex to see any overlap when they called around about Mr. Dolling tomorrow.

She stood up and shoved her things into her bag. "I'm sorry. You're right. Go ahead and see if you can track this kid down too. I mean, you don't need my permission." She took a deep breath before she continued. "Thanks for meeting with me. This was really helpful. I'll let you know at the end of the day tomorrow where things stand," she paused. "I know you know this, but I have to say it. You know you can't print any of this until I say so, right?"

Cari touched her arm. "Of course. Don't worry about it."

Genevieve pulled her bag over her shoulder. "I need to go make sure James Dolling has been reported as missing. Something about this doesn't sit right with me. If you hear from his roommate, please let me know. Actually, did you get his number?"

"I did. I'll text it to you."

"Thanks. I appreciate it," Genevieve said as she put her hand on the doorknob.

Cari nodded. "Same. Drive safe."

"Talk to you soon," Genevieve said as she let herself out. It felt good to make progress on the case. She wished she could have convinced Grusky to sign off on it. She brushed the thought aside and hurried back to her car.

* * * * *

It was close to ten o'clock when Genevieve had rushed out of her apartment. Cari wanted to get her action items for the next day in order before she got ready for bed. She was giving Bob the day off from running tomorrow and decided to take a rest day herself too. They could do an easy jog on Thursday morning and be ready for the 5k on Saturday.

She needed to call Deb or Melia again to ask about the fifth server. She flipped back through her notes some more. Deb was the head server for the party, but Melia seemed more forthcoming with details. She added James Dolling's status next on the list. She knew Genevieve most likely wasn't going to update her midday, but she could look up the state's missing person database and see if his name was on the list. Genevieve had mentioned Gayle worked for a small insurance company in Arizona. Cari wanted to call the owners and see what they knew about their former employee. She wrote down 'friends' next. She couldn't believe someone was living life without a single confidante. Someone out there knew Gayle Smith and at some point, had considered her a friend.

Cari looked at the printout with the six names and email addresses from the guest list. Cari took a picture of them with her phone. She decided to get a leg up on the day and send them each a quick email before she got ready for bed. She identified herself as a journalist for the Beagle and said she would be giving them a call regarding the death of their friend and colleague, Gayle Smith, a.k.a. Natasha Gillespie. Rather than type six separate emails, she just copied the same words into each one and then changed who she was addressing in the body of the text.

Her phone buzzed. She looked at the screen and saw it was reminding her about Dahlia's voicemail message. She sighed. She didn't really have time to put toward the young woman's theories. The young woman's heartbreak was evident. Cari felt guilty ignoring her all evening, so she hit play on the message.

*"Hi again. It's me, Dahlia. I, uh, well, my group and I found some surprising similarities between our loved ones. I think it's rather convincing. If you could call me. I know you're busy. *sniff* We were all shocked when we saw it. I'm not sure I should share*

it in a voicemail. I know that sounds paranoid, but I think whoever did this has some connections. Maybe he can hack into my voicemail. It's just I—"

The message ended before she finished her sentence. Cari looked at her list and then back to her phone. She reluctantly wrote Dahlia's name on the list. She'd barely set her pen down when she remembered her epiphany from earlier. Dahlia had left a message about using her great-aunt's printer. Cari had shrugged it off at the time, but she realized now the young woman must have been telling her the printer cartridge was gone. If the printer had been out of ink when her aunt died, how could she have printed the suicide note? She picked up the pen again and wrote the word printer next to Dahlia's name. Maybe there was more to Vivian Roust's death than it seemed at first glance.

* * * * *

Genevieve called the station on her Bluetooth connection as she drove away from Cari's apartment complex. The dispatch officer picked up immediately and asked her to hold. She drummed her fingers on the steering wheel while she waited for them to reconnect. Rather than drive back to her apartment, she turned her vehicle toward the station. She could just as easily look it up from her computer there.

"Brenington Police Department. Thank you for holding. How can we help you this evening?" An older man's voice asked her.

"Is this Kurt? Sorry, this is Detective Viacorte," she apologized.

"It is indeed Kurt. What can I do for you, detective?" Kurt asked her.

As far as she knew, Kurt had been with the department longer than anyone else. If you needed to know something, he was the one to ask first. He'd started as a beat cop and then switched to a desk job when his knees got tired. Genevieve had met him on her first day on the job. She'd gone to the information desk to get directions to the new officer training. He had walked her to the conference room rather than just rattle off a series of steps for her to follow. She brought him coffee the next day and he became her ally. She smiled as she pictured him sitting behind the desk with the phone cradled between his fuzzy white hair and his big shoulder.

"Kurt, I'm looking for a young man named James Dolling. He might have been reported missing by his roommate earlier this evening," Genevieve told him.

"Let me see," he responded. She could hear his big fingers jamming the keys on his keyboard. "Is that two ls in his last name?"

"Yes, D-O-L-L-I-N-G," she confirmed.

"Nothing in the system, yet. Was the roommate coming here or would he have gone to one of the neighboring towns?" he asked for clarification. "Sometimes it takes a bit for the whole system to update."

"True. I'm pretty sure he was going to BPD, but I could be wrong. I'll make some calls. I appreciate your help, Kurt," she responded.

"Any time, detective. You be careful out there," he said, ending the call.

She parked in the lot and pulled out her phone. Cari had texted her the roommate's contact information earlier. She found the text and touched the number to give Xander a call. It rang three times before an automated voicemail message began. She hit end and decided to text instead.

Xander. This is Detective Viacorte with Brenington PD. Please call me.

She stared at the screen for a few seconds, willing him to respond. She saw the message status go from unread to read, but the little dots indicating someone was typing did not appear. She looked at her watch and saw it was well after ten o'clock now. Maybe the kid was scared and unsure if she really was a police officer. She decided they could try to pay him a visit the next morning instead. Her phone vibrated with an incoming call, startling her even though she'd been staring at it. She swiped across the screen to answer it.

"Hi, Bea. I wasn't expecting to hear from you tonight. Is everything okay?" Genevieve asked her.

"Oh, everything is fine!" Bea said cheerfully. "I know I told Cari we could connect tomorrow, but I thought I'd check in now. Sorry that it's so late. Are you sure you're up for watching the kids? We usually have a high school girl come over, but she's got a date, so we're scrambling."

"It's not a problem at all. I used to watch my little brother all the time," Genevieve said easily. "What time do you need me there?"

Bea clucked her tongue. "Robby said it's a late dinner, so we don't need to leave until 7:30. How about fifteen minutes before that? The kids will have already eaten and bathed. You're really just going to help them wind down and go to bed. Their bedtime is still at eight o'clock, though Hilary is starting to push back on that. Mostly, we just need a warm body here in case of an emergency."

"I get it. It will be fun to see your kids again. They were a big help at the first responders' car wash fundraiser back in May. I think they washed more cars than everyone else," Genevieve responded.

Bea laughed. "Joel is still talking about getting to wash the firetruck and police cars. They'll be excited to see you too. I'm not sure what time we'll get home. Hopefully, not too late. We're all four coming to the 5k and parade Saturday morning too."

"It will be okay either way. I'll see you Friday evening," Genevieve said.

"Thanks again. We really appreciate it," Bea said and ended the call.

Genevieve pushed her phone back into her bag and yawned. Alex was probably already asleep and would be disappointed she was still chasing down leads this many hours after their shift ended. She put her car in reverse and backed out of the parking space. This would keep until tomorrow.

Chapter 13

Ollaman was waiting at Cari's desk when she arrived at the office Wednesday morning. She had hoped to run down to the coffee shop at the corner to get a latte before digging into the investigation that day, but apparently, coffee was going to have to wait. Ollaman had seen her step into the newsroom and was walking her way.

"Turnlyle! How's the story coming? Any new leads? Have your sources in the police department given you the inside scoop, yet?" He used air quotes on the word sources making Cari inwardly groan.

"Good morning, Mr. Ollaman," she said as cheerfully as she could. She continued walking toward her desk even though he had met her halfway. "The chief of police is concerned the case will have too many leaks and has ordered all his people to keep a tight lid on the details of the case."

"Ah, but you have special access, right?" he said with a wink.

"No, I promised Bob we wouldn't talk about the case. It's not worth the risk to his job," she explained, trying not to cringe.

Ollaman's brow knit together. "Huh. What have you found out then?"

Cari reached her desk and draped her messenger bag over the back of her chair. "I got the names of the five servers from the retirement party and one of them seems to have gone missing. In fact, I'm not sure he actually made it to the party in the first place."

"Oh, that is interesting. Maybe he was involved. Good work, Turnlyle!" Ollaman turned and marched off to his office.

She shook her head in disbelief. Her boss' obsession with this investigation was a little odd. Normally, she wouldn't think twice about talking through her progress with him, but his behavior this week was off somehow. She looked back to his office and saw he was on the phone. When he noticed her looking at him, he walked over to the window and pulled the blinds closed. *Surely, he wouldn't leak details to another news outlet, right?* She almost laughed at the absurdity of her thought. Ollaman would never jeopardize the success of his newspaper.

She pulled out her notebook and logged into her computer. Dahlia had been weighing on her mind. Part of her wanted to call the young woman and confirm that she understood her voice message correctly: the printer cartridge was missing. She looked at Ollaman's office again. He'd already berated her once for not focusing on the Smith investigation. She mentally set Dahlia aside and looked at her notebook. First on her list was to talk to one of the servers again. Her gut said Melia would tell her more, so she pulled up the woman's number and punched it into the desk phone. Melia answered immediately.

"I take it you have more questions?" Melia said with a bored tone.

"Yes, this is Cari again…" Cari started to say.

"I recognized the number. I'm rolling silverware today. What's the question?" Melia asked, sounding annoyed.

"Right, sorry. I was able to speak with three of the other four people who worked the party with you on Sunday evening. The fourth, Mr. James Dolling—"

"No, Doll-baby was not at the party. I thought he would be because he seems to usually get assigned when the two teeny-boppers are on duty, but I guess he didn't this time," Melia cut in.

Cari smirked at her nicknames for the other workers. "Do you have a name for the fifth server? I'd like to speak with him too."

"Oh, what was it? It was something boring. Some everyday name. If you hadn't asked me, I could have told you. You know, I'm sure Ted has his information in his computer. He does simple background checks on all his servers for obvious reasons. He doesn't want any pervs working for him. Anyway, I can ask him when he gets back. He's out of the office right now," Melia offered.

"That would be great, thanks," Cari responded as she thought through what Melia was saying. "It's strange though…"

"What's strange?" Melia asked her.

"Ted was the one who gave me the list. Why would he give me the wrong name?" Cari asked her.

"Maybe it was a last-minute change. It happens sometimes. Ted gets busy and forgets to update his system, I guess," Melia surmised.

"Okay, well, thanks again for your time," Cari replied.

"Sure thing. Bye." Melia ended the call.

Cari frowned. It didn't make sense that the owner would spend time calling and confirming the list of workers if one of them hadn't actually been assigned to the event. She wondered if Deb would know why there had been a switch and punched her number in next.

"This is Deb," the familiar voice said into the phone.

"Hi, Deb. It's Cari from the Beagle again. I've been having a hard time tracking down the fifth server from the author's event the other day. It sounds like I might have been given the wrong name by accident. Was James Dolling assigned to the party?" she asked.

Deb clucked her tongue. "He was initially, or so I was told, but this other guy showed up in his place. He had the uniform, so I figured Ted approved it."

"Any chance you remember his name?" Cari asked hopefully.

"Yeah, Edward Butler. He was a big help. No complaints here. He was a much harder worker than the Dolling kid. Speaking of,

I'm glad you called. I need to tell Ted how much I enjoyed working with him. I hope he continues to hire more mature adults. The teens and college kids are just in it for the paycheck. No work ethic," she complained.

"Did you get Mr. Butler's contact information?" Cari asked her.

"Nah, Ted will have it. He keeps meticulous records," Deb told her.

"That's the impression I have of him, too," Cari said thoughtfully. "Which makes it even stranger that he gave me Mr. Dolling's name rather than Mr. Butler's."

Deb clucked her tongue again. "That *is* odd. It must have been a very last-minute change. Maybe Dolling called in sick. I mean, he's a nice kid, but he's not the most reliable sometimes."

"What do you mean?" Cari asked, intrigued by the description.

"He's a smoker and needs to take frequent smoke breaks. I always have to remind him not to smoke upwind of the guests if we're outside. No one wants their fancy clothes smelling like cigarette smoke. Gross," Deb explained. "Did you have any other questions because today is actually my day off."

"Oh! I'm so sorry. I'll try to get in touch with Ted and see if he can connect me with Mr. Butler."

Cari ended the call. She knew Ted wasn't available at the moment, so she looked at her list again. She wanted to get the people from the insurance company on the phone and see what they could tell her about Gayle Smith. It was obviously a small company, so they surely knew more about her than just her name. She looked up the information Genevieve had given her about the company. She had the owners' names and the company name. She typed the man's name into LexisNexis and waited for the results to load.

Oliver Duncan was in his eighties and had been married for over sixty years. He was listed as retired. Cari scrolled through the information and found his phone number. She started to pull the receiver from her desk phone when she remembered the time difference. She couldn't remember if Arizona was in the mountain time zone or the pacific one. She opened a browser window to look it up. The results quickly informed her it was logical not to remember: the state was in one time zone for half the year and another for the other half. They didn't do Daylight Saving Time. *Smart people*. Regardless, it was much too early to call a retired couple at this point. She jotted down the phone number and set it aside for later. She could start looking up the six guests who didn't come to the party while she waited for Ted, the caterer, to call her back.

* * * * *

The coffee carafe was already empty when Genevieve went to fill her mug on Wednesday morning. She sighed and opened the canister of grounds to make more. It took the coffee maker more than ten minutes to brew a full pot. She hit the start button and returned to her desk sans coffee.

"The carafe was empty again. I'm going to go grab a coffee from the truck. You want anything?" she asked Alex.

He held up his mug and took a sip. "No, I'm all set here. We need to leave for the lawyer's office in about half an hour."

"I'll be back in less than five minutes," she told him.

Her phone buzzed with an incoming call as she passed his desk. She pulled it out and saw it was the FBI instructor from the program she completed last month. She swiped the screen to answer it.

"This is Detective Viacorte," she said crisply.

"Viacorte. It's Dureski. Any update for me?" her instructor asked. "We're grasping at straws over here."

Genevieve clenched her teeth and felt her shoulders slump. "Not yet. I found a way in, but it can't happen until Friday night."

She pushed the door to the station open and stepped onto the sidewalk. The wind was howling again and rustled a loose strand of hair into her face. Thankfully, most of her hair stayed in the low bun she'd wrapped it into that morning.

"You're sure you can get something for us then?" he pressed her.

"I feel pretty confident about it," she lied.

"Call me as soon as you have something," he said and ended the call.

Genevieve looked up at the office window and wondered if Alex had been watching her. She shoved her phone in her pocket and stomped over to the coffee truck.

"One hot coffee with half-n-half," she said to the barista. "And a squirt of vanilla."

"Coming right up."

The wind gusted and overturned the truck's assortment of sweeteners and creamers. She grabbed as many as she could and returned them to the little basket. The barista grinned at her in gratitude and slipped the basket onto the other side of the window for safe keeping. Genevieve tapped her card on the payment screen and waited for him to finish filling the paper cup for her.

"Here's your coffee," he said, handing her a cup. "Sugar or sweetener?"

She reached through the window and took a sugar packet from him. Normally, she didn't put sugar in her coffee, but she was in a hurry and didn't want to have to go back to the break room for honey. She thanked him and walked quickly back to the station's entrance. The coffee was too hot to drink, so she blew across the top before taking a sip. It was better than what she'd started in the break room.

Alex was looking her way when she entered the detective's bay. She lifted her cup in acknowledgment and took a seat at her desk. He swiveled his chair to face her.

"Bob called while you were getting coffee," he told her. "They found the charm bracelet."

Genevieve had lifted her coffee to her mouth as Alex spoke. His revelation made her momentarily forget how hot the coffee was. She winced as it burned her mouth. "Ouch! Dang it."

Alex smirked. "Smooth. Anyway, they found it inside her map book."

"Did you say *map* book?" Genevieve asked him.

"I did. It used to be a very common household item, or at least something everyone had in their car. You know what a map looks like, right? Like a paper map?" he goaded her.

She rolled her eyes. "I've seen a map before, Sherlock. I didn't realize they sold maps in books, but you know, olden times and all."

He glared at her briefly before continuing. "As I was saying, they found the bracelet marking the page for the strip in Las Vegas."

Genevieve almost took another swig of coffee, but stopped herself just in time. She blew into the cup and then took a sip. "Vegas! Okay, so we have the ace of hearts and now Vegas. Something must have happened there twenty years ago. She ran away to escape it and whatever it was caught up to her."

"Or *whoever* it was," Alex remarked.

"I believe you mean whomever," Genevieve corrected him.

He rolled his eyes. "It seems like she made an intentional effort to point us in the right direction."

Genevieve nodded. "She must have swallowed the charm and then hidden the martini glass and bracelet when she was inside for the extended period of time. I suppose there could be other hidden clues, but we're going to need to find out more of her background to give us an idea of how to identify them."

"Okay, so we're meeting with the lawyer today and going to her bank. What else?" Alex asked her.

She started to answer when her cell phone buzzed. She checked the screen and saw it was Sharon Chiddy.

"Ugh, it's Sharon," she moaned.

"Better answer it," he instructed her.

"Hi, Sharon. How can we help you today?"

"It's been over forty-eight hours since someone found my sister dead in her home. You still haven't released her body to us *and* we haven't heard a thing about her estate. Who is the executor of her will? Is it Penny?" Sharon asked haughtily.

"Uh, Sharon, we have just started going through her will. We're getting it verified," Genevieve explained.

"She did have a will then. Who is named in it? Siblings? Nieces and nephews? Who?" Sharon demanded.

Genevieve tried to dodge the question. "We, uh, we aren't really at that point yet, Sharon. I'm sure her lawyer will be in touch with you in the event—"

"Nothing?! She left us nothing?! I can't believe it. Of all the ungrateful…" Sharon's voice trailed off and the call ended.

"That sounded pleasant," Alex grinned sarcastically. "Maybe we should tell the lawyer to hire some security when he executes her will."

Before she could respond, her phone buzzed with another incoming call. The caller ID said "Xander" and she quickly swiped to accept the call.

"Xander. I'm glad you returned my call," she said quickly. "Were you able to file a missing person report for your roommate?"

Alex's face twisted in confusion. "Missing person? What?"

She waved him off and listened to Xander. "Can you repeat that? I'm sorry, my partner was talking in my other ear."

He cleared his throat. "I haven't done it yet. I…I…I don't want to get him in trouble. Um, did your friend tell you about his, uh, history?"

"The drug use?" Genevieve asked.

"Uh, yeah, that. I mean, maybe he's just out partying or sleeping one off…" Xander said uncertainly.

"For almost three days, Xander?" she asked incredulously. "He could also be hurt or in the hospital or worse."

Xander groaned. "Ugh. I know. I *know*. I mean, I guess you're police, right? You said you're a detective or something?"

"I am," Genevieve confirmed.

"Can't you just file it? Now that I've called you?" he asked. "Look, I returned the call. I, uh, I gotta go."

Genevieve pulled her phone down and looked at the screen. "He hung up."

"Who? Who is Xander?" Alex asked.

"He's the other server's roommate," she told him.

"The other server? The one we didn't have a number for? You tracked him down?" Alex asked in confusion. "How did I get so far behind on this?"

She hesitated. She didn't want Alex to know about her meeting with Cari last night. "I wanted to talk to the other servers, but we didn't have a number for this guy. The video showed the male server carrying the tray of martinis, so I thought he'd be our best bet of knowing how much the author drank at her party."

"But this was his roommate on the phone…" Alex raised his eyebrows at her. "How did he enter the picture?"

"I got in touch with him trying to reach James Dolling. He said Mr. Dolling left on Sunday for work, but hasn't been home since. He isn't answering his phone or responding to texts."

"And you encouraged him to file a missing person report." Alex connected the dots. "I take it he didn't do it?"

"No. He's worried about getting his friend in trouble. Or maybe getting in trouble somehow himself. It seems like he isn't very trusting of law enforcement. After we meet with the lawyer, I think we need to spend some time finding this kid. The roommate says he's only twenty-one, but the server at the party looked much older," Genevieve told Alex.

"The male server? Yeah, he's older than me for sure," Alex agreed. "We need to get to the lawyer's office, but I agree with you. Something's weird about this kid going missing the same night the author was killed."

"Let me just call down and get the ball rolling on the missing person report. I can give them a name and the roommate's information," Genevieve requested.

He shrugged and she took it as permission to go ahead. She entered the extension for dispatch and waited for someone to pick up. It wouldn't be Kurt as he'd been working the night shift.

"Dispatch," an unfamiliar female voice answered.

"Hi, this is Detective Viacorte. I need to get a missing person report started," she said quickly.

"Name?" came the quick response.

"Uh, James Dolling. Age twenty-one. I don't have a D-O-B," Genevieve responded.

"Mr. Dolling's parents called this morning to report him missing and said they'd arrive by lunch to sit down with someone. I can add you as a point of contact," the woman offered.

"That would be great. I appreciate it." She ended the call and turned to Alex. "The parents decided to make a report this morning. Ready to meet with the lawyer?"

She stood up and tried to grab the keys before he did. His long arm brushed hers aside and lifted the keys from the hook. He dangled them in front of her face victoriously.

"Look up the directions. I'm driving," he said and laughed.

* * * * *

It felt like she'd wasted the last hour and a half. Cari crossed the second to last name off the list of six Genevieve had compiled for her the previous night. Each of the people she'd called so far had been excited to learn she was writing a story about the infamous author. They wondered if she needed any quotes from the woman's contemporaries to put into her piece. Not a single one had missed the party because of illness.

It had taken her about thirty minutes to find a phone number for the absent guests. She grudgingly picked up the receiver to call the last name on the list. What was that definition of insanity? Doing the same thing repeatedly and expecting different results. She groaned and punched in the number. A woman answered on the third ring. She sounded out of breath.

"Hello? Hello?" a voice said breathlessly into the phone.

"Hello! Is this Veronica Stiles?" Cari asked quickly.

The woman exhaled into Cari's ear. "Yes. Yes, it is. Sorry. I was upstairs and had to run downstairs to get the phone. I'll catch my breath in a moment. I noticed the caller ID said Brenington Beagle. Are you a journalist?"

Here we go again.

"Yes, this is Cari Turnlyle with the Beagle. Ms. Stiles, I'm writing a story about Gayle Smith, a.k.a., Natasha Gillespie. I understand you were invited to her retirement party but were unable to attend," Cari repeated her spiel.

"Yes, yes! I was invited. Oh, goodness. What a terrible thing, Natasha, I mean, Gayle being found dead. I've been one of her ARC readers for years and years. She reads for me too," Ms. Stiles explained. "Oh, and please, call me Veronica."

"Veronica, what are ARCs?" Cari asked as she made a note.

"ARCs are advanced reader copies. Authors like to send out their manuscripts to trusted readers in an effort to get a bunch of reviews posted the day the book releases. The more reviews you have, the more your book is seen in the digital world," Veronica told her.

"That makes sense," Cari responded. "It sounds like you and Gayle were close."

"Oh, I don't know if I'd say we were close. We were definitely reliable to each other. I knew I could always get a great review from her on day 1. Did I know her dog's name or if she even liked dogs? No," she stated matter-of-factly. "Gayle was all business, all the time. I sure hated to miss her party, though."

Cari tried to keep the negativity out of her voice. "If you don't mind me asking, why did you miss it?"

Veronica sighed. "I live about five hours away. I would have had to get a hotel and stay overnight or drive in the dark. I couldn't justify the cost. I know she understood, but I still felt bad."

Cari had another thought. "How did Gayle get the ARCs to you? Email? Snail mail?"

"Well, early on, the files were too big for the email servers, so we mailed each other those little thumb drives with the file on it. We'd just send them back and forth, but in the last decade or so, emailing a pdf was no big deal. There are even apps that will do it for you," Veronica laughed.

"Did Gayle ever send anything besides a manuscript? Any other files?" Cari asked.

"What kind of files? Like cover images or something? I'm pretty sure it was always just the book. Why do you ask?"

Cari debated about sharing her theory with a perfect stranger. Could she trust the woman to be discreet? She wouldn't find out if she didn't take the risk. "I have a theory that Gayle left little clues behind to help us figure out who killed her. I was hoping she might have left something in an email at some point, but maybe I'm way off base."

She heard Veronica clap her hands in the background. "That would be *just like her*! She really wrote some great books. I bet you're right. I guess it just wasn't me she picked for this particular clue."

Cari resisted the urge to groan out loud. "Thank you for your help, Veronica. I appreciate your time."

"I hope you find the next Easter egg!" Veronica said encouragingly and then ended the call.

Easter what? She almost dismissed the words as old timey, then remembered she'd heard the reference before when Bob talked about movies. Easter eggs were little hints used in movies that screenwriters or directors used to wink at their audience. Bob pointed out one in an Indiana Jones movie where creator George Lucas stuck a hieroglyphic of R2D2 and C3PO from Star Wars into one frame. Cari added Easter egg to her notes. She knew someone in CSU was probably looking through the author's computer, but with the press being persona non grata right now, she couldn't exactly call them up and tell them to look for a funny attachment. Genevieve had promised to check in later. She could pass the idea along then.

She checked her watch. It was finally late enough she felt comfortable calling the insurance company owners in Arizona. She found the phone number again and dialed it on the desk phone. It rang three times, then clicked, then rang twice before a female answered.

"I'm not sure who you're looking for, but you're about to be disappointed," a female voice said to her.

"Um, hi. This is Cari Turnlyle with the Brenington Beagle. I'm researching the background of a woman named Gayle Smith and was hoping to speak with Oliver Duncan about her. He was her former employer," Cari said cautiously.

The woman sharply inhaled when Cari mentioned Gayle's name. "Well, I did not see that coming. Usually, it's people trying to sign dad up for Medicare supplemental insurance…or solar panels…or extending his car's warranty. I digress. Gayle Smith. Wow. I haven't heard that name in a long time. How is she?"

Cari hesitated. "I'm sorry, you said you're Oliver's daughter, but I didn't catch your name."

"My apologies. I'm Wendy."

"Nice to meet you, Wendy. I was actually hoping to talk to your father or mother. Are they available?" Cari asked her.

Wendy didn't answer immediately. Cari heard her take a deep breath and click her tongue a couple of times. "Sorry for the delayed response. Mom and Dad…well, they aren't going to be able to chat about Gayle. They've both got dementia. Mom's is more advanced than Dad's, but neither one remembers my kids' names, let alone employees from over thirty years ago. I'm sorry."

Cari shoulders drooped. "I'm so sorry to hear that. Well, to answer your question from before, I'm sorry to tell you, but Gayle was murdered Sunday night," Cari said gently.

Wendy gasped. "No! What happened? Was it…? I shouldn't make assumptions. What happened?"

Cari started to blurt out the cause of death and stopped herself. "The police are being pretty tight-lipped about what happened. It's been a struggle to get details. How well did you know Gayle?"

"Well, she worked for my parents. I did too, but I wasn't a great employee at that point. I mean, it was my parents. What were they going to do if I was late? Fire me? Anyway. Gayle was a star employee. She was so good with numbers," Wendy responded.

"She was an actuary, right?" Cari asked for confirmation.

"That's right. She did some risk analysis stuff. I was one of their salespeople, but I didn't make too many sales. Gayle was fun to work with, though. We used to get lunch together during the week or maybe go to a concert in the city if she didn't have other plans. Sometimes I wondered if she just humored me as a friend because she liked working for my parents. But word of her value got around quickly. She started working as a freelance actuary about six or seven years after getting the job with Duncanins. I didn't see her hardly ever after that. I can't believe she's dead!" Wendy exclaimed.

Cari shook her head in disbelief. "Did you say Gayle went to concerts with you? That seems really out of character from what I've learned of her last two decades."

"Oh yeah, we probably went to at least six concerts a year together over in Vegas. They were so much fun. Gayle usually drove us in her car and we'd share a hotel room. We never stayed in the same place two times in a row. She said she wanted to share the wealth or something," Wendy laughed. "Like we had any wealth."

"You said you only went to concerts if Gayle wasn't busy. Did she have other friends? A love interest?" Cari asked, intrigued by this other side of the author.

"I don't know about love interest, but she made frequent trips to Vegas. At least once a month, if I remember correctly. She mentioned a man's name once, but I think it was by accident. I tried to bring him up again later but she clammed up about him. I was like, okay, hands off," Wendy informed her.

"Please tell me you remember his name," Cari begged.

"Hmm…it was so long ago. It was an old man's name. I can't quite come up with it; it's been too long. It might come to me later. I'm sorry," Wendy apologized.

"Wendy, earlier you started to ask me a question about how Gayle died, like you had an idea. What were you going to ask?"

Cari heard a squeaky sound and realized Wendy was sucking her lip into her teeth. "Oh, that was audible. Sorry. That's my nervous tick. Well, I don't want to sound judgmental, but I'm almost positive that Gayle was gambling in some fashion with all her trips to Vegas. I don't know if it was slots or card games or what, but it's kind of, well, a risky thing to do so much, right?"

"Did Gayle go to Vegas with this other friend?" Cari asked.

"That I don't know. I always assumed that's who she was with, but I don't think I ever met him," Wendy responded. "Is there anything else I can tell you about Gayle?"

"I don't think so. I really appreciate your time today. And, uh, I'm sorry about your parents. That must be hard," Cari told her.

"Thank you. Some days are better than others. I still have my memories," Wendy said wistfully before ending the call.

Cari made a note of the mystery man from Arizona. This was the second time someone had mentioned poker or gambling in reference to the author. She and Genevieve had tossed around the idea of Gayle being a card counter the day before. Maybe there was more truth to that than they had originally thought. She thumbed off a quick text to Genevieve to tell her the author used to make frequent trips to Vegas.

Chapter 14

The law office of Taylor Gomez, Esq. sat on Main Street in Brenington, nestled between a restaurant and an insurance office. Genevieve guessed it had previously been a single-family home, which someone subsequently converted into a business. It seemed like the older parts of the city had morphed into their current business classification while the newer portions were built with a specific design scheme in mind. The one-story building had white trim and greyish-blue siding with small planter boxes under the two windows in the front. She imagined it must have had a cute white picket fence to go along with it in its previous life. A faded plastic sign with the words "We're open! Come on in!" printed on it hung on the front door. She twisted the knob and pulled the door open. A very young man with carrot-red hair, skin as pale as a ghost, and freckles for days looked up when they entered.

"You must be the detectives," the fresh-faced young man said to them as he pushed his glasses back in place on his nose. "I'm Sebastian, Mr. Gomez's summer intern. He'll be right with you."

Genevieve smiled and signaled to Alex they should sit in the two cushioned chairs to the right of the front door. She took a seat next to him and gazed around the room. Mr. Gomez had his undergraduate and law school degrees framed on the far wall. He had a psychology degree from NYU and attended law school at Columbia. Below the law degree was a certificate designating the lawyer as a James Kent Scholar for all three years at Columbia.

She wasn't familiar with the classification and started to pull out her phone to look it up when the lawyer entered the room.

"I apologize for keeping you waiting," Mr. Gomez said. The wiry lawyer was over six feet tall with ebony skin and closely cropped black hair. He flashed a friendly smile and gestured toward the hallway. "I'm Mr. Taylor Gomez, Esquire."

Genevieve and Alex shook hands with him. "I spoke with you on the phone. I'm Detective Runimoss and this is my partner, Detective Viacorte."

"Thanks for meeting with us," Genevieve said as they followed him down the hallway. "How long have you practiced law here?"

He pushed open a door on the left and then turned to face her. "About twenty-five years. I initially joined the law practice of a family friend. When he retired, he passed all his clients to me. Otherwise, I'd probably still be trying to pay off my school loans…please, have a seat. Make yourselves at home."

The bedroom-converted-office had a large window behind the lawyer's desk and a closet with two cherry-stained wooden doors. Alex and Genevieve sat in the leather chairs across from Mr. Gomez's desk.

"I know you're busy, so let's get right to it. I received the death certificate from Dr. Green and have begun working with the surrogate's court to validate the will. I also had a copy of it in my files. Have you had a chance to review it?" he asked.

"We've just skimmed it for bits of information," Genevieve told him. "Have you handled Ms. Smith's estate for a long time?"

"About twenty years. She was one of the first people I could call *my* client. She wisely wanted to have a living will and testament drawn up to make things easier on her loved ones at the end of her life," he paused. "I don't think she expected it to be in her sixties. Have you figured out what caused her death?"

Alex cleared his throat. "We can't comment on an active investigation."

The man raised his eyebrows, but didn't press them for details. "Well, her will was fairly straightforward. You'll have to get the exact figures from her bank, but she has a savings account and checking account. I suggested she put some of her savings into the stock market, but she wasn't interested. She said she wasn't a fan of gambling."

Genevieve almost choked but managed to pass it off as a cough. "I'm sorry, could I get a drink of water somewhere?"

Alex gave her a funny look but remained silent.

Mr. Gomez pointed at the door. "Sebastian should have offered you something when you came in. Let me just buzz him...Sebastian, two bottles of water, please. Thank you."

A moment later, the young intern entered and handed them both a chilled bottle of water. "Thank you, Sebastian," she said as she twisted the lid off. "Please continue. Mr. Gomez."

He waited for Sebastian to pull the door closed. "Ms. Smith initially left all of her estate to the New York Public Library. It would have been a significantly larger sum, but when the local bookstore burned to the ground last fall, she felt inclined to help with the rebuilding process."

"Oh really! I wondered what was speeding that along. I thought maybe the new owner was just well off," Genevieve commented.

"She made her donation anonymously through our office," Gomez told her. "Anyway, the remainder of her estate will go to NYPL."

"Nothing to family or a church or...? Alex asked.

"I got the impression Ms. Smith wasn't close with her family, though I didn't know her well," Gomez responded.

"You and everybody else," Alex said under his breath.

"I'm sorry?" Gomez asked him.

"It's nothing. I was just commenting that you aren't alone in not knowing her well. She seems to have been a bit of a recluse," Alex told him.

"Were you aware Ms. Smith was an author?" Genevieve asked.

Gomez shook his head. "I was not. She told me she was self-employed and had saved some money from previous ventures. It sounds like she was rather successful as an author. I read she was a bestseller."

Genevieve nodded. "Yes, I think she had quite a fan base. Is there anything else you can tell us about her?"

Gomez looked up before making eye contact again. "I can't really think of anything. She was not one of my high-maintenance clients. I drew up these papers and helped her with the donation a few months ago…that was about it."

Alex nodded at Genevieve and they both stood up. "Thank you for your time, Mr. Gomez. If we need anything else, we'll be in touch. Here's my card in case you need to contact us."

Gomez came around his desk and opened the door for them to exit. "It was nice to meet both of you. If you haven't had a will put together, please keep me in mind when you are ready to do it."

Genevieve gave him a tight-lipped smile. She had never thought about having a will or living testament made. It seemed like you didn't need to do that until you were old. Alex probably had one.

* * * * *

When Cari went to the breakroom to refill her coffee, she found Bryson and Michelle chatting around the coffee pot. They looked up as she walked into the room and stopped talking. She smiled hesitantly and wondered if they'd been talking about her. They stepped away from the coffee pot so she could fill her mug.

"Hey, Cari. Michelle was just telling me about a little contest you've got going with some of the police force," Bryson said to her.

She flinched. "Contest?"

"Yeah, at the race this weekend. One of the crime scene techs challenged you and one of the detectives or something to that effect?" he explained. "I didn't realize it was a secret."

She blushed, relieved it didn't have anything to do with the author's death. "Oh, that. No! It's not a secret. I didn't know others were aware of it, I guess. Yeah, Chris, he's part of the CSU team…anyway, Chris said he thought he could beat Detective Viacorte and then Bob, *my* Bob, said he thought I could beat both of them…and now we're all four running it. If I win, Chris has to buy the rest of us dinner, I think. If he wins, then maybe Bob has to buy dinner? It's been a month or two since we decided on the terms."

"And where is dinner?" Michelle asked.

"Oh, you know, I don't think anyone declared that part of the bet," she laughed.

"I think we should promote this. I know the event is only a few days away, but I bet more people would show up to see who is faster. A little showdown between the newspaper and law enforcement," he teased.

Cari raised her eyebrows. "I hadn't thought about that. It's a good idea. You should ask Ollaman and see if he's okay with it. I'm kind of regretting taking the day off from running now. The stakes just got higher."

"I'll keep you posted," he said and turned to leave the breakroom.

Michelle grabbed her mug of coffee. "Between you and me, who do you think will win?"

Cari shrugged. "I don't know. Genevieve is a pretty dedicated runner, but Chris is tall. It will be a good race."

"Well, good luck!" Michelle told her.

"Thanks," Cari responded as she turned to walk back to her desk.

She checked her list from the night before. Deb had given her the name of the new employee, so Cari checked LexisNexis to find more information on the man. Opulent Eatery didn't have a long list of employees; they all fit on one screen. She ran her finger down the list, but none of the names were Edward Butler. She frowned. Melia had called the server new. Maybe he just wasn't in the system with the company yet. She decided she needed to talk to Ted Immihan about the server change up. If she had to guess, he hadn't been told James Dolling didn't make it to the retirement party. Otherwise, he surely would have given her the other employee's name. Melia had promised to ask Ted to call, but maybe she forgot. Her hand hovered over the receiver as she debated calling him anyway. Before she could decide, the phone rang on its own.

"Brenington Beagle. This is Cari Turnlyle. How can I help you today?" she asked.

"This is Ted from O-E returning your call," Ted responded.

Ask and you shall receive. "Hi, Ted. I wanted to thank you for the list of names you sent over yesterday."

"Glad I could help," Ted said. "The police were asking about my servers too. Luckily, I'd already gotten the list together for you."

"About the list…the last name on it, Mr. James Dolling. I was able to find an address and phone number for him, but he didn't answer his phone when I called," Cari began.

"Don't take it personally. He isn't answering my calls right now either. He's only twenty-one years old. A lot of my younger employees don't have a strong sense of loyalty or responsibility yet," Ted told her.

"Oh, I get that. I actually went by his apartment to try to speak with him." She explained her interactions with Xander and then her later conversation with Melia and Deb.

"Missing? Oh, wow. I mean, I thought he was just ghosting me, but this seems more serious. He wasn't at the party on Sunday at all?" Ted asked with concern.

"No, an older employee of yours filled in for him, but I haven't been able to find him yet. Deb said his name was Edward Butler," Cari explained.

"Edward Butler?" Ted asked incredulously. "I have no idea who that is."

Cari blinked. "I'm sorry? What?"

"No one by the name of Edward Butler works for me now, nor have they ever," Ted said in frustration. "This is bad. I need to make some phone calls. Thank you for alerting me."

The call ended abruptly. Cari felt bad for Immihan. She knew he background-checked his employees, so having an imposter work one of his parties probably felt like a gut punch. She underlined the name Edward Butler in her notebook. *Who was this guy?*

She picked up her phone to text Genevieve and then remembered she wasn't supposed to be working with her. She set the phone down, but left her hand on it. She didn't want to get Gen in trouble, but maybe she could call the station as a concerned citizen. She grabbed the receiver of her desk phone and entered the number for dispatch.

* * * * *

"What was that back there?" Alex asked Genevieve after they were back in the car.

"What was what?" she asked with a confused look.

"You were surprised or caught off guard when Gomez told us Gayle Smith wasn't comfortable gambling. What gives?" he asked again.

"I did some more digging into our victim's background last night," she said slowly. "It's looking like she maybe had the propensity to go to Vegas and gamble before she moved back here."

Alex threw up a hand in frustration. "You found evidence she went to Vegas? Why didn't you say something?"

"I don't have concrete evidence," Genevieve backpedaled. "It's more of a theory right now."

He relaxed. "Well, it would explain how she had the funds to pay off that huge house."

"I thought so too," she said, looking relieved.

"How late did you stay up last night? Geez. You found out the server kid is missing, and our vic might have had a gambling problem."

"I don't think it was a problem if she was successful, right?" Genevieve countered.

"True, but back to the server. Do we have a photo of him? We need to figure out where he went or what happened. It bothers me that he possibly went missing from a party the same night the author was killed," Alex told her.

"I just texted the roommate for a photo, so we can have a description," Genevieve responded by waving her phone at him. "Here it is. When we get back to the station, let's call the two hospitals and see if anyone fitting his description has come in the last few days."

Alex made a right turn toward the police station's parking lot. He felt like Gen was hiding something from him and he didn't like it. He liked to keep his personal and professional lives very separate. He knew his wife appreciated it, but he didn't like having to play catch up to his young partner the next morning.

"Next time you dig up a bunch of dirt on our vic overnight, let me know first thing," he grumbled.

"Sorry. I'll try to keep you in the loop better," she said.

Alex parked the car and waited for her to get out so he could lock it. He hoped they'd find the kid at one of the hospitals or maybe the roommate knew another friend the kid sometimes crashed with if he was out partying. He heard Gen's shoes clicking along the pavement and realized he'd left her behind with his long stride again. He reached the door and looked at his watch.

"We've got a little less than an hour before we go to the bank. Call and see if they've checked with the hospitals yet," he said as he opened the door for her. "Let's track this kid down and figure out who the other server was if we can," he said quickly. Gen was slipping her phone back into her pocket. Her face looked troubled. "What is it?"

She pulled her lips tight and didn't respond right away. "I got an alert regarding the missing person report. James Dolling hasn't been showing up for work all week. His employer reported an unknown man served in his place at the party on Sunday."

Alex balled his hands into fists. "Let's call Dr. Green. I have a bad feeling we're going to find this kid in the morgue."

He pulled open the door to the station and followed her inside. She already had her phone up to her ear. They went straight to the stairs. Genevieve turned and pointed at the phone. She mouthed, "It's ringing."

"Dr. Green? Yes, it's Detective Viacorte. Runimoss and I are headed down to see you. Do you have any unidentified bodies in the morgue right now?" she asked as they hurried down the stairs. "Yes? Male? Yes. We need to take a look at him."

Alex pulled open the large door that led to the CSU hallway, the morgue, and Dr. Green's office. Dr. Green was walking down the hallway toward them. He ushered them into the morgue.

"We got a body Monday afternoon. Drug overdose. The needle was left in the young man's arm. The EMTs who brought him in said he was already dead when they arrived," Dr. Green said as he walked along the row of drawers. He checked his clipboard and then slid one open.

"Here he is. No identification. I hadn't had a chance to do an autopsy yet with the other case taking up so much time," he explained as he unzipped the thick, dark bag to reveal the man's face. "Is this your missing person?"

Genevieve pulled out her phone and enlarged the photo Xander had sent a few minutes before. Alex looked over her shoulder at the screen and then at the person in the bag. It was definitely James Dolling. He punched his right fist into his left hand in frustration.

"I guess we found the missing server. Dr. Green, we need you to start on his autopsy. Viacorte, did they say if the parents are on their way?" Alex asked her.

She nodded in confirmation. "They're supposed to be here by lunch."

He checked his watch again. "Let's get over to the bank. Dr. Green, can you ask them to have the parents wait in the family room if they arrive before we get back?"

Green nodded and zipped the bag closed. Alex watched as he pushed the drawer closed and then rested his hand on the outside. He looked at Genevieve and saw her eyes were shiny.

"Hey, this is not our fault. We had no way of knowing this kid was even missing. It's possible it's not related to our case. Didn't you say the kid had a history of drug use?" Alex asked her.

She nodded slowly. "It has to be related, Alex. How did the other person know to show up and work the party for him? The owner doesn't even know who the old guy is!"

He knew she was probably right. "It still doesn't change the fact that this is out of our control. It happened before we even knew about the author. Come on. Let's go talk to the bank. Maybe she has a co-signer on her account that we can interview."

Genevieve shook her head. "We need to find this other guy. We don't even know his name!" She pushed past him. "I need to make a phone call."

Alex watched her stomp out of the room. He was as frustrated with the case as she looked. They just needed to keep following the evidence. They could find this guy.

Chapter 15

Cari almost jumped when her phone started vibrating. She'd been looking at the video with the older server and comparing his image to social media photos she found of people named Edward Butler. She knew it was a long shot as the name was extremely common. She looked at the screen and was surprised to see Genevieve's name.

"Gen? What's up? I didn't expect—"

"Did you get his name?" Genevieve interrupted her to ask.

"Uh, the mystery server?" she asked in confusion.

"Yes. The old man. What is his name? Did you find it?" Genevieve asked in a frustrated tone.

"Yes. It's Edward Butler. That's what Deb, the head server told me. You sound upset. What's going on?" Cari asked.

"Edward Butler? Butler? Are you kidding me? Ugh. That's not his name," Genevieve groaned.

"That's the name Deb gave me," Cari argued.

"Butler? As in, 'the butler did it?'" Genevieve explained.

"No way. I mean, that seems a little…conspiracy theory to me, Gen," Cari disagreed.

"Look, we're pretty sure this guy killed the other server in order to take his place at the party. I have to go," she said, and the call ended.

Cari stared at her phone screen for a moment in disbelief. If his name wasn't really Edward Butler, how was she going to find him? And did Genevieve mean the young server was dead? She clenched and unclenched her fists. She wished they didn't need to sneak around to talk about the investigation. She wasn't ready to give up on the name Edward Butler yet and wondered if Wendy would recognize the name or if it would jog her memory of the man's real name. She pulled up Wendy's phone number and touched the call button.

"Hi, again, Cari. I take it you have a new lead?" Wendy asked when she answered the phone.

"Does the name Edward Butler ring a bell?" Cari asked hopefully.

"Hmmm…I can't say that it does. The name was kind of common. Like I said, she only mentioned his first name. I'm sorry, but Edward doesn't really sound familiar to me. Did you find someone with that name?" Wendy asked her.

Cari sighed. "No, not exactly. I'm sorry to be vague, but I can't really get into details. Thanks for taking my call."

"No problem. Good luck with your search," Wendy replied.

Cari ended the call. The name Edward Butler had seemed like such a promising lead. Now she was back to square one. Her phone started buzzing again before she put it down. She looked at the screen and saw Dahlia's name again. She looked over at Ollaman's office and cringed guiltily. Ollaman would be angry if he caught her looking into this young woman's story during the workday again. She let it go to voicemail.

She looked over her notes again and her eyes rested on the name of the one author who lived too far away to attend the party. She seemed to have known Gayle as well as anyone else. She at least communicated with her regularly. She dialed Veronica's number again and mentally crossed her fingers.

"Ms. Turnlyle, you're calling again sooner than I expected," Veronica said cryptically.

Cari's brow furrowed. "I'm sorry?"

"Oh, don't sound so suspicious! I just didn't expect you to find another mysterious Easter egg this quickly," she said cheerfully.

"Veronica, do you know something you haven't told me?" Cari asked pointedly.

"Not at all, dear. I'm sorry. I probably do sound like I'm up to something. And I probably sound way too cheerful right now, but Bloody Marys will do that for you!" she giggled. "How can I help?"

"Well, I came across a name of someone, possibly someone from Gayle's past. Is the name Edward Butler familiar to you?" Cari asked her.

She whistled, bringing Cari's hopes up. "Can't say that it is. You said it's from her past? Like before she became an author?"

Cari swallowed back a groan. "I'm not sure how far into her past. I was hoping you would know."

"Edward Butler, huh? What a plain name. Did Gayle leave it hiding somewhere? Maybe it's an anagram!" Veronica suggested.

"An anagram? Where you rearrange the letters?" Cari asked.

"Yes, that! It's a fun little plot gimmick, right? So, Gayle left this name for you to find? Where? It wasn't in her latest book. I read that," Veronica told her.

"No, it wasn't Gayle who gave me the name. It was…someone else," Cari said slowly as she thought about the letters in the name. "I suppose it does have several common letters and could be rearranged into another name. Thanks for the idea."

Veronica didn't respond for several seconds and Cari wondered if the call dropped. She checked the screen and it said it was still connected. "Are you still there, Veronica?"

"Just a sec. I think I got it. Um, oh…hmm. This is a lot harder when you're tipsy. No, that won't work. Sorry. I thought I'd found another name in there, but I guess not. It was worth a shot. Any other questions?" she asked.

"That's it for now. I appreciate your help," Cari said and ended the call.

She wrote *anagram* in her notebook. Maybe she could play around with the letters later and see if she could form them into another name.

* * * * *

The line for the tellers was fairly long when Alex and Genevieve entered the bank. Luckily, Alex had the name of the banker he'd spoken with the day before and her nameplate was visible from the lobby. They crossed the room and got her attention. She rose from her desk to greet them.

"Hello, detectives. Why don't you have a seat while I get Ms. Smith's account information pulled up?" Helen Maroney suggested. She was a petite woman with light brown skin and dark brown eyes. Her straight black hair was clasped with a large barrette at the nape of her neck. She quickly typed on her keyboard and then clicked her mouse several times.

"Here it is, Gayle Smith. It looks like she had a savings account, checking account, and safety deposit box with us," Ms. Maroney told them.

"Ms. Maroney, would it be possible for us to see the contents of her box?" Genevieve asked.

"Certainly, though, her lawyer was here on Monday to access the box. He may have already cleared it out," Maroney said.

Genevieve and Alex exchanged a glance. "Her lawyer was here on Monday?"

She rotated her screen around. "A Mr. Taylor Gomez came first thing Monday morning and requested access to her box. He's listed as a signee for the box. Is there a problem?"

"Does he have to show identification or how do you approve the request?" Genevieve asked her.

"It says he provided a valid New York driver's license," Maroney responded after turning the screen back to face her.

Genevieve looked at Alex, who nodded once. "Ms. Maroney, we need to see your security footage from Monday morning. My partner is going to call Ms. Smith's lawyer, but we just spoke with him and he made no mention of visiting your bank on Monday. In fact, I think he was out of town."

The woman's face paled. "Of course. I'll make a call and we can get that pulled up for you. Did you still want to access the box?"

Genevieve nodded. "Yes. We also need statements for her accounts or digital access to them."

"I can get you digital access, no problem," Ms. Maroney replied as she lifted the phone receiver to her ear. "Just one moment."

Her knee bounced rapidly while she waited for the banker to speak on the phone. She looked across the lobby and found Alex pacing while talking on the phone. He looked irritated, but that wasn't new. He closed his little flip phone and rejoined her at the desk.

He leaned in and whispered, "Gomez didn't even know Smith had a safety deposit box. He says he's never been here before."

Genevieve nodded in understanding and whispered back. "I'm not surprised. Ms. Maroney is getting someone to access their security footage for us. Then we can look at the box."

"Okay, detectives," she said as she wrote something on a sticky note. "Here's your access to her accounts. If you'll follow me, my colleague is pulling up the video from Monday."

They followed Ms. Maroney down a narrow hallway to another office. An older man was sitting behind a wall of monitors and typing on the keyboard in front of him. He tapped a few more keys and then turned to speak with them.

"This view shows the hallway leading to the boxes," he explained, pointing at the monitor nearest him. "This one shows the view from the teller where Mr. Gomez requested to access the box."

Genevieve looked at the second monitor. The person had on a baseball cap, which cast a shadow over their eyes. They looked masculine but definitely white.

She smirked. "For someone who has clearly done their homework on many aspects of Gayle Smith's life, they sure didn't do a lot of research into her lawyer. Mr. Gomez is decidedly not Caucasian."

"He's quite a bit taller than the person in this image too," Alex commented. "Do you have a camera in the room where he looks at the contents of her safety deposit box?"

"We have one in the vault," the man said. "Let me key it up."

He hit a few more keys and then pointed at the monitor in front of him again. Genevieve watched as the man posing as Smith's lawyer removed the box and opened it on the table. He sifted through a few items and then grasped something with his right hand.

"Wait, what was that?" she asked. "Can you rewind it and slow it down? Possibly zoom in on his hands?"

The technician did as she requested and started the video again at a slower speed. She leaned in and watched as the imposter moved various poker chips out of the way to reveal a small thumb drive. He grabbed the drive and two chips before replacing the lid. Then he slid the box back into the wall, locking it into place.

"It looks like he stole some chips and a thumb drive," Alex commented. "I wonder what was on the drive. Do you have a list of the contents of the box? Like for insurance purposes?"

"That would be in the possession of the owner," Ms. Maroney told him. "Does she have a will?"

"We have a copy of it. We'll take a look," Genevieve responded. "I don't think any of these angles capture the man's face well."

"Agreed. Still, we need a copy of these files for our CSU to look through. They might be able to pull something we didn't see," Alex told the two employees.

"Coming right up. Do you have an email I can send them to?" the technician asked.

Genevieve pulled out a card and handed it to him. He quickly keyed in a few command strokes and then pulled up his email program.

"Done. What else can I help you with today?" he asked.

"I think that's it. Ms. Maroney, could we see the box now?" Alex asked her.

"Right this way," she said as she guided them out of the office and further down the hallway.

"Viacorte, we need to get CSU over here to dust that box for prints. I was surprised to see him not wearing gloves, but maybe he thought it would make him seem too suspicious," Alex told her.

"I'll call them now," she agreed and pulled out her phone. She entered the extension for CSU and waited for someone to pick up.

"Bob! It's Detective Viacorte. We're over at Ms. Smith's bank," she said and explained the situation to him. "Can you or someone else come over and pull some prints?"

"I'll be right over," Bob responded and then ended the call.

Alex turned to Ms. Maroney. "We need to secure her box and get our crime tech back here to print it."

"I'll go let the tellers know to bring your person back here once they arrive," she said and exited the vault.

"I feel like we might finally be getting somewhere with this case," Genevieve said to Alex.

"Don't count on it. We don't even know if there are prints. Even if there are prints, it doesn't mean they're in the system," he cautioned.

"Don't be such a pessimist. Something has to break our way, right?"

* * * * *

Cari yawned and stretched her arms over her head. The day was dragging and she felt like she was spinning her wheels on the investigation. Getting the name *Edward Butler* seemed like such a strong lead, but Genevieve had really downplayed it. Veronica had suggested it was an anagram. Cari wrote the name in block letters and tried to rearrange them into a new name, but she'd never been very strong with word scrambles. She came up with *Bear* and then crossed it out.

"Turnlyle!" Ollaman barked, making her jump and drop her pencil.

"Sir?" she asked in surprise.

"What are you doing now? Yesterday, you were scrolling through social media and today, you're doing word puzzles?" he growled. "Did you find the missing server?"

"I was able to speak with his roommate," she explained the course of events. "I found out earlier today that he's dead."

"Darn it. How did he die? Is it related?" he peppered her with questions.

"Uh, I...I'm not sure. I haven't heard an update," she stammered.

"Well, what else do you have?" he asked with his hands on his hips.

She bit her lip. Her boss' behavior was really off this week. She didn't want to anger him more, but his micromanaging was getting frustrating. "Sir? My apologies, but is something wrong with my work lately?"

He narrowed his eyes and then coughed. "No. Why?"

"You don't normally take such an *active* interest in my investigation process for these stories. I know I was a bit behind after my vacation, but I'm not sure what this is," she said moving her hands between them.

He sighed and ran a hand over his head. "This," he said, mimicking her hand movements, "is you getting to the bottom of the story. Not doing word puzzles."

Cari willed her eyes not to fill with tears and barely succeeded. "I understand."

"One other thing," he said and drew in a breath. "The photographer is going to get a photo of you and the three law enforcement people tomorrow morning at eight o'clock. Millar said he mentioned it to you earlier. Dress, uh, sporty."

He stomped off. She had thought he was about to apologize for a second. She looked at her watch and decided to call it a day. It was just a bit before five o'clock. She could finish her *word puzzle* at home. She stuffed everything into her messenger bag and shut down her desktop computer. Ollaman had his door closed with the blinds drawn, so she walked silently past his office to the elevators.

When she stepped into the parking garage, she caught a movement out of the corner of her eye. She whipped her head around to see who it was. A young woman waved at her frantically.

"Miss Turnlyle! Cari! I'm so glad I caught you. I came early because I wasn't too sure what time you leave work each day and I'm so glad I did because here you are. If I'd come later…" The young woman spewed the words out almost faster than Cari could understand them. Cari recognized the voice: Dahlia.

"Dahlia? What are you doing here?" she asked dumbfoundedly.

"You haven't returned my call. We made a big discovery and you need to know about it," she pouted.

"I'm sorry, Dahlia. I've been chasing this story fairly exclusively this week. My boss has been riding me to get answers for some reason, so I can't do any outside stuff while I'm at the office," she explained as she gently guided the young woman away from the elevator bay.

"Well, you're not in the office now!" Dahlia exclaimed. "Here's the thing! We were chatting, in the group that is, about our loved ones and they were all readers!"

Cari resisted the urge to roll her eyes.

Dahlia continued. "And they were all reading the same book! When they died, that is. They were all reading or had just finished reading the same book. What are the odds?! It has to mean something."

Cari almost hated herself for asking. "What book?"

Dahlia's eyes lit up. "All. In. Murder," she said dramatically.

Cari blinked. The title was familiar. "Wait. Is that by—"

"Natasha Gillespie! Yes! The local author! Don't you see?!" Dahlia almost shouted.

Cari stopped mid-stride. "That is…interesting, but she was a very popular author. A lot of people read her books."

Dahlia's face dropped. "I thought you of all people would see the connection. No one believes us. This wasn't suicide. It couldn't have been."

She turned and walked away. Cari started to put a hand out to stop her but hesitated. She didn't have time to chase this other story right now, though this new piece of information possibly tied it into the Gillespie/Smith investigation. Still, the connection was pretty thin and she felt like she was finally getting somewhere in the other investigation. She looked down at her hand and saw she'd grabbed her locket. She released it and pulled out her phone instead.

"Grandmother? It's Cari," she said slowly as she unlocked her car.

"You sound sad, dear. What's wrong?" her grandmother asked.

"I feel like I'm letting this young woman down. She's begging me to prove her great aunt was killed and I just don't have time. Ollaman is asking for updates constantly and I can't talk to Bob about it because it's about the case and I set a boundary." She got in her car and pulled the door closed. "Genevieve must have thrown in the towel on the restriction though. She came over to talk through the investigation last night."

"Did she get permission?" Grandmother asked.

Cari pursed her lips. "No, I think she just wants answers. It's just really hard to find any. The woman had no friends. All she did was work."

"It's unfortunate when people are unable to have balance in their lives. You miss out on a lot of the fun things in life without friends," her grandmother commented.

Cari brushed a tear from her eye. "I want to help, but I have to finish this story first and I can't chase down every conspiracy theory that comes my way. I found out the name of someone suspicious from the party, but Genevieve discounted it as fake immediately. It feels like I'm still fighting to be taken seriously."

"I'm sorry to hear that, Cari. You can only do so much. Do you know how to eat an elephant?" Grandmother asked.

Was she losing her mind? "Um, an elephant?" Cari asked in confusion.

"Yes, an elephant. Do you know how to eat one?" she repeated.

"I'm not sure I've ever heard of people eating elephants," Cari responded. *Or why we're talking about it.*

"You eat an elephant like everything else: one bite at a time," her grandmother explained. "This story…this investigation seems insurmountable, and you can't figure it out all at once. You have to do it one step at a time. Just keep taking the next best step and you'll get there."

Cari smiled. "You're right. I can only do what I can do. I need to stop focusing on what's out of my control and take care of the things I can control. Thanks, Grandmother. I have to get going. I love you."

"I love you more."

* * * * *

Genevieve tossed her bag onto her sofa. She wanted to grab one of the cushions and scream into it. This case got more frustrating by the hour. Discovering the young server in the morgue had angered her. She knew he'd died before they even caught the case, but it felt so unfair. She could still see the anguish on Mrs. Dolling's face when they broke the news to her about her son. Her gut was telling her the other server was responsible for the young man's death, but they didn't have any evidence to back that up yet. She wasn't even sure where to look next, but she certainly wasn't giving up.

Alex was telling her to have better boundaries between her work life and her personal life, but she didn't even have a personal life, minus running and gardening. Those weren't even social activities; they were solely for her mental health. She pulled her laptop from her bag and set it on the coffee table. While it started up, she went to the kitchen to fill up her water bottle and grab some crackers for a snack. Maybe she'd order a pizza later. For now, she wanted to dig into the case more. Cari would be home by now or at least on her way, so she pulled out her phone to call her.

"Hey, are you free right now?" she asked after her friend answered.

"I was just about to call Bob to make our running plans for the morning. We need to go early because of the, uh, photoshoot," Cari responded.

"Right. I heard about that too. Whatever," she said flippantly. "I called because I want to talk through things on this case some more. Want to join me for some pizza? My treat."

"I already ordered delivery, sorry," Cari said.

Genevieve frowned. "Well, let's do this over the phone then."

She heard Cari exhale and wondered if her friend was going to lecture her about boundaries too. She had a persuasive response to throw at her when Cari spoke up.

"Okay, well, I called the insurance company owners. The Duncans? Duncanins, or whatever. They both have dementia, so they couldn't talk to me."

Genevieve groaned. "Why can nothing be easy in this case?!"

"But!" her friend cut in. "I reached their daughter Wendy and she knew Gayle when she was an employee."

Genevieve listened as Cari shared the conversation she'd had with the daughter. "I told you Edward Butler wasn't the guy's name."

"To be fair, she never met him, she just heard about him. Anyway, one of the authors who didn't attend the party had a good idea about the name being an anagram," Cari explained. "I've tried rearranging the letters on my own, but haven't gotten anywhere yet."

"Seems like a waste of time," Genevieve told her. "We've got another dead body in the morgue because of this guy."

"So, you're certain the imposter server killed him?" Cari asked.

"Green is doing an autopsy, but it can't be a coincidence. How did the old guy know they would be short a server? How did he get a uniform?" Genevieve laid out the obvious signs.

"That's a good point. That poor kid," Cari agreed. "This old guy has done his research. It's like he thought of everything."

"It sure feels that way. He even went to the bank and took something from her safety deposit box. He posed as her lawyer to do it. I don't know how he found out her lawyer's name, but he did. We can see on the security video it isn't the lawyer, but we can't get a good image of his face to figure out who he really is. I'd bet money it's our old server, though. CSU fingerprinted the box and its contents. None of the prints matched anyone in our system. I sent them over to my contact with the FBI, so maybe they'll have more luck," she said more hopefully than she really felt.

"This is kind of an out of the box idea, but…" Cari paused. "you're going to have to hear me out for a bit."

Genevieve listened to Cari talk about Dahlia, the young woman who wouldn't accept her loved one had committed suicide. It sounded horribly sad, but she wasn't about to doubt someone else's police work.

"I'm sorry, but this woman is just experiencing grief. She's in denial and trying to find a way out of it," Genevieve said dismissively.

"Part of me completely agrees with you, but there's a little part of me that doesn't want to fully discount it," Cari told her.

"You're welcome to spin your wheels on that all you want. I think you're wasting your time," Genevieve said. "There has to be another way to figure out who this guy is."

"Oh, I almost forgot," Cari said with enthusiasm. "The author I spoke with today, uh, Veronica. She thought our author might have left little clues behind, like Easter eggs. Is Chris digging through her devices? Laptop, computer, phone?"

Genevieve nodded her head even though Cari couldn't see her. "Yeah, we got her contacts, a copy of her will, that kind of stuff."

"Maybe she has a hidden file somewhere. Maybe in an email or a secret drive or…I don't really know much about computers, but Chris or Bob probably do," she suggested. "I feel like she left that martini glass for us to find, you know?"

"That's a great idea. Chris usually works late. I'm going to text him and see if he's still working. Thanks, Cari," she said as she hung up the phone.

She thumbed off a text to Chris and stared at the screen for a minute, waiting to see if he had read it. The status didn't change and she sighed in frustration and let the screen go dark. She could ask him about it in the morning. Her stomach rumbled. She hadn't ordered the pizza yet. Maybe she'd just throw together a salad instead.

Chapter 16

Thursday morning was muggy. Cari felt the humidity as soon as she stepped outside to join Bob for one last run before the race. She saw him pull into the guest parking space for her unit and waved.

"Tell me the weather will be nicer on Saturday," Bob begged. "This feels like a swamp."

"I haven't checked. But, hey, it's only three miles, right?" she joked.

"Only? How far is it today?" he asked.

"How does two miles sound?" she offered.

"Like torture, but I'll take it. Remind me to keep my mouth shut next time," he groaned.

"Do you need some water first or are you ready to go?" she asked.

"Let's just get it over with."

She started her watch and they jogged out of the apartment complex and toward the park down the street. It had a nice hike and bike trail. After a few windy days early in the week, the air was completely still and felt like a wet blanket.

"Hey, weather man, is it supposed to rain today?" she asked Bob.

"It sure feels like it, but I didn't look," he responded wearily. "Are we there yet?"

"You're doing great, Bob. Think how good it will feel to finish on Saturday!" she encouraged him.

"I still can't believe I got talked into this. And to pile on, we're out here almost before the sun so we can get our photo taken first thing this morning. Like I don't have better things to do," Bob griped.

Cari decided to change the subject. "Dahlia has been calling me all week. She is fully convinced the police were wrong about her great aunt."

"It has to be hard for her. It sounds like they were really close. Kind of like…" Bob trailed off.

"Like what?" Cari asked him.

"Like with your grandmother," he said quietly.

"But she's in great health and happy. She is always encouraging me and would never…" Cari started to argue. "I guess I see your point. No one wants to experience that."

"Death is never easy, regardless of how it happens," Bob agreed.

"I think I hurt her feelings last night," Cari told him.

"Your grandmother or Dahlia?" he asked.

"Dahlia. I told her Ollaman was really on my case about…well, you know, and I didn't have time to help her. She took it as another person who doesn't believe her and just walked away," Cari said sadly.

"You can't please everyone," Bob replied.

"I feel so guilty. In fact, I downloaded the…uh…this book she is convinced is a major clue to what happened with her aunt and started skimming through it to see if I could find anything," Cari said, avoiding the author's name.

"What book?" he asked.

"Uh, it's called "All in Murder," I think," she said vaguely, not wanting to accidentally tread into a discussion on the case.

"Why is that familiar?" Bob asked.

"I think it's a bestseller, which makes it less significant, as I explained to Dahlia last night," Cari said. "Oh, look! We just hit two miles. Ready to do a cool down walk back to the apartment?"

* * * * *

Genevieve quickly threw her running clothes into her gym bag and slipped her dress shoes on. She thought the photoshoot was a huge waste of everyone's time, but understood why people wanted to do it. The proceeds from the race went toward the fire department's benevolent fund, which offered assistance to those in crisis. They supported the soup kitchen Cari and Bob volunteered in, too, so it was for a good cause. She wrapped her hair back into its usual bun and grabbed the gym bag.

Instead of going straight to her desk, she took a detour to the CSU. She knew Chris was in already as he had to be in the photo too, and she wanted to ask him about their victim's computer and email history. She knocked on the door as she pulled it open.

"Hello?" she called out as she entered the labyrinth of cubicles.

A chair rolled out into the walkway and its occupant spun around to face her. It was Chris. "Hi, Detective Viacorte. I saw the text you sent last night. What emails or files are you looking for exactly?"

She followed him back to his desk. "I'm not sure. Someone mentioned mystery writers like to leave little bread crumbs or clues in their books to help the reader solve the case before it's spelled out for them."

"Oh, like Easter eggs in movies," Chris said enthusiastically.

"Right. I thought maybe there might be something on her computer that might point us in the right direction."

He touched the mouse pad on the laptop at his desk. "This is her laptop. We've gotten it unlocked, so let me just wake it up."

The machine whirred to life. Chris hit a few keys and then opened the little file folder icon at the bottom of the screen.

"Here are all her files. Lots of manuscripts and drafts. She had a folder for each book she wrote," he explained and clicked on one folder. "Like, here's her last book. It has all the drafts, edits, and formats for the book as well as the cover files and ads. I didn't expect to see so many files just for one book."

"Are there any different files in that folder versus one of the older books?" Genevieve asked.

He picked a random folder and opened it too. "It looks like more of the same."

"What about in the deleted items? Maybe the killer accessed her laptop and deleted something? Or maybe she deleted it hoping we'd notice?" she suggested.

He right-clicked and found the trash can. It was empty. He looked at her for another idea.

She wracked her brain for a different strategy. "What about her email then? Maybe there's a funny attachment that's larger than it should be or something else out of place?"

Chris opened her email application and went to the sent folder. "I mean, there's hundreds if not thousands of emails in here. It could take days to go through all of these."

"Well, ask Bob or some of the other CSU people for help. It can't be another dead end. I think it will be recent too," she told him.

"How recent?" he asked.

"Just start with the most recent and work backward. Can't you copy this somehow and share it with others?" she asked.

"We'll look into it. By the way," he said, flicking his head toward Dr. Green's office. "Dr. Green said he finished the autopsy on the kid you identified yesterday. I think Runimoss is on his way down here now."

Genevieve looked through the small window in the door and sure enough, Alex was striding down the long hallway toward Dr. Green's office.

"Thanks for your help, Chris. Keep me posted." She turned and walked quickly to catch up to Alex.

"Alex, wait up!" she called out.

He stopped and looked her way. "I wondered where you went. I thought maybe they wanted you for extra photos or something."

She rolled her eyes. "No, I was just following up on a hunch with Chris."

"Care to fill me in?" he asked as they reached Dr. Green's door.

"I asked him to look for a hidden email attachment or file on the victim's laptop. I thought she might have left a clue somewhere in the event she died unexpectedly."

He raised his eyebrows. "You think she knew she was going to be killed?"

"Maybe. The martini glass in the bedside table is weird. Why would it end up there? If someone poisoned her with it, wouldn't they take it so the evidence couldn't be found? Maybe she was hiding it in hopes we'd figure out what happened," Genevieve suggested.

"Couldn't she have just written it down for us?" he asked, dumbfounded.

"Not if she was worried the killer was going to come into her house. Or maybe she did write it down and he took it," Genevieve argued her point. "It's worth a shot."

"What are we arguing about now?" Dr. Green asked as they entered his office.

"Nothing," Genevieve said quickly. "You finished the autopsy?"

"I did indeed," he answered as he got up from his desk. "As I suspected, he overdosed on heroin. Let me show you a few things."

Dr. Green put on a pair of latex gloves. He pulled out the same drawer from the day before and unzipped the bag the whole way this time. He moved the white sheet off of the victim's left arm and pointed to some marks.

"See these? These marks are old needle scars. This young man had used intravenous drugs before this past weekend, but it had been a while. These scars are healed. I would estimate it had been close to a year since he put a needle in his arm," Dr. Green told them.

"His roommate mentioned a previous drug problem, but seemed to think he'd quit for good," Genevieve replied. "Do you think he relapsed or did someone inject it for him?"

"I can't say for certain. The EMTs who brought him over found him with a needle in his *right* arm, rather than his left. The parents say he was right-handed. The EMTs bagged the syringe and we dusted it for prints," Dr. Green said.

"Victim's prints or someone else's?" Alex asked.

He hit a few keys and pulled up the results. "Victim's, but they were somewhat smudged. If you look at the positions of the prints on the syringe, they don't align in a way one might expect if the victim injected himself...but that doesn't mean he didn't do it himself."

"Where was he found?" Genevieve asked.

Green looked at the report. "In an alley near his apartment building. Walking distance from his building."

She made a note. "Who reported the body?"

"A woman called it in on Monday morning. She was on a walk with her son, and his ball rolled into the alley. They went to retrieve it and discovered the young man," Dr. Green read from the report. "He'd been dead for a while when the EMTs arrived. One of our patrol officers took her statement."

"When was his time of death? The roommate said he'd been missing since Sunday afternoon," Genevieve commented.

"My best estimate is between four and six p.m. on Sunday," Dr. Green answered her.

Alex sighed. "We can't release the body to the parents yet. The connections to the other case are too strong to ignore for now. We'll let you know." He turned to Genevieve, "Let's go back upstairs and see if we can shake anything loose in this case."

* * * * *

Cari had the author's last book open in an e-reader program on her work computer. She continued to skim the pages, but nothing was jumping out at her. It was impossible to know what she should be looking for. She had to admit, it did seem like more than a coincidence that each of the people in Dahlia's group had been reading the same book when they died. She wondered how many of them had finished it. Ollaman was still in the conference room chatting with the photographer and copy editor about the blurb for the 5k ad, so she wasn't worried about him looking over her shoulder for the moment. She pulled out her phone to text Dahlia.

How many of the loved ones from your group finished the book before they died?

Dahlia responded promptly.

Ill find out xo

Cari grimaced at her lack of punctuation and then set her phone aside. She paged through the book some more, but she still couldn't find anything of interest. She heard the door to the conference room open and minimized the book on her screen just in case. Ollaman went straight to his office, and she exhaled in relief. She hated hiding things from him but didn't want to press him on his behavior any more than she already had. Before she could enlarge the book again, her cell phone buzzed with an incoming call. *Veronica!*

"Hi, Veronica. Did you think of something else about Gayle?" Cari asked hopefully.

"Oh, no. Not about Gayle, but I think I might have solved your anagram!" she exclaimed.

"Oh, wow. I hadn't realized you were going to keep working on that. What did you find?" Cari asked her.

"Walter Redbud. It uses all the letters once," she said proudly.

Cari hesitated. "When you brought up the idea of the anagram and Easter eggs, it was from the perspective of Gayle, not this other person, though."

Veronica clucked her tongue. "That doesn't mean he didn't do something like this with his name! He's obviously got a deceptive personality. What is it they say make the best lies? When you have a little bit of the truth in there too. It's still his name, just rearranged."

"That's true. I'll look into it. Maybe we'll finally figure out who the guy was," Cari responded. "Thanks for your help."

"No problem. I love word puzzles," Veronica said and ended the call.

Cari opened LexisNexis and entered the name. It was still a very common-sounding name and produced thousands of results without any other information. She added New York as the state and reduced the number significantly, but still had over one hundred names on the list. When she added Brenington, the results went to zero. She frowned and removed the city name from the search parameters. She entered their county name instead and hit enter. That cut the list to sixteen names.

Each name had the person's age included in parentheses. Cari could eliminate two because they were deceased and another because they were under the age of twenty. She opened the remaining profiles one by one and looked at the image files. She was starting to doubt Veronica's theory when she opened up the eleventh name on the list. Walter Redbud #11 looked a lot like the imposter. She took a screenshot of the information and emailed it to herself. Then she opened the email on her phone and downloaded the attachment. She texted it to Genevieve. She knew this had to be the guy, and as much as she wanted to go find him herself, she knew he was far too dangerous.

* * * * *

Alex patted his pocket when he heard the vibration, but his cell phone was still. He looked over at Genevieve and saw her furtively glance away. He knew his young partner didn't like the restrictions their chief had placed on this case and wondered how closely she was following those rules. This seemed to be his answer.

"Are you gonna check that?" he asked her in what he hoped sounded like a casual tone. "Maybe it's your FBI contact."

Her face belied her surprise at his suggestion. "Right, let me check."

He watched as she unlocked the screen of her smartphone with her face and then touched an app from the homepage. Rather than make her uncomfortable, he refrained from rolling his chair to her side to look over her shoulder. Her eyes grew wide and she looked up at him from the screen. He felt guilty for silently accusing her of breaking the rules.

"I think we found him," she said quietly. She chewed on her lip. "Open up the database and type in 'Walter Redbud' and leave the city field blank, but include our county and New York and an age range above fifty-five," she instructed him.

"All this from your FBI guy?" he asked as he pecked at the keys.

"Uh, I can do this faster myself," she grumbled and he heard her fingers smoothly rolling across the keyboard. "Got him. Walter Redbud, age sixty-three. He's renting an apartment nearby."

"In Brenington?" Alex asked, surprised. He had suspected the person wasn't local.

"Not Brenington. I put the address into my phone. Let's go talk to him," she said as she pulled the keys off the hook.

"Whoa, hold up. We need to talk to Grusky. Tell him what we found," Alex said, putting a hand on her arm.

"Call him on the way. I'm driving," she said as she shook his arm off and marched toward the exit.

"Just wait a second, will you?" he grumbled.

She came to a halt. He rapped his knuckles on their lieutenant's door.

"Come in," Grusky barked from inside.

Alex poked his head into the office. "We think we've located the mystery server from the party. We're going to go talk to him now."

"Be careful. It sounds like this guy is unpredictable. Call for backup if anything seems off," Grusky told him and waved him on.

Alex jogged out of the station and caught up to Genevieve as she was starting the car. He got in the passenger seat and buckled his seatbelt. She jammed her phone into the display mount on the dash.

"Keep track of the directions. It says it will take us a little over twenty minutes to get there," she told him.

"The FBI really came through for us. I had my doubts. I thought they'd just blow us off," Alex commented as he watched the directions on the phone screen.

Genevieve grimaced and gave a slight nod. "Something had to go our way eventually."

"I put in a call to the two casinos whose chips were taken from the safety deposit box," Alex told her. "They wanted an image of the chip so they could verify it was one of theirs, so I asked Chris if he could get a clean image for us from the security video."

"That's a good idea. It's been at least twenty years since she was there, though. It's probably a long shot someone still works there and remembers her," Genevieve replied. "It's not like they keep track of outstanding chips or something, right?"

Alex realized she was right. "I guess they probably don't. From what you told me, it sounds like she went pretty often though. Like once a month or something?"

"That's what the co-worker said. Maybe even twice a month sometimes," she responded. "It's almost like she was a completely different person back then."

"What do you mean?" Alex asked her.

"The friend or co-worker, she described her as someone who went to concerts and traveled to Vegas with a friend regularly. That doesn't mean she was outgoing, but she did at least *get out*."

Alex nodded in agreement. "That is pretty different from the picture I have of Gayle Smith, the author. I wonder what happened to make her become so reclusive?"

Genevieve shrugged. "Part of the mystery we haven't learned yet, I guess."

They drove in silence for a few minutes with only the navigation system speaking directions to them. Alex wondered how the older man would respond to them arriving on his doorstep. He'd been so careful and methodical; maybe he didn't think they'd catch him.

"When we knock on this guy's door, let's not get too close. He apparently likes to stick people with needles or drug them. Who knows what he'll do when we show up at his home?" Alex said to her.

"I bet he isn't even there," Genevieve responded.

Alex looked at her incredulously. "What? Why are we going to his apartment then?"

"We have to at least check, right? But I bet he's cleared out. I think part of him probably wanted to stick around and watch us spin our wheels, but the smarter part knew he needed to leave," she told him.

"I hope you're wrong," Alex grumbled as the GPS announced their arrival.

The apartment was on the ground floor and had an exterior door. The complex looked to be on the older side, but all the units had a fresh coat of paint. Genevieve parked in a visitor area near Walter Redbud's unit. Alex banged on the door and took a step back. They both leaned in slightly to listen, but the apartment was silent. He stepped forward and knocked again. Genevieve had her hand on her sidearm and was watching the door attentively.

"Brenington Police, we're looking for Walter Redbud," Alex said assertively and pounded on the door again.

A door opened two units down from Redbud's and a man in a cheap suit stepped out. He walked over to them and put out his hand.

"John Wolfry. I'm the super for these units," he said and they each shook his hand. "The man in this unit moved out the other day. He only lived here ten days or so, but paid for several months up front. I just went through it yesterday to see if it was ready to be shown again and it's completely cleaned out. Like he was never here. I think he cleaned it better than my staff does."

Alex felt his shoulders sag in disappointment. "Did he leave a forwarding address?"

The super looked away quickly and then back at Alex. "Well, uh, he paid for the space in cash. I usually require a background check and a credit check, but he had the money ready, so, uh, I looked the other way. What is he guilty of?"

Alex shook his head. "We aren't at liberty to discuss that right now. Can we get a copy of the lease he signed?"

The man looked sheepish. "Well, uh, I, um, I mean…"

"You didn't make him fill one out," Genevieve spat the words out.

"I needed the renter. I didn't know he was a criminal," the super whined.

Neither do we. Alex thought. "It's fine. We don't have time to talk to the housing authority about this right now, but rest assured, Mr. Wolfry, you will be hearing from them."

They turned and walked back to the cruiser. They'd been so close, but it was another dead end.

"Chin up, Alex," Genevieve said. "We know two aliases now. We're closing in. We're going to find him."

* * * * *

Cari rubbed her eyes as she paged through the e-book. It was longer than she'd expected and the monotony of just scanning the pages and swiping to the left was getting hypnotic. She stood up to stretch her legs. She'd left the office early to avoid another interrogation by Ollaman. She told Michelle to say she was tracking down a lead and would be back the next day. It wasn't a complete lie. Earlier, she'd made herself a peanut butter and jelly sandwich for dinner, then ate a slightly expired yogurt from her fridge. She hoped she wouldn't regret it in the morning.

Something tickled her memory. She tried to relax and let her brain find whatever it was searching for. *Myra McIlvain.* The woman had seemed nervous when they met for lunch. Cari thought it would become clear as she investigated Smith's death, but nothing seemed out of place. She got out her phone and gave Myra a call.

"This is Myra. How are you, Ms. Turnlyle?" she asked softly. "I thought you might call me again."

"I'm sorry to bother you, Myra. I know it's been a hard week, but I got the feeling you didn't tell me everything you know about your boss," Cari prodded her.

Myra sighed. "I thought maybe you didn't notice. I almost called you several times this week, but there's been very little in the news…even in the tabloids, I had to be sure."

Cari squeezed her hand into a fist in anticipation. "Be sure about what, Myra?"

"That the police were going to investigate her death. If I left it…if I hadn't taken it…they wouldn't have tried to find the killer," Myra said, her voice barely above a whisper.

"What did you take, Myra?" Cari asked.

"A note. There was a typed note on her table. She said she realized during her party that she didn't have any friends, her family didn't really care about her and she was too lonely, so she had to end it. It had her signature on it, but I knew she didn't type it. She was always fastidious about things. She had this little stamp she'd use for her signature. This letter was signed in blue ink. She never used blue ink. Only black. I know it's just a little thing, so small, I didn't think the police would believe me. So, I took it. I took the letter," Myra choked back a sob.

"Did you keep it?" Cari asked.

"I put it in a bag and hid it in my closet. Are you going to turn me in?" Myra asked in a shaky voice.

Cari hesitated. On the one hand, the police *needed* to know about this letter. On the other hand, she wasn't supposed to be talking to them. "I don't know what to do. It could have fingerprints on it, Myra. It could help them find the guy who did it. You should take it to them."

"They'll arrest me for tampering with evidence!" Myra cried.

"Maybe, but maybe not. Just be honest with them. They're good people. Ask for Detective Viacorte. She's a friend of mine," Cari told her.

"Okay. I'll think about it," Myra replied and ended the call.

Cari ran her fingers through her curls. This made Dahlia's theory much more relevant. She didn't want to get Myra in trouble, but if Genevieve found out she knew about the letter, she'd be really angry. She'd give Myra a day to turn it over, then she'd let Genevieve know about it. She hoped the woman would do the right thing.

She remembered getting a text from Dahlia earlier, but forgot to read it as she'd been talking to Veronica at the time. She got her phone from her messenger bag and opened her messaging app. Dahlia responded that it was a mix: four people had finished it, three were just close to finishing it. Cari was curious. She was feeling guilty for brushing Dahlia off all week and not giving her theories any merit. She hit the call button and waited for it to connect.

"Ms. Turnlyle! I didn't think you'd call again…you seemed…well, never mind. Did you have another question?" Dahlia asked.

Cari cleared her throat. "I'm sorry for being, well, flippant about your ideas, Dahlia. I do find it interesting that each of these people were reading the same book around the time they died. The ones who finished the book, did they happen to leave a review?" Cari asked.

"Oh, yes! The only man in the group. He is older, like my Aunt Vivian, but he always reviewed books he read and he sometimes posted about them on a book site. It's kind of like Reddit, but it's called Commented. It's not very well-known," Dahlia replied.

"Commented? Hmm, I haven't heard of it. So, did he post about the book there?" Cari asked interested to see if the man's words caught someone's eye.

"I'm not sure. We were all throwing out activities our loved ones did and trying to find commonalities. I only sort of remember him mentioning the site. I can ask him," she offered.

"Thanks, I appreciate it," Cari responded and meant it.

"Uh, talk to you later, I guess," Dahlia said and ended the call.

Cari went back to the e-book. If the book was somehow relevant, then whatever triggered a reaction from the possible killer was near the end of the book. She hesitated as she started to page backward through the book. It seemed really far-fetched that someone would be killed over reading a book, but the author's recent death made the idea feel more relevant. Still, how would someone know a specific person had read the book? It was a bestseller; literally thousands of people must have read it. She touched the page to shrink it and then scrolled the pages across quickly to see when the book was published. The copyright was listed as April 2026, so it had been close to three months. Was this the only book the readers had in common? She cringed and thumbed off a text to Dahlia to ask rather than call her again. Dahlia responded quickly.

This was the most recent one they all read

Cari chewed the inside of her cheek. She went back to her e-reader and returned to the page she'd been on before checking the copyright. As she flipped from page to page, she tried to think of some indicator, some recognizable feature other people could see. She frowned. She felt ridiculous; this was most likely a big conspiracy theory and she was wasting her time. She didn't have any other leads to follow though. Genevieve had texted to say the man she'd identified had already cleared out of his rented apartment. They didn't know where he'd gone.

She looked at the e-book again. What element or feature was unique to one person versus another? She swiped back a few more pages and it hit her: the highlighting feature. Not everyone used it, but maybe there was something everyone highlighted near the end of the book that set someone off. She flipped through the pages some more and found a large passage with seven highlights. Goosebumps rose on her arms. She took a photo of the page with her phone and texted it to Dahlia.

Did all of your loved ones highlight this passage?

I will ck

Cari yawned and looked at her watch. It was almost ten o'clock. She decided to get ready for bed and look into the idea more in the morning. For once, she felt like she might be on the right track with the investigation.

Chapter 17

A buzzing sound awakened Cari the next morning. She blinked several times and finally realized it was her cell phone. She managed to grab it and swipe across the screen to answer it just before her voicemail would have picked up.

"Bob! I thought I told you we had a rest day today?" she asked him groggily.

He laughed. "You did. I thought you might want to get coffee together before work this morning. Seems like I woke you up, though."

She yawned and stretched her arms overhead. "Oh, that sounds like a great idea. I just need to take a shower first. What time is it anyway?"

"It's just before seven o'clock. Do you think you can be ready in half an hour?" he asked.

She threw off her covers. "Not if I keep talking to you on the phone. Are we meeting at the place near my office?"

"That works," he answered. "I'll see you there. Love you."

"See you there! Love you!" she shouted at the phone before ending the call.

She didn't need to wash her hair, so she could take a fast shower, throw her hair into a bun, and be out the door more quickly than usual. She checked her phone for texts. Dahlia hadn't responded to her text from the night before, so Cari set the phone aside and focused on getting ready for the day.

She was out the door in record time and even managed to look fairly professional despite her hastiness in putting herself together.

She jumped into her car and took off for the coffee shop. She saw Bob had already arrived when she pulled into the parking lot. Cari grabbed her messenger bag from the front seat and locked the car behind her. Bob was waiting for her at a table with two coffee mugs and two scones.

"Scones! Perfect. They won't be as good as the ones in Wisconsin, but they will still be delicious," she cooed. "Thanks for buying me breakfast, Bob."

"My pleasure. Is this good for carb-loading for the race tomorrow?" he needled her.

She laughed. "It's definitely carbs, right?"

Her phone vibrated with a text. She checked her watch and saw it was from Dahlia. She gave Bob a sheepish look and pulled her phone out.

"Sorry. I just need to see what Dahlia has to say," she said as she unlocked the screen.

"Dahlia, huh? Did you find something interesting in the book she told you about?" Bob asked.

Cari hesitated after reading Dahlia's text. The two cases seemed tightly linked unless she was wrong and this was just a wild goose chase. "Sort of. It sounds like each person in her group, or whatever you call it, highlighted the same passage in the book. I'm not sure what that means or if it's possible to get that kind of information."

"They highlighted it in the e-book?" Bob asked for clarification.

"Yes. All seven of them highlighted the same set of paragraphs," Cari responded.

He scratched his head. "What was in that section of the book?"

"Well, it was near the end. The detective in the book was explaining how he solved the case…like the specific steps the killer took to murder his victims," Cari told him between bites of her scone. "This is a close second to the scones at your aunt's place."

"It's a fictional book, though, right?" Bob asked, steering the discussion back to Dahlia's story.

"Yeah, I think it's the last book in the series," Cari replied. "I'm just not sure someone would know *who* highlighted something in an e-book. Usually, it just says how many people highlighted it, right? Not who they were?"

"That sounds right. I mostly read in-print books, though," Bob admitted. "You could call the e-reader company and ask them if the information is accessible somehow."

"That's my next step. Hopefully, I won't have to sit on hold for too long. Ollaman is already grumpy about my attention to this other story…" she trailed off.

Bob nodded knowingly. "So, with Dahlia's story…your theory or her theory is someone was angered by seeing this unveiling of the killer and his motives, actions, et cetera, and decided to track the people down to…silence them?"

"It sounds crazy when you say it out loud," Cari agreed. "But it's the only connection. If I show her people can't be tracked in this way, maybe she'll let it drop. Or maybe she's right and this will give her some peace."

Bob looked at his watch. "Well, we'd better get to work. Thanks for meeting me. If I don't hear from you again today, I'm still planning on picking you up at seven for the race tomorrow."

Cari stood up and pushed her chair in. "Right. I'll be ready. Love you, Bob."

He dipped his head and kissed her goodbye. She stacked their dishes and set them in the return bin. She was ready to connect the dots in these cases. Despite what she said to Bob, she really thought she was onto something.

* * * * *

The message light was blinking on Genevieve's desk phone when she arrived at her office Friday morning. She picked up the receiver and entered the passcode to retrieve the message.

"Hi, Genevieve. It's Chris. I think I found the file you were talking about. It was embedded in an email attachment Ms. Smith sent to her publicist a few weeks ago. She hid it well, but the file size made it stand out. I forwarded a copy to you and Alex. Let me know if you have any questions. Bye."

Genevieve sat down and booted up her computer. After coming up empty at Walter Redbud's apartment, she was ready to cast frustration aside and figure out who this guy really was as well as where he was hiding. She opened her email application and found the message from Chris. She double-clicked to open it just as Alex sat down at his desk.

"You look hyper-focused this morning. You didn't even get coffee yet," he commented.

She looked over at him. "Remember how I told you about asking Chris to look for a hidden file somewhere in our victim's devices?"

Alex nodded. "You got lucky?"

She looked back at the screen. "I don't know about lucky, but Chris found something. He emailed it to you too. I was just about to read it."

Alex stepped over to her desk to look over her shoulder. "It's some sort of document? Did the email mention it?"

Genevieve minimized the document and clicked on the email again. "No, she was responding to her publicist's congratulatory email about her latest book. The book hit number one on the first day and stayed there for over a week. Ms. Gummill said she didn't know how *Natasha* always managed to come up with such unique bad guys. Ms. Smith responded by saying sometimes she's just had the right life experiences. Chris wrote in his email that the file was embedded in the word 'life'."

"I didn't even know you could do that. I can barely attach a document to an email in the normal fashion," Alex admitted.

She laughed. "I know. Let's see what it says."

Dear Janice or whomever finds this,

This is my confession of sorts. Twenty-one years ago, I moved back to New York to run away from a life I'm not proud of. In Arizona, I had a friend, more of an acquaintance really, who recognized my skills with numbers. He talked me into joining him in Vegas. He was a dealer for several casinos and worked shifts at each of them in some sort of rotation. He told me he could help me win big at Texas Hold 'Em, and we could split the pot after I cashed out. It sounded pretty lucrative. I knew it was most likely illegal, but when we started, I was only twenty-three years old. I had almost no money to my name. Even though I had a good job, it sounded exciting to enter this world of risk and fortune. He said we could start small and keep an irregular schedule and no one would catch on. The first night, we split just five thousand dollars, but it seemed like a million to me. We kept at it and we were careful. We switched casinos each month and rarely worked the system more than once a month. Sometimes I won more than $20,000.

Over the next almost twenty years I lived in Arizona, we split over two million dollars in winnings. It was exciting and felt like such a thrill every time we got away with it, but one night, someone recognized me. I don't know who the man was, but he'd been at a table with me at some point before. He didn't realize it at first, but my friend, my conspirator as you might call him, noticed the man's reaction. He signaled me to call it a night and I quit the game. I cashed in my chips and left the casino. I went back to my hotel and couldn't sleep. I was so afraid the police were going to show up at my door at any moment. Around two in the morning, my cell phone rang. It was my friend; he needed a ride home. He lived within walking distance of the casinos and didn't have his own car. I threw on some clothes and met him in a neighborhood about five miles from the strip. He was sweaty and scared out of his mind. I asked him what happened, were we caught? He said it had been close, but he'd 'taken care of it.' That scared me. I asked what he meant, even though part of me didn't want to know.

He explained how he realized this other man was onto us and our play against the game. After I cashed out, the game went on for a few more hands and this man ended up winning. He went over to the bar to celebrate. My friend joined him—he was easy to be around, you know? Friendly, handsome, seemed safe. The man said we were lucky he won the pot. He knew we were cheating, and if he'd lost, he was going to report us. He'd already had a drink or two during the game and wasn't at all sober. My friend, I didn't realize this until much later, but he planned for every contingency. He had no desire to go to jail and no intention of ever being caught. He had some kind of drug with him. He didn't tell me what it was, just that it would make the guy seem more drunk than he really was. He put it in the man's drink when he wasn't looking. When the man started struggling to keep his eyes open, my friend helped him out to his car and offered to drive him home. The man agreed and off they went. He helped him into his house and his bed.

I'm not sure he went there with the intent to kill him, but he saw a gas-powered space heater in the man's bedroom. He disabled the carbon monoxide detectors in the house and did whatever you do to make it leak carbon monoxide into the air. Then he waited outside for an hour. When he went to check on the man, he was dead. He kept his airways covered with a wet bandana and then wiped every surface he'd touched down in the house and the car. Then he locked up the house and called me from outside. I was terrified. By picking him up, I was certainly an accessory to the crime. I told him it was too close of a call, and I wanted out. We'd made our money and it was time to part ways. Several times during his confession I begged him to stop telling me and he told me the story was his insurance policy. He was already in my car, smelling of gas. He assured me if I ever went to the police or told anyone about this, I would meet the same fate as the man from the casino. I told him to forget he ever knew me. I was moving away and he'd never hear from me again. I wouldn't tell anyone, but our partnership was over. I kept that promise until this book. I couldn't live with the secret anymore and while it's a coward's way of confessing, that's what I did. If you've gone looking for this, then I'm probably dead. I'll do my best to leave clues behind for you to find the man who did it. His name is Walter Redbud.

Genevieve put her hand up to her mouth. "If only we'd found this sooner, we could have gotten to him on Monday!"

"He cleared out of town as soon as he took that thumb drive from her safety deposit box at the bank. She probably hoped her lawyer would find it first, but as she said, this guy planned for every contingency. He just wasn't computer savvy enough to find this file in her email account," Alex told her.

"How do we find him now?" Genevieve groaned. "If he left town, where did he go? Back to Nevada?"

"We can start there, but let's search the DMV for people with his name and age range. More than likely, he moved away from Vegas too."

"I'll call my contact at the FBI and see if they can help us locate him. It's possible he has another alias or two," she told him.

"Good idea. We're close now, Gen. He's not getting away this time," Alex assured her.

The door to the detective bay swung open. Dana, who was basically the gatekeeper of the station, stood next to the housekeeper they'd met at the author's house a few days earlier.

"Ms. McIlvain. I didn't realize we had a meeting scheduled. How can we help you?" Genevieve asked.

The older woman swallowed and lowered her eyes. She had a large bag clutched to her chest. She slowly walked over to their desks.

"I'm very sorry about this. I shouldn't have done it. I know it was wrong, but I just didn't know what else to do," she told them.

Genevieve put her hand on the woman's arm. "Have a seat, Ms. McIlvain. What is it you think you've done?"

The woman opened her bag and pulled out a clear, plastic, resealable bag with a sheet of paper inside it. "I took this. I took it from the table at Gayle Smith's house."

Genevieve gently took the bag from her and looked at it. The paper was a typed note. She skimmed it and gasped. "It's a suicide note. Ms. McIlvain! Why would you take this?"

"Because she didn't commit suicide. And you know she didn't. I talked to…someone…and they encouraged me to come forward now that you know she was murdered. I'm sorry. Are you going to send me to jail?" she broke down into tears.

Alex reached over and took the package from Genevieve. "I'll take this down to CSU. They can run prints."

"Ms. McIlvain, I don't think you're going to go to jail. I'll talk to the DA. There will be some sort of punishment. Let's go talk to my boss. He'll know how best to handle this. Thank you for bringing this in. You did the right thing."

She stood up and led Ms. McIlvain over to Grusky's office. Three days ago, the letter would have looked very different. She understood why the woman didn't want them to find it, but she couldn't condone what she'd done either. Hopefully, Grusky knew what to do.

* * * * *

It had been almost seventy minutes since Cari called the technical support line at the e-reader company. She put the call on speaker and allowed the elevator music to play quietly while she worked on other things. The city was already starting to make arrangements for the annual fall festival. She reached out to the Brenington Chamber of Commerce to request a list of businesses that planned to participate in the annual duck painting contest. Most businesses enjoyed the good-natured contest, which required you to paint a ceramic duck in a unique style and display it in front of your place of business for the month leading up to the festival. People voted with their money and some of the proceeds covered advertising costs for future BCC events, while the majority of it supported the local shelter and food pantry.

Cari kept a close eye on Ollaman's office while her call was on hold. She didn't want to anger him further and wasn't sure how she'd explain the phone call to him. Luckily, he'd been in and out of the office for various public relations opportunities that morning. She had to hand it to him, he was very dedicated to the 5k event and raising awareness for it. She sent her email and crossed it off her to-do list. The elevator music continued to play from the phone. She glared at it, willing someone to pick up. Unfortunately, the door to Ollaman's office opened first and Ollaman looked her way. Cari grabbed the receiver so he wouldn't hear the hold music. She mouthed, *"I'm on hold"* to him and he nodded, but continued walking toward her desk.

"Turnlyle, feel free to take the call when it connects. I, uh, well…" he paused and ran a hand over his bald head. "I wanted to apologize for my behavior this week. You see, my wife is a huge fan of Natasha's books. She even calls her by her first name, well, I suppose it's her pen name. Anyway, she has been hounding me for information all week and I let her frustrations spill over onto you. I know you're doing a good job with the story. I'm sorry for micromanaging you. I, uh, well, I'll leave you to it."

Cari started to respond when the phone finally made a clicking sound and started to ring, indicating someone was answering it. She nodded her thanks and pointed at the phone. Ollaman lifted his chin in understanding and turned back to his office.

"Technical support, this is Jeremiah. How can I help you today?" a young, male voice said.

"Hi, Jeremiah. My name is Cari. I'm doing some research on people who prefer e-books to print books and have a technical question for you."

"Go ahead. I've seen just about every problem you can encounter with an e-reader," Jeremiah bragged.

"One feature a lot of e-book readers like is the ability to highlight phrases or paragraphs in books they read. I've noticed the e-book sort of keeps track of frequently highlighted sections by putting a dotted line below them with a number to indicate how many readers highlighted it," she began.

"Yes, it is a popular feature," Jeremiah agreed.

"Would it be possible for someone to figure out *who* highlighted something in an e-book?" Cari asked him. "Some people who prefer print books have expressed concern about their identity being stolen through this feature."

Jeremiah choked back what Cari assumed must be a laugh. "Uh, wow. Uh, I didn't expect that question. I've never heard of anyone wanting to know who else highlighted something. I mean, who cares?"

"Right, it does seem like a silly thing to look for, but if someone wanted to, could they get that information?" Cari probed further.

"I mean, we would never give it out. I'm not sure…I'm sorry, what? My apologies, Cari, my colleague was eavesdropping and is talking to me at the same time. Steve, what did you just say?" Jeremiah asked quietly.

Cari strained to hear the other person's words, but whoever Steve was, he was too far away from Jeremiah's headset for his words to transmit to her ear.

A new voice came on the line. "Cari is it?" the voice asked.

"Yes, I'm Cari," she responded. "You're Steve?"

"Yes, this is Steve. I'm sorry to take over your tech call, but I couldn't help but overhear Jeremiah's responses. I had a similar call a month or so ago. I assured the caller we do not track this information," Steve told her.

"But, do you have the information?" Cari pressed him.

"Uh, well, just a sec. Let's just pick a book at random and I'll walk you through what we can see on our side," Steve offered.

"How about 'All-in Murder'?" Cari suggested.

"Great. Let me pull it up…okay. In the data for the book's history, we can see there were eight hundred and ninety-seven highlighted segments," Steve told her.

"Okay, what about the section on page 386?" Cari asked. "On my side, it says it was highlighted seven times."

"386…got it. Yes, seven times," Steve agreed.

"Is there something in your database that says which readers highlighted that?" Cari asked.

She heard Steve click away on a few keys. "I can find their user number, an identity tag each customer is assigned when they start using our app or e-reader."

"And in theory, you could trace those numbers back to real names?" Cari asked and leaned forward.

"I guess so, but I don't think anyone—" Steve started to say.

Cari interrupted him. "Can you just see if anyone, besides you of course, has accessed this list of numbers for this highlighted section?"

"Uh, sure, but I seriously doubt…" his voice trailed off. "Oh. Well, it looks like it was accessed from a remote location."

"Like someone hacked into your files?" Cari asked.

Steve clicked his tongue. "This probably isn't going to be very reassuring to your readers, but yes. I'm going to need to alert our security team to this."

"Wait, Steve. I have a confession. I'm not actually researching what I said. I'm investigating a series of murders. I need you to screenshot everything you've found and forward it to an email address I'm going to give you. It's for a police detective in Brenington, New York. I need you to find the IP address or whatever it is that tells you about the person who accessed your system. Get a screenshot of it. Get a screenshot of the user numbers. Then look up their names and send those to the detective too. Are you ready for the email address, Steve?" Cari asked him pointedly.

"Uh, wow. Uh, yes. Go ahead," Steve said in a shaky voice.

* * * * *

"Did you see the DA walk out with the housekeeper?" Alex asked Genevieve.

"Yeah, I'm almost afraid to ask what happened," Genevieve responded.

"It took a lot of courage for her to bring that letter in," Alex remarked. "Hopefully, they'll be lenient."

Alex's phone rang and he put it on speaker. "Detectives Runimoss and Viacorte. You're on speaker, but Viacorte's on hold with someone else, so she might not say anything."

"Just a quick call from us," Bob said. "The letter didn't have any prints except for the housekeeper's. We probably wouldn't have checked it for prints if we'd found it on Monday."

"I guess our guy wore gloves," Alex commented.

"Seems like it. That's all I've got for now," Bob said and the line clicked dead.

A ping sounded from Genevieve's computer. She wedged the phone receiver between her shoulder and her ear to free up her hands. She was on hold with one of the casinos that used the chips Mr. Redbud had removed from the safety deposit box.

She and Alex had found who they thought was the original Walter Redbud in an old DMV record from the state of Nevada. He looked quite a bit different back then. His face was narrower, he had a full head of black hair, and his eyes were light blue. The newer Redbud was balding with a round face and brown eyes. He was in the right age range, so they were giving him a closer look. Unfortunately, the license had expired five years ago and was never renewed. They weren't sure if he had created a new alias, moved to another state, or both. Her contact at the FBI had promised to email her if they found a match in their system.

She navigated to her email system and saw a new email from someone named Steve Tate with the subject line "Murder Case Evidence." Mr. Tate's email was registered as though he worked for the popular e-reader company, but she didn't read e-books. Her initial reaction was his email had somehow made it through the department's screening system even though it was most likely spam. She cautiously highlighted the email to see what Mr. Tate wanted. He addressed her as Detective Viacorte and said he'd been contacted by an investigator who enabled him to discover a hack within their system that gave a person access to seven people's names and addresses. She frowned. This was not really her problem. She started to delete the email when the phone call connected. She minimized the screen so she could focus on the conversation.

"Detective Viacorte?" A woman's voice sounded in her ear.

"This is she," Genevieve responded.

"I was able to access old employment records and yes, we did have a Walter Redbud working with us from the mid-eighties until the early 2000s. He was part-time," the woman told her.

"Did you get a forwarding address?" Genevieve asked hopefully.

"We pay our employees electronically, so we had no need for him to give us a new address. I don't know if he moved away. He just stopped working for us about eighteen years ago," she responded.

Genevieve tried a different approach. "Can you tell me why he quit working at the casino?"

"It just says he put in his two-week notice and that was it. His employee reviews were very good. He was a dealer and seemed to be well-liked by everyone. I guess he was just ready to move on," she told her.

"Okay, thank you for your time," Genevieve said and hung up the phone. "Alex, I got an email from some guy named Steve Tate."

"Who?" Alex asked. He rolled his chair over to her desk.

"Exactly," she laughed. "Let me pull it up."

She enlarged the email and waited for Alex to read it.

"An investigator told him to email you? What?" Alex remarked.

"Yeah, it seems fishy," she agreed and moved the mouse up to click the delete button.

"Wait! Did you see this last part?" Alex asked, pointing at her screen. "The book he's referencing is by our dead author."

She looked at the last paragraph of the email. Mr. Tate said the investigator told him to mention the hacker had accessed the names of people who highlighted the conclusion or dénouement of the murder in the book "All-in Murder" by Natasha Gillespie. Tate listed the items he attached which included screenshots of the people's information as well as when it had been accessed. He claimed the investigator said all seven people were now dead.

"The person accessed this file multiple times," Genevieve said when she opened one of the screenshots.

"It looks like he found four people the first time and then came back three more times for names," Alex agreed. "Who are these people?"

"Let's look them up," Genevieve responded.

Alex scribbled down their names and rolled back over to his desk. One of the names had a New York address, so she queried their database for their name. The person's information popped up on her screen. She scanned the results and her heart sank when she saw the person was deceased.

"Vivian Roust was a New York resident. She lived in our county. She died by suicide...melatonin overdose..." her voice trailed off.

Cari had mentioned something about a young woman wanting her to disprove that her loved one had committed suicide. She looked at Tate's email again. *An investigator*. It must have been Cari, but she hid her identity to keep Genevieve from getting in trouble.

"When?" Alex interrupted her thoughts.

"When, what?" she asked him.

"When did she die?" he asked.

"Oh, it was recently," she said, reading from the screen.

"The first person I looked up is dead too. Also suicide and with melatonin," Alex told her. "This guy, he attached an IP address? Can we use that to find him?"

"I don't know how, but I bet Chris or Bob do. I'll forward this to them while you give them a call."

She quickly typed an explanation to Bob and Chris, then sent the email off. Alex had the phone to his ear and was pantomiming 'hurry up' with his hands. He was always so impatient. She stepped closer so she could hear what he was saying.

"…we're on our way down. You got the email? Great. We'll explain more when we get there…wait, what?" Alex stopped talking for a half a minute then hung up the phone. "Chris and Bob knew exactly how to track the IP address. They say it's in Pennsylvania. The IP address belongs to one Drew Derault. They emailed us the information."

"What? Drew Derault? I need to see how that's spelled," Genevieve said and grabbed a pencil. She opened the email from CSU and wrote the man's name down on some scratch paper.

"Okay, I'm totally lost. Obviously, this somehow relates to our case as this book was written by our dead author, but who are these seven other people?" Alex asked with his brow furrowed.

Genevieve was only half-listening to him. She crossed out the letters one by one. "It's him. It's Walter Redbud. It's another alias. He rearranges the letters in his name to make new names. Look."

Alex looked at the paper she held up. "Okay, so, this guy killed the author and seven random people who read her book?"

"If you look at the evidence Mr. Tate sent us, these seven people highlighted the part of the book where she gives up the murderer's method. Remember the letter she sent to her publicist? She said she copied his technique or whatever in her latest book. He must have gotten wind of it and tracked her down," Genevieve mused.

"He didn't know who he was looking for until she announced who she was on the Today Show. But these seven other people? Thousands of people read the book, right?" he asked.

"It was a bestseller like the others, so I assume so," she responded.

"And they bothered him more because they highlighted this part in their e-book?" Alex scoffed.

"I mean, the guy obviously has problems. Let's get Grusky to help us. We can't just drive to Penn and arrest this guy. He might not even be there," Genevieve reasoned.

"Oh, he's there. I can feel it," Alex said and patted his chest. "He thinks he's invincible, but we've got him now. Grusky can coordinate with their locals to bring him in while we drive over there to get him. This is our guy, Gen. I just know it!"

* * * * *

Dahlia had tears in her eyes as Cari reported the news to her. She felt awkward as the young woman's tears spilled over onto her cheeks. After discovering the e-reader company's files had been accessed remotely, Cari had called Dahlia to see if she could meet.

"I just, I can't thank you enough for this. I knew Aunt Vivian was murdered." She blinked. "Wait! I need to tell the others!"

She pulled out her phone and unlocked the screen. Cari put her hand out and gently rested it on the young woman's arm.

"Dahlia, I told you, we can't share this publicly yet. The police have to find the guy and finish their investigation first, remember?" she asked delicately.

Dahlia let the phone drop into her lap. "Oh. I...I thought you meant I couldn't share, like, on my social media. I can't tell the others either?"

Cari shook her head. "No, not yet. Hopefully, soon. We don't want this guy to realize he's caught before they catch him. Does that make sense? He might destroy evidence or go into hiding."

Dahlia nodded. "I understand. I can't believe you did it. I mean, I knew you could do it, if anyone could do it, but I thought you'd given up. I thought you thought I was crazy."

Cari's head dipped a bit before she raised her eyes to meet Dahlia's. "I'm sorry I didn't believe you at first, Dahlia. I thought you were in a state of denial. I was wrong."

Dahlia pulled Cari into a hug. "It's okay. It's all okay now. Thank you for helping us."

* * * * *

Genevieve rolled her head around in a circle to work out the kinks in her neck. The two-hour drive to Pennsylvania had seemed to stretch on forever. Alex pulled into the police station and put the car in park. They went inside and checked in at the front desk.

"Detectives Runimoss and Viacorte, Brenington PD. We're here about a Mr. Drew Derault," Alex told the man behind the desk.

"One moment please," he said and picked up his phone. "The detectives are here."

The inner door opened and an officer in uniform extended her hand. "I'm Lieutenant Salovin. We've got your guy in an interrogation room with our detectives. We thought you'd want to sit in on the interview."

"Appreciate that. How did it go when they picked him up?" Alex asked her as they followed her down a hallway.

"He was pretty nonchalant about it. Like we had the wrong guy or something. He was like, 'sure, let's go clear this up," she told them.

"It's pretty clear who he is," Genevieve said. "I'm glad you were able to pick him up."

"Here we are," she said and gestured to the door in front of them.

Alex opened the door and let Genevieve go in first. One of the other detectives nodded at them, got up and left. The other one shook their hands. He was sitting down, but Genevieve could tell he was quite a bit shorter than Alex. He had blonde hair and brown eyes. She looked at the man across the table. He wore a bemused expression.

"I'm Detective Brown. My partner said he'd watch from the other room. You guys go ahead. We just barely got read in on all this," he told them. "Mr. Derault has been read his rights. He waived his right to an attorney for now."

They sat down in the two empty chairs. The man continued to smirk at them. Genevieve couldn't wait to wipe that grin off his face.

"Mr. Derault, or should I say Redbud…or is it Butler?" Genevieve asked him.

The man's expression faltered momentarily. "I'm not sure who those other people are. My name is Drew Derault."

"Cut the crap. You're all of these people. We have your fingerprints now and we matched them to a safety deposit box in New York. It's over," Alex said with a sneer.

The man's face paled. "I don't have to talk to you. I change my mind. I want a lawyer."

"That's completely within your rights. By the way, unfortunately, you made the choice to kill people in multiple states. That means we had to talk to the FBI. Fortunately for the rest of us, I know some people with the FBI, so I already called them and they're enroute as we speak. I have to hand it to you, Mr. Derault, you were clever. No one connected the dots right away, but one of the people you killed has a rather persistent niece. And she got the attention of a rather persistent journalist. You just never stood a chance," Genevieve said with a smirk. "Now, do you have a lawyer you'd like us to call for you, or is this going to be a public defender case?"

Chapter 18

The race course wrapped around the city park and along the hike and bike trail before ending in front of City Hall. Cari could see Genevieve up ahead of her by about two blocks. She'd passed Chris just after the second mile marker and had been gaining on her friend over the third mile. The finish was less than a quarter mile away, so she really needed to speed up if she was going to win their contest.

She picked up her pace some more even though the muscles in her legs were already fatigued. She was at least four inches taller than Genevieve, so she could gain more in one stride than her short friend. The course had a final right-hand turn and then three blocks along Main Street to City Hall. Cari curled around the turn and was astonished to see Genevieve crossing the finish line already. She must have sprinted the last quarter mile! She could hear the race announcer reading off people's names as they approached the finish line.

"And next we have our very own Cari Turnlyle of the Brenington Beagle! As many of you know, she and Detective Viacorte had a little side competition going on for the race today. Well, Ms. Turnlyle, in case you missed her, the detective had your number today. Great race, ladies!" the announcer said with a smile. "And coming down the stretch, we have another one of our city employees, Chris Luvenon…"

Cari grabbed a cup of water and looked around for Genevieve. She didn't think she could have gotten too far away already.

"Looking for someone?"

Cari whipped her head around and saw Alex grinning at her. Genevieve was standing next to his collapsible chair, drinking a cup of water too.

"Great run, Gen!" Cari said and gave her a high five. "I thought I might be able to catch you with your short legs, but you really finished strong. Did you see your time?"

Alex cleared his throat. "All results can be found by simply entering your bib number into the little machine on the table behind you."

Genevieve rolled her eyes. "I got under twenty-two minutes. It's a really flat course, but it's a great time for me. You did a good job too."

"Cari! Aunt Cari! Over here! Over here!" A small voice called out.

She looked over Alex's shoulder to the crowd gathered outside of City Hall. Joel and Hilary were waving at her from the sidewalk. She walked over to join them.

"Hey, guys! I'm glad you could come to the event today. Are you having fun?" Cari asked them.

Joel had a stick of blue cotton candy and a sugar smile. "It's the best. My dad bought me this cotton candy and my mom said we can do some of the games in the park in a little bit."

Hilary gave a shy nod. "It's really loud, but it's fun. I guess you didn't win the contest, huh?"

Cari grinned. "That's okay. Genevieve is really fast. I had no idea she was this fast. Want to go say hi and meet her partner?"

Joel looked at his mom. "Can we, Mom?"

Bea nodded her consent, so Cari walked with them over to the two detectives.

"Ms. Genevieve! You did it! You won!" Joel called out as they crossed the barricaded street.

Genevieve smiled. "Hi, kids. Looks like you found the cotton candy already. Hilary, Joel, this is my partner, Detective Alex Runimoss."

Alex stood up to shake their hands. "Nice to meet you, Hilary and Joel. How do you know my partner?"

Cari wasn't certain, but it looked like Genevieve's face flushed.

"She was our babysitter last night! Wasn't it lucky that she was over at Aunt Cari's house when my mom called to see if she could watch us last night?" Joel asked Alex.

Cari gulped. She saw Alex's face flash in surprise before he smiled at her nephew. "That is lucky, Joel."

"Next year, my mom said I could try running this race too," Joel said triumphantly.

"No, she said you could try doing a fun run. Like a mile run," Hilary corrected. "This race is over three miles."

Joel's face dropped. "I could do it. I'm really fast. Just wait. You'll see me running it next year for sure."

Cari heard a phone vibrate and looked at her watch to see if it was hers. At the same time, Genevieve pulled her phone from her pocket and stepped away from the group.

"I need to take this," she called over her shoulder.

Cari looked back at the finish line and saw Bob rambling toward it. She jogged up the street with the kids to cheer for him.

"Let's go Bob!" they yelled.

He smiled in response. He crossed the finish line and bent over at the waist for a moment before standing up straight again.

"Way to go, Bob! You did it! I'm so proud of you." She stood on her toes and gave him a quick kiss on his cheek, even though it was a bit sweaty.

"Ugh," he panted. "I finished it. Phew. No more running. I'm cooked."

The two kids laughed in amusement. Cari chuckled too. She walked with him to Alex's water station. Bob grabbed two cups of water and walked to the nearby curb to sit down. Bea called out to Hilary and Joel to come back to the sidewalk, so they waved their goodbyes. Cari turned back to Alex.

"I heard you guys had a quick road trip yesterday," she said to him as she turned to join Bob on the opposite side of the street.

Alex raised his eyebrows. "You heard that, huh?"

She nodded and took a step back in his direction.

"Listen, I'm not sure who kept you connected on this case—" Alex started to say.

"I didn't force my way into this, Alex," she told him.

"It could have been dear, sister Sharon for all I know," he said sarcastically. "I know you have your job to do and we have ours. I also have my suspicions that you made sure we got the information we needed to solve this murder and apparently seven others."

"And you found the guy in Pennsylvania," Cari reminded him.

"We did. I know Viacorte gave you the inside scoop already. She got permission from Grusky to fork it over."

Cari smiled. "Then relax, Alex."

"I am relaxed. I'm passing out water to all you crazy runners from the comfort of my own chair," he told her then frowned. "I can't believe you tracked that guy down from an e-reader. He was so cocky. Man. He thought he could get away with anything."

"It sounds like he got away with murder for two decades," Cari remarked.

"Well, not anymore," he grumbled. "Enough about the case. I'm not comfortable discussing it. I told Gen…she…your friend isn't very good at boundaries."

"She's an adult. She doesn't need a babysitter," Cari retorted.

Before Alex could respond, Bob let out a loud groan from over on the curb. They both looked his way as he painfully pushed himself off the curb.

"I am going to feel this tomorrow. Whose idea was this anyway?" he said with a hint of sarcasm.

Cari grabbed another cup of water and walked over to Bob. "Drink some more water. It will keep your muscles from cramping."

"Too late," Bob moaned and rubbed his calf. "At least I can serve as a distraction. It sounded like you and Alex were getting into it over there."

Cari felt her face flush, but shook her head in disagreement. "We were discussing boundaries. I was making sure he knew Genevieve can take care of herself. She doesn't need a babysitter."

* * * * *

Genevieve walked back to the water table where Alex was sitting. She watched as Cari helped Bob rub his calf over by the curb. On the opposite side of the street, Joel waved goodbye to her as his dad tugged him along the sidewalk. She returned the gesture.

"I thought you were on the phone," Alex said.

"It was a quick call. It's done," Genevieve responded.

"All week, I thought you were sneaking off to call your newspaper friend here, but clearly, that wasn't the case," Alex observed.

"I guess you don't know everything after all, Alex," Genevieve said shortly. "I've told you; you can trust Cari. You can trust me."

Alex's mouth stretched to a thin line. "I never said I didn't trust you, Gen. And I'm trying with…Cari. See? I just used her name instead of newspaper chick."

Genevieve tried to smile, but her heart wasn't in it. "Look. I know I've been a little secretive lately. I'm sorry, but I was trying to look into some things for my contact with the FBI."

"You mean Dureski? He's kind of like your mentor from the program or whatever?" Alex asked for clarification.

"Yeah. When he saw I worked for Brenington PD, he approached me about a case they've been slowly working for several months now."

"Yeah? That sounds good for you, right? He must have seen that you're a good detective and investigator."

She shrugged. "Maybe, maybe not. I think this is more of a location, location, location benefit."

Alex gave her a confused look. "I don't follow."

"It's about Robby and his company. I'm not sure how to tell you this," Genevieve said slowly. She casually looked Cari's way before continuing. Her friend wasn't paying any attention to her and Alex. "The FBI is investigating Robby's company for involvement in a string of murders."

Alex's face paled. "Robby? As in your friend's brother-in-law? The accountant? Murder?"

The End

Thank you for reading "Unwritten in Death". I hope you'll take a moment to leave a review!

I left you with a cliffhanger, but never fear, the next book will be out before you know it! Cari's brother-in-law, Robby is becoming increasingly worried about his job with New Technology Systems. On more than one occasion, he's been asked to process billing codes which are suspiciously identical to the initials of local business owners who have died in freak accidents. The time of the payment requests align with the dates the two people died. Fearful he's somehow involved in paying off a hitman, he reaches out to Cari for advice. Is Robby being paranoid or is there something more sinister going on? Find out in Book 6!

Visit https://leslieapiggott.com for more information and to join my e-newsletter list.

Acknowledgments

No book would be complete without a big shoutout to my friend Desiree. Thanks for your endless help with each of my books. I can't thank you enough!

A big thank you to Jennie Rosenblum, my amazing editor! Thank you for always pushing me to be better.

Congratulations to fellow author, Myra McIlvain for winning my contest! I hope you enjoyed the experience.

And finally, to all of my readers: thank you for your dedication and support.

About the Author

Leslie A. Piggott lives in the Austin, Texas area with her husband and their two children. She is a scientist-turned-mom who received her doctorate in Biomedical Sciences from the University of Texas Health Science Center at Houston. In addition to writing, she also enjoys running marathons, quilting, knitting, singing in the church choir, and watercolor painting. She has previously published two watercolor and poetry books, both in 2021: *Poems in the Pandemic*, and *Art in Words*. Her first novel, *Rising Pressure* was published in January of 2022. To sign up for her e-newsletter, you can visit her website at https://leslieapiggott.com.